DAMAGED GOODS

A BUCKNER THRILLER SUSPENSE

KATHY BENNETT

ALSO BY KATHY BENNETT

THE DEADLY THRILLER SERIES

A Dozen Deadly Roses

A Deadly Blessing

A Deadly Justice

A Deadly Denial

A Deadly Beauty

A Deadly Prayer (A Novella)

A Deadly Blood Moon

THE BUCKNER THRILLER SUSPENSE SERIES
(A TRILOGY)

Collateral Damage

Damaged Goods

Damage Control

STANDALONE WORKS

The Gunfighter – Short Story - The Black Car Business Volume 2

Much of this book was written during the Covid-19 pandemic.

I dedicate this book to all the first responders, police, fire, doctors, nurses, medical specialists, support staff, and caregivers of the elderly who worked tirelessly to save lives. May God blue you all!

ACKNOWLEDGMENTS

While I often tell people (tongue in cheek), "I know everything, just ask me," nothing could be farther from the truth. And the longer I'm retired from the LAPD, the less I know how the department is currently being run. Additionally, there are other details, stories, or policies that occurred before I pinned on my badge. That's why I reach out to others to help get the details straight.

The following people were generous enough to help me with those pesky details in *Damaged Goods*. It should be noted that any mistakes in the book are mine.

Huge thanks for your input: Keith Bushey, Connie Castruita, Paul McLaughlin, Manny Mojarro, Jill Niles, Cliff Shepard, and Eric Solter.

PROLOGUE

The rookie cop stood outside the 7-Eleven convenience store sipping his coffee. The heat from the paper cup warmed his hand against the dampness of the 3:00 a.m. air in mid-town Los Angeles.

A pair of black and white LAPD Crown Vic's sat backed into spaces several stalls apart from each other.

Two partnered veteran officers, plus the rookie and his training officer, stood in a circle. They talked. They joked. They laughed. Their formation ensured a 360-degree view of their surroundings. Their eyes never stopped scanning—passing cars, apartment rooftops, and the shadows in the night.

The rookie raised his arm for another sip of coffee. His training officer slapped the cup from his hand, causing what little caffeine remained to go flying, splashing the pant leg of one of the veteran cops next to him.

"What the hell," the splashed cop yelled, jumping back.

The rookie gaped at his partner.

"Didn't they teach you anything in the academy...*boot*?"

He tilted his head, not sure what he'd done wrong.

"You *never* hold something in your gun hand when you don't have to." The training officer's eyes narrowed. "You've been standin' out here for fifteen minutes slurping your cuppa joe, and if we got attacked, you'd be holding your damn coffee."

"Better than him man-handling his dick," the spattered officer joked.

His face flaming, the rookie nodded. "Yes, sir."

The joking cop's partner turned to him. "Keep it in your pants, pal. The gangsters around here have a bounty for shootin' the po-po in the pecker."

Not sure if the seasoned cop was kidding, he said nothing but bobbed his head in acknowledgment.

"Let's hit the bricks," his training officer ordered. "These two hyenas need to do some police work."

Minutes later in the quiet of the patrol car, the rookie found his voice as they drove down an alley that paralleled Wilshire Boulevard. "I'm sorry. That was a dumb mistake. Keeping your gun-hand free is a primary thing you learn as a recruit."

"I didn't think you'd ever drink enough of that brew so I could get your attention without covering Cordova with hot coffee."

He hung his head and pretended to write in the log. "Uh, sir?"

The street-schooled veteran gave him a sidelong glance.

"I heard some guys talking in the locker room about throwaway guns." Warmth crept upon his face again. Luckily, in the car's darkness, his partner couldn't see.

His training officer scoffed. "You know what it is, don't cha?"

He nodded. "A gun that can't be traced back to you. Usually acquired from a suspect."

"Acquired. You're quite the scholar, aren't you? I bet you've even got a college degree."

He bit the inside of his cheek. "Criminal justice."

The veteran sighed. "So why do you want to know about a throwaway?"

"Should I get one?"

His training officer drove in silence at least a half-mile on the empty street. "Nah. You're the kind of cop who's going to do minimum time in the field and then find some cushy desk job. You may be a good guy, but you ain't no warrior, and you'll make a lousy street cop. Your heart isn't in it."

His partner's words hurt, and he wondered if the veteran officer was right.

"Aw, what the hell. Tell ya what, kid. I've got two deployment periods left before I retire. On my last day, I'll give you my throwaway. I won't need it—I'm movin' to Florida—land of bikinis, babes, and booze."

PART I

1

ROY

22 years later

Leaning against the kitchen island, Roy Buckner watched as his wife, Amber, performed a chamber check before sliding her Glock into the holster of her spit-shined Sam Browne gun belt lying on the table.

"Are you nervous?"

She looked up at him. "A bit."

"I'm sure you'll do fine."

She blew out a breath. "I hope my training officer isn't a jerk."

Inwardly, he cringed. He didn't personally know Amber's TO, but he'd asked around, and Duane Sutton was known to be hard on probationary officers—especially the women. But why give her something else to worry about on her first night as a cop?

"Mama." Their son, Gage, toddled into the kitchen. He lifted his arms to his mother. "Up."

She bent and hoisted the boy onto her hip. "Who's mama's big boy?"

The eighteen-month-old grinned a drool-filled smile. "Me!"

Roy tried to ignore the fear causing his stomach to rumble. His mind cast Amber in all the dangerous situations he'd experienced on the streets of Los Angeles as a policeman and barely survived. How would she ever get through?

As always happened when he questioned Amber's fortitude, he remembered two years ago. She was more than capable of taking care of herself.

You've got nothing to worry about. She's probably more prepared and experienced to face trouble than ninety percent of the cops on the job.

She gave her son a hug and sent him off to fetch his favorite stuffed dog, which he called Teddy. Then she turned to him. "You'll be dropping off Gage at my parents' house in the morning, right?"

"Yep, and I'll pick him up after work."

"Are you driving downtown or riding the train?"

"I'm taking my truck. I don't want to stay late and not have a way home."

She frowned. "You can't leave him with my parents for hours on end. You have to get off on time."

He sighed. "I told you I would do my best to get him by

five. But I have job responsibilities too. What more do you want me to do?"

They stared at one another—an experience happening all too often in their marriage these days.

Amber broke the standoff and retrieved her gun belt and war bag. "Okay, I'm off to the station."

Roy stepped from behind the kitchen island and stood before her. He wrapped his arms around her and tried not to feel hurt when she tensed. "I love you. You'll be fine." He kissed the top of her head, inhaling the coconut scent emanating from her hair. "Just be careful. Gage and I would be lost without you."

2

____

AMBER

Amber pushed open the door to the women's locker room at LAPD's Topanga Division. She had about an hour before roll call and was glad to find the space empty. She walked past the rows of metal compartments, many decorated with photos of children, husbands, and pets. A few of the cabinets held wire hangers displaying towels air drying.

Her locker was located against the back wall. She undid her padlock and scanned her belongings she'd organized the day before.

Roy had built her a shelving unit that fit below her pressed uniforms. In magnetic frames, pictures of him and Gage smiled from inside the metal compartment. She didn't want to display her family to others who entered the area.

Donning her uniform, she tried to calm her nerves. She was as nervous as on her first day of nursing in the neonatal

ICU. Those days seemed decades ago, although it had only been two years. Here she was in her early thirties, starting a new career as a cop.

The door opened and a curvy female officer entered. She eyed Amber. "How ya doin'?"

"Fine. How are you?"

"I'm breathing. I haven't seen you here before at Topanga."

"My first day—here or any station. I'm Amber Buckner."

The other woman chuckled. "Welcome. You can call me Barb. Who's your TO?"

"Sutton."

The other officer made a face and sighed. "That's unfortunate. He's a dick. Especially to females."

She groaned. "Wonderful."

"No need to stress. You may have a couple of tough months working with him, but then they'll take pity on you and put you with someone better." Barb opened her locker and removed a toothbrush and toothpaste. "Learn what you can from him and don't let him rattle you."

"Good to know, thanks."

In the roll call room, following tradition, Amber sat alone in the front row. She wasn't surprised when the watch commander asked her to define probable cause. Roy had told her what to expect, and she'd prepared to be quizzed on some of the most basic of laws, policies, and procedures. He'd told her that if she appeared to be knowledgeable, they probably wouldn't ask her again.

She responded error-free, so the lieutenant moved on to reminding the night shift they needed to check the e-learning portal for some new training orders.

After the briefing was over, she hustled down the stairs to be at the front of the line for equipment from the kit room. She still hadn't met her training officer, Sutton.

Casting a glance at the name tags on the uniforms surrounding her, she didn't spot him.

After collecting their vehicle keys, radios, shotgun, the beanbag shotgun, Tasers and fingerprint gear, she spotted an officer swaggering down the hallway. Styrofoam cup of coffee in hand, he sauntered toward her. About ten feet away, he yelled to her.

"You Buckner?"

"Yes, sir!"

"Get that equipment out to the black and white. I'll be out in a few minutes."

She eyed the pile of equipment she needed to move, grabbed the radio and Taser she'd checked out for him. She hurried over to him and held them out to him.

"Is that your tube against that wall unattended? You don't leave a firearm abandoned—ever."

Her cheeks warmed, looking at the shotgun she'd set next to her war bag. "Yes, sir. It won't happen again."

"It won't happen again, who?" Sutton smirked at two cops standing next to him as he took the offered equipment. The other officers appeared to be enjoying the show.

"It won't happen again, *sir*."

Her partner sipped his coffee. "Go on now. Get the car set up."

"Roger that, sir."

She turned away. From the heat on her cheeks, she knew her face flamed.

A young officer who'd finished signing out his gear

nudged her with his elbow. Without a word he slung the beanbag shotgun over his shoulder, hoisted his war bag containing the radios and Taser on the other one. His hands were left free to carry the print kit and the 12 gauge.

Following suit, she trailed the young officer out the rear door.

"I'm Mike," he said as they made their way to the parking lot where the patrol vehicles stood waiting in the stalls.

"Amber," she replied, looking at the tag on the keys for the vehicle number.

"It sucks you got partnered with Sutton. He's a prick. But on the plus side, he knows what he's doing."

"Thanks."

"Good luck. You're gonna need it."

During the early hours of her shift, her partner drove around their assigned area pointing out the problem locations and quizzed her on "what-if" scenarios.

She thought her responses were credible, but her TO chided her, telling her she was way off.

They eventually got a radio call of a residential burglary. They needed to take the report.

Sutton took the lead, explaining as he went how to conduct the investigation and what signs to look for. The point of entry was easy—someone had broken a rear window. But he also showed her to check for pry marks on any likely points of entry. "If everything else is locked up, usually breaking the glass is the way they get inside. In rare cases, if they've used tools and left impressions, and we catch a suspect with his tools, we can match them."

She listened as he advised the homeowners which

possessions they shouldn't touch because if the burglar hadn't worn gloves, there might be fingerprints.

He directed her to start the burglary report and get a list of items taken.

Back at the station, she handed her completed investigation to the watch commander, who reviewed it and told her she'd done a great job.

It was after eleven when they returned to their patrol vehicle.

"Let's head over to Pancho's for Code 7. Best place in the division for Mexican food."

She picked up the mic to ask for their lunch break.

"No. Don't request yet. Wait until we're there. We only have a half hour, and we'll kill thirty minutes driving there. Get to where you want to eat, *then* contact the dispatcher."

Once they pulled into the parking lot of a taco stand, he nodded to her.

"21A1 requesting Code 7 at Topanga and Roscoe."

"21A1, okay 7."

While they ate, Sutton asked if she had questions about anything they'd done.

"At the burglary, why didn't we take the fingerprints ourselves? We have a print kit."

He swallowed the last of his second taco. "We're lucky. We've got a couple of old-timers at the station whose only function is to lift prints. They're as good, if not better, than the SID guys."

"Then why bring the print equipment?"

He shrugged. "So if I get a chance, I can teach you. But you don't need to think about prints on day one. I need you to be capable of writing a report." He looked at his watch. "21A1 show us clear."

"21A1 handle the shooting just occurred Sherman Way and Variel at the Bounce House. Handle Code 3."

Pumped with adrenaline, Amber chucked her trash and drink into a nearby trash barrel, then keyed the mic clipped to her shirt. "21A1 Roger."

As they jogged to their car, she called out to Sutton. "A bounce house is open this time of night?"

He jeered as they jumped into the vehicle. "It's a strip club."

3

———

ROY

After watching the evening news, Roy wondered for the hundredth time how Amber was doing at work. He turned off the TV.

"Okay, Gage. You need to get ready for bed."

The toddler, surrounded by toys, continued to play with his train set.

"Did you hear me?"

The little boy shook his head.

He smiled but forced more authority into his voice. "Gage. It's time for night-night. Put your choo-choo away."

"No."

"What did you say, young man?"

"No."

He marched over and squatted down next to his son. "You don't tell Daddy no." He grabbed several of the train cars and tossed them into the big plastic container where they were stored when not being used.

The boy howled in protest.

He took in the toddler's distressed face with tears streaming down his cheeks. He kept his tone soft. "Stop."

"Twain."

"We're done playing with trains today. You need to get clean before bed."

"No," Gage wailed.

He frowned and then forced his features to relax. "I have a great idea, but you have to stop crying before I'll tell you."

The boy struggled to stop his tears and calm himself into gulping hiccups.

"What if you didn't have to take a bath, but we gave you a shower instead? Like Daddy."

The child's face lit up. "Sower?"

"Like a big boy."

"'K."

"But before the shower, we have to put away the toys.

The toddler picked up a train car and threw it in the box. Then he hurried to collect the others.

A half hour later, he was showered, in his pajamas, and wearing a dry diaper.

Roy had his son stand on the toilet lid while he combed his hair. "How about a bedtime story now?"

Gage nodded.

He swept him into his arms and carried him into his bedroom. A rocking chair sat near the window, and the crib was against the wall. He set the boy down and pointed to cubbies along another wall that held a few toys and dozens of kid books. "Pick out which story you want me to read."

He waddled to the cabinet and pulled out a book with fire trucks and police cars on the front.

"That one?"

The little boy nodded. "Binky."

He eyed the pacifier on top of the shelving. "Do you need a binky? You're a big boy. You took a shower."

"Binky."

At least he's not crying for a bottle. Choose your battles, Dad.

"Okay. Get the binky."

Gage grinned and stood on tiptoes to reach his prize. He popped it into his mouth and toddled back to him.

"Okay, Son. This is an exciting story about firemen and police officers and the good work they do."

4

———

AMBER

As they tore through the city streets to the shooting, Amber watched for inattentive drivers who might pull out in front of them.

Lights and siren blaring, they approached intersections, and she looked for approaching cross-traffic from her side of the car. "Clear right!" The noise, lights, and speed had her adrenaline level running as fast as their patrol vehicle.

Sutton keyed the mic on his uniform. "21A1, is there a suspect description, and where they were last seen?"

"21A1, suspect is a male Hispanic, gray shirt, black jeans, twenty to twenty-five years. Last seen fleeing the rear of the location. No further."

"21A1, roger." Sutton glanced at her. "Got that?"

"Male Hispanic, gray shirt, black jeans."

"21A43, show us Code 6 in the area of A1's call."

Her TO smirked. "Fish and Rudy."

Several other units notified communications they too were en route to the incident.

"Shooting at the titty bar, and everyone wants to roll."

As they approached the location, she saw citizens waving their arms and pointing frantically toward the Bounce House.

He pulled their patrol vehicle in front of a barber shop across the street. "Keep distance between us. Any one of those *borrachos* might have a gun."

Amber did as she was told, trusting he knew how to deal with a drunk crowd. Far away she heard another siren that she recognized as a rescue ambulance—or RA.

Her partner approached the people. "Is the manager here?" He scanned the group, who stared back at him. "*Donde esta el jefe?*"

A Hispanic man with a ponytail and wearing well-worn cowboy boots stepped forward. "Me. I'm in charge."

"What happened?"

"One of the girls was giving a guy a private dance in the champagne lounge. Some other player comes in and starts yelling at the dancer. The customer is pissed and squares off against the dude interrupting his fun. The guy shot him, then ran out the back door."

"Describe the shooter."

"Male Latino, dark shirt, and black pants. Some kind of ink on his neck."

"You sure about the tattoo? Could you tell what it was?"

The man shook his head.

"Where is the guy who was shot?"

"Still in the VIP room."

Another unit rolled to the front of the gentlemen's club, and the two officers exited their vehicle.

Sutton called out to them. "Hey, will you get FIs and statements from these guys? We've got to find the victim."

The officers pulled out Field Interview cards and started asking for ID.

"Buckner! Come on." He pushed through the crowd into the strip joint.

She followed him to a smaller chamber off the main showroom area.

They pushed aside a red velveteen curtain and saw a man writhing on the floor, groaning.

Her partner yelled for someone to turn on the overhead lights.

Seconds later the room was filled with light. The black painted walls looked chalkboard gray. The purple and pink neon lights that circled the ceiling were washed out, as were the spotlights that lit the forefront of the customer's plush chair.

Several scantily clad females in platform stilettos surrounded the downed man. As the cops approached, all but one of the girls scattered.

Amber could see the victim had been shot in the shoulder.

"Ahhh, *estoy muriendo*," the injured guy moaned.

"You're not dying," Sutton said with disdain. He looked at her. "Get an FI on him." He touched the elbow of the girl who stood looking down at the wounded customer.

The stripper startled, and when her gaze landed on him, her eyes widened.

"Miss, I need some information from you."

The woman edged away. "I...I don't know anything." She turned and strode on her seven-inch platform heels toward a black-painted door hidden in the wall.

"Hey, come back here."

The girl continued to walk.

"Hey! You get the hell over here."

He marched after her and grabbed her by the arm.

Amber looked up from where she knelt next to the victim.

"Sutton!" A sergeant stood at the red velveteen-curtained entrance of the VIP area.

Her partner paused.

The stripper pulled away and bolted through the door.

The supervisor motioned to Amber. "Go get the dancer. Bring her out here so you're within sight of Sutton while you interview her." He walked over to her partner. "You grab the victim's info. The paramedics are on their way in."

She hastened to follow the girl. The passage led to the area behind the stage in the main showroom.

The sound of heels clicking on the cement floor alerted her to where she could finally catch up to the stripper.

"Ma'am? I need to speak with you for a minute."

The young woman stopped. "I won't talk to that other officer."

Amber smiled. "Half the time *I* don't want to talk to him. I have to get your contact information, but I must return to my partner. Can you please come with me?" She saw hesitation in the entertainer's eyes. "I promise. You won't have to deal with him. You can interact with me."

The young woman gave a slight nod.

"After you," she said, motioning the girl to walk down the

hall. Relief filled her that she'd convinced the woman to comply.

In the private lounge, the paramedics worked on the man on the floor.

Sutton and the sergeant started toward Amber.

The dancer turned. "I'm outta here."

She placed her hand on the stripper's arm. "Wait. I'll take care of it."

Meeting the two men halfway, she looked at her training officer. "I'm not sure what her problem is, but she doesn't like you."

His gaze shot to the girl, who stood nearby biting the cuticle on her index finger. She turned her back to him.

"Sutton, you ride with the victim to the hospital. I'll stay with Buckner while she gets witness statements."

Her TO frowned. "Are *you* working with Buckner, or am I?"

"As your supervisor, I'm telling you to go with the victim in the RA. Buckner will get the girl's statement, and I'll follow her while she drives your vehicle to the ER."

Sutton turned on his heel, muttering under his breath.

The sergeant looked at her. "Lesson one. As a TO, don't challenge a supervisor in front of a probationary officer. You'll always lose. Lesson two. If an arrestee, victim, or witness gets under your skin or refuses to talk to you, let your partner give it a shot."

He glanced at the girl, who watched them carefully. "You're up. Write an FI on her and get her statement about what she saw. I'll listen in and if you miss anything important, I can follow up at the end. Got it?"

"Yes, sir."

Minutes later she didn't have too much more than what the guy in front of the bar had told them, other than the dancer's contact information.

The sergeant reviewed the FI and stepped slightly forward. "Miss Jubilee, this information is all correct?"

"Yes."

"Your *real* name is Jewel Jubilee?"

She gave a wry smile. "My mother was an exotic dancer too."

"Have you ever seen the suspect before—here in the club, or anywhere else?"

The stripper shook her head. "No."

"What about the client you were dancing for? Was he a regular? Had you danced for him before?"

The dancer shrugged. "He's not a regular. I've been doing this a long time. After a while the customers all look alike." She hesitated. "Although I do remember the ones who are big tippers."

Amber paid rapt attention to the questions he asked. She hadn't thought to ask Jewel any of them.

"What were they arguing about?"

Interesting. He's asking the same question I asked earlier. She assumed he was checking to see if the woman gave the same answer as when *she'd* ask the dancer.

"The private customer wanted me to do more than a lap dance. We're not supposed to do anything *extra*. The other guy came in from the main showroom, saw what was going on, and flipped out."

"Then what happened?"

She shrugged. "My client got in the dude's face and pulled

a gun. Then the other guy had a piece and shot the customer."

That's exactly what she told me.

"So, the victim had a firearm and displayed it before he was shot by the second guy?"

"Sure did."

The sergeant shot a look at Amber. "Did you guys find a pistol?"

"No." She looked at the dancer. "Did you see what happened to the customer's gun?"

"Yeah. When he got shot, he dropped it. The dude who shot him picked it up and boogied."

The veteran officer lifted his gaze to the ceiling and circled the room. "Do those security cameras work?"

The stripper shrugged. "I didn't even know this place had them."

5

———

KATIE

Katie was sandwiched between Wiggins and Roy Buckner as they walked through RHD.

She knew why she was sent there and wondered what *his* story was. How did he rate such a cushy assignment?

"Here's where the CCU murder books are kept." The sergeant ushered them into a small room with rows of metal shelves filled with large blue notebooks. "Take a look at the cases and see what captures your interest." He looked at his watch. "If you have any questions, you can ask me or any of the detectives working Homicide. I've got conference call. Gotta run." With a quick wave, he was gone.

Katie appraised her partner. He was a ruggedly handsome man. His cleft chin was framed by prominent dimples, giving his brawny appearance a boyish charm. Assessing him to be in his mid-forties she was surprised to catch herself looking for a wedding ring. More surprising, she was disappointed when she saw the gold band on his finger.

He smiled and looked at the shelves. "Shall we look in some of these books and find a case?"

"Sure. That's what we're here for."

She hated the small talk when working with a new partner. She didn't feel like sharing her personal history—even with a handsome man who, for the first time in ages, had caught her attention.

He walked to the last shelf at the back of the room. "Ah, the older cases are on this end. Is there any particular homicide you'd like to check out?"

She shrugged. "No. I don't care." Was he looking at her funny, or was her anxiety kicking in? She tried to take some deep breaths without being obvious.

He marched to the shelves, pulled out a notebook, and carried it to a table. He opened it to the cover page.

Katie stood to the side, watching for a moment, then grabbed a book for herself and brought it to the table.

"This murder is a working girl who was found in an alley in Southwest Division," he said.

"I've got a homicide that occurred in West Valley during a burglary—at least that's what the original detectives thought."

They flipped through the cold case notebooks for a few more minutes.

He closed his notebook and put it back on the shelf. "I'm starving. Are you hungry? We could grab a bite to eat and get to know each other, then pick a case we'll both want to work."

"Sure. You think it will look bad if we take off for lunch so soon after arriving?"

He winked at her. "Nah. They'll think we've picked a case and are out chasing clues."

His flippant attitude concerned her. But it was hard to resist that wink.

"Okay. You name the place. I'm not that hungry."

6

ROY

Roy hadn't slept well. When his alarm blasted, he shot out of bed and hurried to the kitchen to get some caffeine going. He drank half the mug before he hopped into the shower. Toweling off, he got a burst of energy as the coffee kicked in. He donned his best suit for his new assignment. He then shifted into daddy mode to get his son packed up and dropped off with his in-laws.

Amber came home while he was packing the diaper bag. He asked to hear about her first day on the job, but she'd told him she was too tired to talk about it and wanted to go to bed. Then she'd gone to her bedroom and shut the door.

He had no choice but to gather up Gage, his things, and head out.

As they usually did, George and Ceci Granville watched him with disapproving eyes as he parted ways with his son.

"You listen to your grandparents. They're in charge."

The little boy stood quietly, sucking his pacifier.

"You hear me?"

The toddler nodded, then yawned, dropping the device onto the shiny wooden floor.

Ceci stooped and snatched the plastic mouthpiece and held it with two fingers as if it were a dead carcass.

"Binky," Gage said, holding his arms up to his grandma.

"No." She shook her head. "You're a big boy now. You don't need a pacifier."

"Binky," the toddler repeated as tears filled his eyes.

Roy knelt beside him. "Hey, buddy, let's take you inside. I brought you a banana and some cereal for breakfast. I'm sure Grandma and Grandpa won't mind watching cartoons while you eat."

George gave him a withering glance but remained silent as they made their way into the kitchen.

After kissing Gage and telling him he'd be back later, Roy headed out of the kitchen to the sound of his son's screams. Facing a man with a gun would be easier than having his heart ripped out as he left his child with his judgmental in-laws.

As he hit the freeway downtown to the Police Administration Building, better known as PAB, he sucked high-caffeine coffee from his travel mug. He forced himself to put Gage's cries behind him and focus on his new assignment.

He hadn't even arrived, and he hated his job. He wasn't the kind of cop to work behind a desk, but a year ago, when his wife announced her intent to become a police officer for the LAPD, he'd pledged his support. Unfortunately, Gage hadn't been consulted either and their little boy was also paying a price for his mother's career change.

After Amber had been kidnapped, Roy could understand her wanting to feel safe and encouraged her to take self-defense classes and learn to shoot a gun.

Then one day she dropped the bomb she wanted to become a police officer. He never thought she'd follow through with her idea, and even if she did, he didn't think she'd stick with it through the academy—but she did.

Seven months later, she was graduating, and he was assigned to the Cold Case Unit at Robbery Homicide Division (RHD). Normally, a street officer wouldn't be allowed to be a part of such a prestigious detail, but he was given special treatment.

After his wife's rescue, the chief of police had told Roy if he ever needed anything—no matter how small—to reach out.

Amber's career change meant he had to make adjustments too, and he'd taken the top cop up on his offer to help.

It was his suggestion that Roy should work cold murder cases because it would allow him the most flexibility with his schedule. He'd even winked and said, "The CCU doesn't get scrutinized at COMPSTAT so if you need to adjust for childcare issues, it shouldn't be a problem."

Roy had sighed and agreed. In his heart he was a street cop, and there was a trace of resentment that Amber had changed the course of his career with her desires.

After parking a few blocks from the police headquarters, he weaved between the homeless tents pitched on the sidewalk.

He journeyed to the fifth floor which housed RHD. He was met at the elevator by a tall black man.

"Roy Buckner?"

He nodded.

The tall sergeant extended his hand. I'm the captain's adjutant, Darnell Wiggins. Follow me over to Cold Case Unit —also known as the CCU."

He'd expected to be led to a separate office but instead was ushered to a vast squad room fitted with rows and rows of cubicles.

"You and your partner can set up here. "The sergeant said, pointing to a pair of empty workspaces. Above the desks a black plastic sign with white lettering read Cold Case Unit. He looked across the broad space. "Ah, here comes the skipper with your partner now."

He followed Wiggins's gaze and saw a petite Asian woman trailing a tall, curly-haired, smiling, white guy wearing a captain's badge.

The man stepped away from the woman to shake his hand. "Glen Haywood. You must be Buckner. We've heard a lot of good things about you. Welcome to RHD." He turned to the female. "Do you two know each other?"

They shook their heads.

"Kada Nanako, this is Roy Buckner." Their boss beamed. "You guys will be partnered up."

"Actually, I prefer to be called Katie."

Haywood nodded with enthusiasm. "I hear you loud and clear. We can do that, can't we, Darnell?"

Roy shook Katie's hand. "Nice to meet you." She had a firm grip but didn't say a word.

The captain slapped him on the shoulder. "Let's go have a chat." He glanced at Wiggins. "Show Kada—I mean Katie, around and help her get settled."

Roy followed his boss along the perimeter of the boxy work areas to an office midway along the wall.

Haywood ushered him into an office with floor to ceiling windows on the exterior wall. He had a unique perspective of the CalTrans headquarters across the street. Prior to this view, Roy had never noticed the building looked like a giant cargo container perched at the corner of 1st and Main.

"Take a load off," said the captain. He gestured toward a vinyl, padded seat in front of his desk. "It's great to add you to our team." He sank into his black leather executive chair.

"Thank you, sir."

"Hey, when it's just you and me, you can call me Glen."

He smiled at his boss, wondering why he was coming off so buddy-buddy.

A somber expression took over Haywood's face. "I'm sorry that you and your wife had to go through such a devastating experience a couple of years ago." His expression brightened. "However, I understand she's overcome it, and recently graduated from the academy."

"Last week."

"Where is she doing her probation?"

"Topanga Division," he replied warily. *Why the hell do you care?*

The captain nodded. "That's not too bad. Probably close to home?"

Roy smiled and nodded.

"Well, you're a good man to allow his wife do what she

needs to do to heal. I think you've got a young son now, right?"

The patronizing attitude about his family caused him to clench his jaw. "Yep."

"Good. Good." He leaned forward. "Let me tell you a little bit about what we do here. We look at unsolved homicides with fresh eyes. We re-interview witnesses, re-test DNA, all in the hope that something new will result allowing us to catch the killer and close the case." He smiled. "Most of the detectives who come into Homicide Special want to crack the big cases. You know, they think they'll solve the Black Dahlia or who *really* killed Nicole Simpson and Ron Goldman." He gave a caustic laugh.

Roy forced a smile.

"Anyway, since you and Kada are fresh to the unit, you can choose any homicide you'd like."

"I think she wants to be called Katie."

The captain grinned and waved a dismissive hand. "Whatever. Wiggins will show you where the CCU murder books are located."

"Great."

Haywood rose, indicating their meeting was over. "Cold cases are an easy gig and the perfect assignment for you and Kada. You each needed a low-stress, flexible spot. We're happy to have you both."

"Thank you, sir." *Why aren't you telling me what's wrong with my partner? I know why I'm assigned here. What's her problem?*

The men shook hands, and he made his way back to his cubicle, where Katie and Wiggins stood chatting.

The adjutant looked up at him. "Ready to solve some cases?"

"Captain Haywood mentioned something about the cold case murder books," Roy said.

The adjutant smiled. "Yeah. Follow me."

7

———

AMBER

Loud pounding woke Amber out of a deep sleep. Disoriented, she stumbled like a drunk and weaved down the hallway. As she got closer to the front of the house, she could hear her son's voice.

She squinted at the clock on the fireplace mantle. One o'clock. Weren't her parents supposed to keep Gage until three? She opened the door.

Her parents' dour demeanor told the story. Her little boy, on the other hand, was thrilled to see her.

"Mama!" He raised his arms for her to hold him.

She scooped him up while motioning her parents inside.

They followed her to the kitchen, where she set Gage down and threw a pod into the coffee machine.

She looked at her mom and dad. "How'd it go?"

"It was fine, dear. But the baby was getting cranky, and we

didn't want to put him down for a nap and then have to wake him to bring him home at three, so we brought him back a little early."

"It's okay, Mom." *Heaven forbid you let him sleep past three.*

Her father came to stand beside her as the coffeemaker distilled the brew into her mug. "How was your first day? You look tired."

She told them about the shooting at the strip club.

"I don't like the fact you've given up a perfectly safe career taking care of babies to roam the streets at night with a gun."

She sighed. "Gosh, Dad, you make it sound like I'm out marauding instead of trying to catch crooks." She held up another coffee pod. "Anybody want some?"

Her mother shook her head and put an arm across her shoulder. "Your father doesn't mean any disrespect. We worry about you."

"I appreciate your concern, but there's no reason to be anxious. I'll be fine."

"There was an officer killed last night in New Orleans," her father said, his tone clipped.

"I understand, Dad. But I've had some of the best police training in world."

"Well, I don't like it and I never will. You should have stayed a Neo-natal ICU nurse. You were a damned good one."

Her mom glided to her husband and placed her hand on his arm. "George, you mustn't get yourself all worked up."

Then she looked at her daughter. "Listen, dear, we want to help you as much as we can, but we won't be able to babysit little Gage like we'd thought. It's too disruptive to our schedule."

She stared at them in disbelief. The three of them had

talked about the arrangement for months. They'd agreed to watch the boy after Roy went to work so she could sleep after working for twelve hours each night. "What am I supposed to do? I need the morning to get rest."

"I know, dear, but Daddy golfs two times a week, and volunteers at the hospital on Wednesdays. I have my mahjong group on Tuesday mornings, and my bowling league early on Fridays."

Amber ran a hand through her hair. "Can you at least watch him until we find someone else?"

Her mother frowned. "I guess so. You know we want to help, but we're well beyond our parenting years."

"Okay."

"Mama." Gage wrapped his arms around her thigh.

"Let's go, Ceci." Her father looked at her. "Will Ray be home before you leave for your job?"

"I'm not sure. I've been asleep all morning...and you know his name is Roy. I'll call him in a little while and see what's up. But to play it safe, you'd better plan to watch him when I go to work."

"All right, dear." Her mother smiled at her. "Maybe you can put the boy down for his nap and get more rest for yourself."

Sure, Mom. After a cup of strong coffee, sleep will come easily.

Relieved when her parents left, she gave Gage a snack and worried how she was going to make the scheduling fly...and how she'd appease her crusty partner.

8

———

ROY

Roy and Katie grabbed a radio and signed out on a white board that kept track of which detectives were in the building or out.

He slipped on his sunglasses against the overcast glare. "Any preferences on where we go to eat?"

"No. I'm not hungry, but Justice in Little Tokyo has good eats, and it's a short walk."

"Never been there. Lead the way."

A few minutes later, they were in a corner, tucked at a table for two.

"Hello. I'm Steven, and I'll be your server. Can I bring you something to drink?"

"Iced tea for me," Roy said.

"Chardonnay, please."

Great. First day back, and my partner is drinking on duty. He gave her a fixed stare and arched an eyebrow.

"Oh, relax. It's a glass of wine. I'm not getting tanked. I just want to smooth the edge of returning to the job and being shipped downtown."

"What do you mean being *shipped downtown*? Are you being disciplined?"

Katie sighed. "No. I've been off for a while. What about you? How is it a P-3 working patrol is assigned to Homicide Special in the Cold Case Unit? You either have dirt on someone or somebody owed you a big favor."

He shook his head. "Neither. They gave me a pity assignment."

The server returned with their drinks and took their food order.

"You were telling me how you wound up at RHD," she said, after taking a sip of her wine.

"My wife is Amber Buckner. Two years ago, she was kidnapped by Seth—"

"Seth Farley, whacko cop and serial murderer. Oh my God. I didn't make the connection. I'm sorry. How is she doing?"

"Well enough that she joined the LAPD, and her first shift was last night."

"Wasn't she a nurse or something...and pregnant?"

He nodded. We have an eighteen-month-old boy, Gage."

"And being a cop?"

"That's how I wound up working at RHD. After the Farley thing, the chief told me if I ever needed anything, to let him know. With Amber on probation, I had to have a job with steady hours and with little possibility of overtime."

"Why not give you a spot in a detective unit closer to home?"

He chuckled. "That's what I asked. Commuting downtown isn't my idea of a fun time." He added sugar to his iced tea. "The chief told me it would be a good career move and a lot less stressful. We handle cases that have nowhere to go but up."

Katy smiled. "In other words, if we fail, no harm, no foul."

"I guess that's one way to look at it."

"What about you? It sounded like you didn't want to work downtown. What's your story?"

"Well, I—"

The server appeared, plates in hand. "Here we go. Chopped salad for the lady, and the spicy salmon for the gentleman. Do you need anything else?"

"No thanks." He returned his gaze to Katie. "You were about to tell me how you wound up at RHD."

"It's not something I want talk about."

How should he respond to her statement? He didn't like it. If he was working with someone who was unstable or physically limited, he had a right to know.

"Look, Katie, I'm not trying to pry, but you indicated you weren't especially happy to be assigned downtown. I've no doubt there are people in the department who have the information you want to keep from me. It won't be hard to find out what you're not willing to share, but I'd rather hear it from you without all the spin others will put on the story for effect."

She'd dropped her gaze to her salad as he spoke. When she looked up, her dark brown eyes were filled with pain.

"You wouldn't even have to ask around. You could do an

internet search and find me." She sipped her wine. "I killed my husband and my son."

She searched his gaze for a reaction.

He hoped he kept his expression unreadable. "Tell me about it."

Her mouth formed a thin line, and she blinked away tears. Her gaze fell on her glass, and she gulped the contents.

"My husband was a pharmacist and was returning from a convention in New York. His plane was arriving at one thirty a.m. He'd planned on using Uber to get home, but I wanted to surprise him. I packed up our little boy, Koji, and headed to LAX." She gave a small smile. "My son was so sleepy but would wake any time I stopped for a red light."

She put a childlike tone into her voice. "Are we there yet, Mommy? Is Daddy here?" A lone tear rolled down her cheek. "Not yet. I'll tell you when we get there.

"Hiroki was so surprised to see us at the baggage carousel. He grinned from ear to ear and held us both so tight." She smiled again. "Of course, he scolded me for us being out so late in the cold. It was November."

She signaled to the server to bring another glass of wine. "I was driving. My husband was telling me about his trip. Koji was asleep in his car seat in the back seat." She paused and licked her lips. "A drunk ran the light and T-boned us. It was a roll-over, and we crashed into an electrical pole. They were both killed. I was banged up but lived." She bowed her head, discreetly wiping away the tears rolling down her cheeks.

Roy couldn't imagine the pain and guilt she must carry every day—especially when she'd see a little boy her son's age.

His heart went out to her. She was forever damaged, and nothing could correct the situation.

"I'm so sorry," he mumbled, feeling lame.

Their server appeared. "Here's that glass of wine," he enthused as he slid the drink across the table. "Can I get you anything else?"

9

____

HAYWOOD

Glen Haywood gazed through the window in his office, which faced the detective squad room. The newbies, Buckner and Nanako, were coming in from somewhere. He'd have Wiggins find out where they'd been and what they were working on.

He wasn't happy when his unit got stuck with problem children. He couldn't very well tell the chief no, but he hated the responsibility of babysitting a couple of special cases. He didn't have too much concern about Buckner, although it must be plenty embarrassing to try to rescue your wife from a maniac only to fail and get shot in the process.

The female, Nanako, didn't seem quite right. Even though the department's chief psychologist had deemed her fit for duty, he wasn't convinced.

When he'd met with her this morning, she'd seemed in a

daze, as though nothing around her was registering. Her eyes seemed to be huge zeros.

He studied the pair as they shuffled into the storage area containing the dead-end murder books.

He opened his office door and motioned to Wiggins.

The adjutant ended the call he was on and responded.

"The newbies, Null and Void. Where'd they go and what are they working on?"

"I think they went out to lunch. I don't think they've chosen a case to work yet. I can go see what they're up to, if you'd like."

"Nah. Hit them up at the end of the day. I want to be sure they've picked something to fill their time and do their job."

"Got it. Anything else?"

"Keep your eye on them."

10

ROY

"Hey, Katie," Roy said as they entered the murder book storage area, "I think I know the case I'd like to work on, unless you have a preference."

She shrugged and shook her head.

He wondered if she truly didn't care, or was her deference a result of the two glasses of wine she'd downed at lunch?

He walked the shelves of the notebooks, searching the victims' names. "It's the homicide of a policeman. He was a probationer of mine. Adam Lowe. Good kid and a better cop. Shot in front of his house as he returned home after his shift."

"They couldn't solve it?"

"Nope." He pulled a binder from the shelf. "Here it is. Let's see why not. Maybe we can get justice for Adam." He slid a chair to the table and motioned Katie to pull her seat next to his.

Once settled he turned to the chronological log. The form was a record of events documenting the investigation thus far, and the detective authoring the entry. He read from the log.

Katie had a pad of paper and jotted notes. She chewed a minty piece of gum.

"Okay, the murder happened eleven years ago. Adam Lowe, age twenty-six was gunned down outside his house in West Hills after returning home from work. Two body shots. No sign of robbery."

"Any wits?"

Roy turned to the crime report in another section of the binder. "Nothing listed here. Let me check further in the chrono log. Maybe they turned up someone later."

He thumbed back to where he started and skimmed all the entries. "Well this sucks. Apparently, there were no witnesses."

"Any mention of video?"

He perused the log entries. "They looked, but it was a residential neighborhood. Eleven years ago home cameras weren't as popular as they are now." He sighed. "I'm familiar with this area. This is way on the west side of the Valley off Roscoe Boulevard. It's nothing but homes.

Even if they'd wanted to canvas commercial cameras, there aren't any businesses in that particular area. You couldn't ask for a better location to commit a murder where it was unlikely video would be a factor—and even if there was video, eleven years ago they weren't very sophisticated—resolution was terrible."

"What about suspects?"

He perused the binder. "Looks like the previous detectives eliminated the wife. They talked to a brother and recent partners, but nothing came of it. They were looking at a couple of gangsters from the South Side Slayers but didn't come up with anything solid."

Katie leaned back in her chair. "So, we've picked a homicide with no clues to go on. Excellent choice."

He flipped the notebook closed. "You don't wanna work this one, fine. You pick a case. But I can guarantee you none of these cases are going to be easy. They're cold for a reason." He stood. "I've got some e-learning to catch up on. Let me know when you've found something easier."

He left her with the notebooks and walked with purpose to the cubicle they shared and sat at his desk. He turned on his computer and logged in.

A minute later she entered their workspace, slid into her chair, and swiveled to face him. "Hey, I didn't mean to make you mad."

"I'm not angry, but I was hoping to have a partner who wasn't afraid to put in some effort. Adam Lowe was a cop—one of us. Someone hunted him down in the middle of the night and killed him. I want to find out why. I bet his family would like to know too."

"Okay. That's fine. We'll handle the Lowe case." She glanced at the e-learning screen on his computer. "Besides, anything is better than frying your brain on Assisted Outpatient Treatment training. I'll go get the murder book."

PART II

SUTTON

As Duane Sutton changed from street clothes into his uniform, he delighted in the fact he had a new female probationer to toy with. He didn't care that she'd survived a kidnapping and rape. In fact, that made her an easier target. She was damaged goods. He didn't trust her. No matter how well she performed as a police officer, because of her trauma, there would always be an unknown trigger—a trigger that could cost him his life. The sooner he got rid of Amber Buckner, the better.

"Yo, Sutton. How you doin' with your P-1? She give you a blow job yet?" Laughter filled the locker room.

He smiled good-naturedly. He could afford to be magnanimous to his co-workers. As the most senior officer on the watch, he didn't have to answer to anyone. The watch commanders respected his time on the job and pretty much left him alone. Except for that sergeant who'd just transferred to Topanga. Last night he'd made him look bad in front Buckner. He planned to meet up and have a chat with the supervisor and set him straight.

Young officers fresh off probation looked to Sutton for his knowledge and experience and rightly so. He knew better than anyone how to pad a log, engineer overtime, or take credit for an arrest he didn't make.

But probationary officers feared him. He was known as *The Axe*. If a probationary officer wasn't doing well, he was their worst nightmare. And if the probationer was female, she could expect to do twice the work of a male P-1 *and* get criticized for taking so long to do it.

Then there was his newest trainee. He knew all about her. Kidnapped and raped, she'd managed to dispatch her captor all by herself.

The captains, lieutenants, and sergeants, even regular cops treated her with a god-like reverence. Yeah, she'd killed a guy. So what? That didn't mean she could cut it on the street. She'd have to prove herself—just like everyone else.

He finished dressing and strolled into the break room to grab a cup of coffee. He wasn't surprised to see his closest allies on the shift already shooting the breeze, coffee in hand.

"Hey, D, how's it going?" Neville Bass, known around the station as Fish, raised his paper cup to him as Sutton entered. "Another day. Another dollar."

Rodolfo Gomez, another P-2 nodded. "This shit sure gets old, doesn't it? I'd rather be home boning my wife—no wait. I'd rather be boning that new waitress at the Country Kitchen."

"Yeah, in your dreams, Rudy. I hear that waitress has been

screwing her way through day watch," he said. "By the time you nail her, somebody will have given her crabs, the clap, or worse."

Rudy made a face. "Don't ruin it for me. I've been jerking off to her for the past two weeks."

"And that's about as close to her as you'll ever get." Fish laughed.

"Yeah, as if you could do any better," Rudy grumbled.

"God, you two sound like an old married couple," he muttered.

Rudy grinned. "Did you see the stacked red-head at the Bounce House last night? Tits out to here." He raised his hands in front of his barrel chest.

Sutton frowned. "No. That new sergeant had *me* ride with the victim in the RA. *He* stayed with my partner to interview witnesses. If you ask me, I think he wants a taste of the Buckner pussy."

Fish smiled. "So, what's the story with her? Did she tell you about what happened with Seth Farley?"

"Nope. I didn't ask her about it, and she didn't bring it up. I figure that the moron who mentions it will have her running to supervision and making a claim about harassment."

Rudy threw his empty cup in the trash. "Did she seem to be okay or is she whacky?"

Duane made a face. "It was only one night. We'll see how things go." He sneered at his buddies. "But I won't make it easy for her, that's for sure."

12

____

KATIE

Driving home, Katie reviewed her day. She'd really blown it. She'd broken down and cried in front of her partner. Of course, her emotional lapse was probably due to the two glasses of wine she'd had at lunch. What was she thinking? What must he think of her?

She'd have to find the right moment to explain how nervous she'd been and how hard it was to talk about losing Hiroki and Koji.

She was unsure about Roy. He seemed like he was no-nonsense, and it was obvious he didn't like being challenged. She'd been joking about his choice of case, but she'd been insensitive. To him it was about a friend being murdered. He knew the man who'd died personally. For him it wasn't a joke.

The only way to make it up to him is to work hard and find something to solve the crime.

The drive from downtown to her condo in Santa Clarita was brutal—especially this time of day. She'd have to talk to him and see if they could agree on a start of watch where they'd both miss most of the traffic.

One of the perks of being assigned to the CCU was they'd been given the privilege to choose their working hours. They might as well take advantage of the offer. Roy had childcare issues. She'd defer to him. She had no similar responsibilities.

She thought of her little Koji. *Don't go there. You've been there once today. That's enough.*

She turned her mind to the Adam Lowe case. A cop goes home after working all night and is murdered in the driveway outside his house. No one sees anything, and no one hears anything. No clues, no suspects, no witnesses. *No chance in hell we're going to solve this homicide.*

13

ROY

Dealing with George and Ceci Granville was the price Roy had to pay for loving their daughter. They hated him—and had since they'd first met him.

George had groomed his daughter to be a nurse so she could meet and fall in love with a prosperous doctor. Someone with a status rivaling his own as prestigious heart surgeon.

Instead, she'd introduced her parents to him—a divorced street cop. And they hadn't been happy.

On the front porch of the Granville home, he shifted his mental state from lowly civil servant to tolerant son-in-law. Then he knocked.

When his father-in-law responded, his features were taut. "It's after six. I thought you got off work at five."

"May I come in?"

George drew the opening wider, allowing him to enter.

"My end of watch is at five. But I'm driving from downtown now. There's a lot of traffic."

The older man closed the door and stomped deeper into the house. "We had traffic in Phoenix too. I didn't need over an hour to get through it." He flounced into the family room and plopped into his favorite chair.

Roy kept his pithy response to himself. Thankfully, Gage spotted him and ran to him at full speed.

"Da-da!"

He swept his son up into his arms and held him close. "Were you a good boy for Grandma and Grandpa?"

The toddler nodded.

Ceci came from the kitchen. "Evening, Roy. How did your new job go?"

His gaze swept the den where toys were scattered and throw pillows dotted the floor. "Apparently, a lot less eventful than the activities here."

Ceci fixed a tight smile on her mouth. "The boy can be quite a handful. Small children and tidy homes don't go hand-in-hand."

Uh oh. You insulted her. Fix it! "Tell me about it. We have a heck of a time keeping things neat at our place. No sooner is one toy put away than he brings out two more."

The firm lines relaxed a bit. "Have you heard from Amber?" She lowered her voice. "Last night she was in a strip club. We simply must make her quit this ridiculous notion of being a police officer."

He shook his head. "Good luck with that. She's determined to struggle through."

George turned off the television and rose from his chair

and faced them. "Well, you need to do something else about the boy. Ceci and I are too old to care for a little one all day. We told Amber that this morning."

Aw, shit.

"We told her we could finish out this week," Ceci said quickly. "We're just so busy." Her gaze searched his as she spoke quickly. "Do you think that she'd quit the LAPD if there was no one to care for Gage?"

"You're wasting your time. She worked long and hard to get through the academy. I think we all know she's not a quitter."

Ceci let out a breath. "Surely there's something *you* can do or say to encourage her to go back to nursing." Tears formed in his mother-in-law's eyes. "Officers are getting killed almost every day somewhere in the country. I don't want my little girl to be one of them."

He sighed. "I'd be lying if I said I wasn't worried and afraid. But she's had excellent training. She persevered through an experience that most people wouldn't have survived, man or woman." He took Ceci's hand. "You've got to trust her. That's what I'm doing."

14

———

AMBER

Amber's stomach gurgled as she made her way from roll call down to the kit room, where she checked out the equipment she and Sutton would need.

By the time he strolled outside, she had their tools and accoutrements in the SUV, the gas tank topped off, and had logged onto the car's computer. She'd parked their patrol vehicle near the back door.

He looked annoyed that she was prepared and waiting for him. He opened the rear cargo compartment and threw his war bag inside, then slid inside the driver's seat.

"Did you check the lights and siren?"

"Uh, no sir." *Damn. I won't forget that again.*

He blew out an irritated breath and flipped a switch to test the safety apparatus, then quickly shut them down. "Let's hit it," he said, pulling out of the station parking lot. "Show us out to the station."

She punched a button on their computer, alerting the dispatcher they weren't available for radio calls.

Sutton drove to a small mom-and-pop cafe in a strip mall. One other police vehicle was already parked in front. "A good cop never goes hungry. You want to eat early because you might not get another chance if it gets busy."

If you were smart, you'd eat before you came to work. She tempered being smug because although she'd had coffee during her drive to the station, she was still tired from not getting enough sleep. While her partner ate, she could consume more caffeine.

Entering the restaurant, they spotted two officers sitting in a booth near the back.

Her TO motioned she should enter the booth before him. He plopped down beside her.

She noticed the officers' name tags. Bass and Gomez. She extended her hand across the table. "Hi. I'm Amber Buckner."

Bass and Gomez hesitated. Bass cleared his throat. "Neville Bass, but everyone calls me Fish." He gave her hand a quick shake.

"You can call me Rudy," said Gomez, barely giving her hand a squeeze.

The server came and took their order.

Sutton and the others asked her about her stint at the academy and quizzed her about some of the instructors *they'd* had when in training. Then they told her how much harder the academy was when they'd gone through.

"Yeah, the department's gone to hell in a hand-basket. They'll let anyone in these days," Gomez said.

She sipped her coffee, knowing they were hoping to upset her. She wasn't bothered in the least and didn't see any point to calling them out.

"21A1, are you clear?"

The dispatcher was looking for them. Amber glanced at her partner.

He keyed his mic. "We're at the station until further. We'll be clearing shortly."

"Roger." The dispatcher's tone carried annoyance.

She knows we're not at the station.

"21A43, are you clear?"

Fish responded. "Negative. We're with A21. We'll clear shortly."

She swallowed a sigh. *So, this is how police work is done.*

15

HAYWOOD

A few blocks from police headquarters, Glen Haywood strode into The Cherry Pick Cafe. He caught the eye of the plump server he always flirted with, and she waved him over to a table by the window where he sat down.

"Mornin', Glen. You by yourself, or are you expecting someone?"

"Today, Violeta, I'm meeting with a co-worker."

Marnie Vega walked through the front door.

"In fact, there she is now."

Violeta turned to eye the trim woman giving Glen a pretty smile.

"You always break my heart, Glen. You always say they're co-workers, but their eyes and smile say something completely different." She winked at him and placed two menus on the table. "Two coffees?"

"Yes, please."

Marnie smiled at Violeta as the server scurried away.

She slid into her seat. "Did you order coffee?"

"Yes, and I highly recommend the omelet, although the French toast is excellent if you're not watching your carbs."

She smiled at him again. "You tell me—do I need to watch what I eat?"

He laughed and shook his head. "Oh no. I'm not dumb enough to fall into that trap." He watched a homeless guy pee outside the window and wave his dick at Marnie. "So, why are you downtown today?"

"The chief wants to meet with all the Valley command staff." She shrugged. "Probably a pep talk for us to reduce our crime numbers and reach out to the community more."

Violeta brought their coffee and took their order, then hustled to the kitchen.

Marnie stirred creamer into her cup. "What's going on with you? I haven't seen you for over a week."

"Same old shit. They keep pulling my detectives for specialized units, but then send me replacements who are problem children."

"Why would RHD get problem children? You guys handle the high-profile crimes in the city."

"Because I can stick them into the Cold Case Unit. The brass has pretty much cannibalized my command anyway, so any bodies we receive from other divisions at least keeps the CCU active."

The server brought their food—French toast for him, and an omelet for her.

He broke off a piece of bacon and popped it into his mouth. "The two I got yesterday are both head cases. One is a detective who was driving her car with her husband and kid. They were hit by a deuce, and the spouse and child were killed. She's been on the rubber gun squad and off the job for over a year."

Marnie's jaw dropped. "She's mentally unstable and they let her come back?"

He lifted his hands as though surrendering. "The department shrink swears she's fit for duty, but I gotta tell you, when I look in her eyes, I see nothin' there. She's like a friggin' zombie."

Marnie swallowed a bite of egg. "I don't get it. Although, I guess the city figures that a zombie detective is better than none—especially if she's tucked away where she'll have little contact with the public and not be under any stress." She took a sip of coffee. "You got two. What about the other one?"

Haywood sighed. "He's a patrol guy who needed a spot where he wouldn't have to work a lot of overtime due to childcare needs. You might remember him, Roy Buckner. His wife is the one who was kidnapped by Seth Farley—"

"Oh, I know all about it," she said, nodding. "His wife graduated from the academy last week, and they shipped her to *me*. She's assigned to Topanga."

He rolled his eyes. "Ah, yes. He told me that yesterday. I didn't make the connection." He grinned at her. "You've got a piece of the Buckner mess as well. Have you met her?"

She shook her head. "As her captain I suppose I should. But it's kind of awkward. Do I come across as sympathetic, or should I go more hardcore? Do your job and, by the way, rape victim or not, you're not getting any special treatment. Although, apparently the Buckners already are benefiting if we're giving them assignments based on childcare issues."

"Well, he seemed okay." He scoffed. "Poor shmuck dealing with a head case at home *and* the job. Before you know it, he'll be ready for the rubber gun squad too."

16

———

ROY

Roy sat at his desk, running a rap sheet. The Lowe murder book sat open next to his computer.

"Well, aren't you the early bird," Katie said, setting her purse on her desk and taking a sip of coffee from her stainless-steel coffee mug.

"Traffic was moving this morning. No clue why."

She leaned over his shoulder and looked at his computer screen. "Who is Antonio Lima?"

He swiveled in his chair to face her as she moved over to her desk and turned on her computer.

"I thought we should take another look at the notation on the chrono log about the two gangsters from the South Side Slayers."

"Did you find something unusual?"

He sighed. "No, but from all the info in the murder book,

that info at least holds some potential of being connected. Let's face it, the Slayers are stone cold assholes and wouldn't hesitate to assassinate a cop."

Katie sat and sipped from her mug, then smiled. "So, who is Antonio Lima?"

He turned back to his computer screen, where a rap sheet was displayed. "He's been popped and convicted several times for possession of a firearm and ADW, along with a number of burglary arrests, and narcotics sales." He squinted at the screen. "He served two years at the state prison in Lancaster for ADW with a firearm. He was released about three weeks before the Lowe murder."

She rolled her chair closer to his computer. "Was there a connection between Lowe and Lima? Did Adam ever arrest him?"

"Previous detectives say no, but I think we should double check, don't you?"

She nodded. "Absolutely. But I think we should start from the very beginning and re-interview everyone and check everything for ourselves."

"I totally agree." He turned to her. "Before we start, we need to talk about our schedule. On patrol, I worked the 3/12 schedule, unless I was on a mid-watch."

Katie smiled. "That's one of the best perks of working patrol. A three-day workweek, with 12-hour days."

He returned her smile. "The detective schedule of a 4/10 seems long. What would you think about taking Wednesdays off? We'd work Monday and Tuesday, off for one, then come back Thursday and Friday, then be off for the weekend."

"I guess that's okay. Of course, if we get a lead or something, we might not want to be off in the middle of the week."

"Of course, if we're jammin' on the case, we'll continue until we either arrest someone or can't go any further."

She grinned. "This is great. That means we're off tomorrow."

He frowned. "Yeah, and I'll spend my day trying to find childcare." He blew out a breath. "But that's for tomorrow. Let's focus on finding Adam Lowe's killer.

"Eleven years ago, Topanga Station had just been built. The Lowe residence was located in the division. He was working mid-PMs which was a 4/10 schedule. The night he was murdered he and his partner worked late on a DUI arrest. The station video showed him driving out of the station at 3:42 a.m."

"Okay, did anyone see him after he left?"

"The reports say no." He flipped through the pages. "I will give the previous detectives credit. They obtained video from businesses along Lowe's route home to see if he was being followed and nothing appeared unusual."

Katie sighed. "I think we should look at that video."

Roy nodded and kept reading. "A man walking his dog found Lowe's body next to his car in the driveway at approximately 5:35 a.m."

"And no one in the neighborhood saw or heard anything?"

"Not a thing."

"Okay. Let's take today and look at the videos, listen to the 9-1-1 call to Communications, and maybe we'll see or hear something others have missed."

They viewed the forty-eight seconds of video showing Adam Lowe leaving Devonshire Station.

He'd walked to his car, a modest Camry, climbed inside

and drove out of the station parking lot. When the electric gate rolled open, there was no one waiting outside the gate to tail the young policeman.

A brief thirty-second clip of video taken from the front of the station showed the Camry drive by alone. Next were three video clips that had captured him along the route as he drove home. Again, no one trailed him.

"Okay, so he wasn't shadowed from the station," Roy said.

"That doesn't mean a suspect wasn't lying in wait at his house."

"Exactly."

His cell phone vibrated on his desk. The screen displayed *Amber.* "I need to take this. I haven't seen my wife to talk to her for a couple of days."

Katie nodded and rolled her chair to her side of their shared cubicle.

"Hey," he greeted his wife. "How's it going?"

"Okay. I'm really tired, but I think it's the stress of a new job."

She *did* sound tired. "What's up?"

"I wanted to thank you for getting Gage up and taking him to my parents. I know it's not easy on you."

"Apparently not for them either. They say they're too old to watch him and we need to get another sitter."

"Yeah, they told me. What are we going to do?"

"I've arranged with my partner for us to have Wednesdays off. So, tomorrow, maybe before you go to work, we can check out some preschools for Gage. I don't want him in a private home with strangers."

"I agree, but I doubt I'll have enough time. I do have to sleep."

He counted silently to ten in his head. "I really think you should go with me." He rose from his chair and walked away from Katie, who he was sure could overhear every word.

"Besides, I purposely chose Wednesdays off so we could continue working with Doctor Stevens. Not tomorrow, but maybe in the future we'll get a set appointment for Wednesday mornings."

"How do you expect me to keep a commitment like that while I'm on probation? You know there will be overtime, court appearances, and eventually, I'll have to work the day watch." Her tone was sharp.

"I remember what it's like. I lived the long hours with little rest. But everything else in your life goes on too. We'll do what we can to minimize your responsibilities around the house but cutting our visits to the psychologist shouldn't be one of them. I'd eventually like to sleep in the same bed with you again."

There were a few seconds of silence, then she sighed heavily in his ear. "Fine. We can check out preschools. We'll have to discuss the shrink visits later." Then she disconnected the call.

17

AMBER

When Amber got home from her job, she immediately went to bed. No telling when her parents would show up with her son.

She had no trouble falling asleep, but in the early afternoon, a door-to-door salesperson had woken her, and she couldn't go back to sleep.

She threw on some jeans and a long-sleeved shirt and drove to her parents' house to collect her toddler.

Her mother greeted her wearing a lime-colored, coordinated warm-up suit. Her hair was swept into a ponytail, and pearl stud earrings dotted her ears.

She knew the ensemble was as casual as it got for Ceci Granville. "You look nice, Mom."

Ceci closed the door and motioned her to follow. "I'm a wreck and you know it. Your father left for the country club extra early. It's been a real strain on him to have the boy here all day."

"Look, Mom, I appreciate all you and Dad are doing. Tomorrow before I go to work, Roy and I are going to go look at pre-schools. We'll get him enrolled and this will all be over next week."

They entered the kitchen and Gage pushed himself to his feet and ran to her. "Mama!" He threw his arms around her knees. "Up."

She lifted her son and kissed his cheek. "Have you been a good boy for Grandma?"

"I've told you not to call me that." Ceci's tone was sharp. She reached over and pinched her grandson's cheeks. "You've been the best boy ever for Mimi, haven't you? Well, other than breaking the crystal carafe this morning." She released his flesh.

"I'm sorry, Mom. I can replace the piece."

Her mother's lips formed a thin line. "Not on your salary." She offered Amber a cup of coffee.

She shook her head.

"Honey, why don't you give up this dangerous and ridiculous job and go back to being a nurse? I mean, look at what it's doing to your family. Your husband has to drive hours every day to his job downtown, Gage is bounced around like a ping pong ball, and your father and I are exhausted."

Her cheeks heated as her anger built. "Why can't *you* understand that this is something I want—no—I *need* to do for myself. I think I've done pretty damn well with putting my trauma behind me, but that's because I've set up boundaries for me and the people in my life. You're either with me or you're not."

"It's not about whether we're with you. We're always behind you. But you need to worry about your husband. Married couples shouldn't sleep apart."

Surprise must have shown on Amber's face because her mother hurriedly continued.

"I've known for months that you and Roy have separate bedrooms. Now he's given up his job so you can turn yourself into some kind of female Rambo. You have to ask yourself, what's in it for him?"

"First of all, *Mom*, our sleeping arrangements are none of your business. Second, he hasn't given up his job. He still works as a cop. He's just doing something different. And what he gets out of it is living up to his vows when we got married. The same way I'm trying to do. You have no idea what we've been through."

"I know that turning your family's world upside down on a whim is a dumb bunny move."

The child looked between his mommy and Ceci, taking in their loud voices. His little chin quivered, and he broke into wailing tears.

"Well, don't let this dumb bunny's whim ruin your busy life. Tomorrow you'll be free. Roy is off. He'll watch Gage. Thursday and Friday, I'll bring him over right before I go to work. He won't be dropping him off in the morning anymore. Thanks for babysitting."

She hugged her son close, turned on her heel, and charged out of the house.

18

———

HAYWOOD

Glen Haywood had spent much of his day in front of the chief of police in the monthly COMPSTAT meeting, where computer statistics determined how well a commanding officer was running his or her command.

Everyone knew the exercise was a waste of time because managers under pressure found creative ways to make their crime stat numbers look better than they were.

Nonetheless, every month the brass would show up and go through the motions of putting their top leaders under the microscope. It was a game they'd been playing for almost two decades.

COMPSTAT day made him cranky. It was even worse this month because the chief had caught him unprepared. He hadn't expected the top cop to ask what case his two new detectives were working.

But knowing how these meetings turned into "gotcha" sessions, he always had his adjutant listening on the phone so he could quickly get an answer to an ambush question.

Almost immediately, Wiggins had texted: *Murdered LAPD Officer Adam Lowe.*

Haywood recovered and provided the answer and enough details of the case that he was sure he'd convinced his boss he was on top of what Null and Void were working on all along.

But the chief's inquiry also alerted him to the fact that upper management was taking a special interest in the pair, so he made a mental note to keep an extra close eye on them.

As he breezed back into RHD, he was pleased to see his right-hand man still at his desk talking on the phone. "Darnell, come in and have a seat."

Inside his office he sat behind his desk and unlocked the lowest drawer. He reached for a bottle of scotch, but his gaze fell on the fake ID and credit cards he'd used when he worked Vice right before he was promoted to captain. He retrieved the identification, remembering his fake name and how he looked with a beard. "Those were the days," he whispered. "What other job do you get paid to drink on duty and then follow it up with a massage?"

There was a quick tap on the door and Wiggins entered.

He dropped the plastic of his past and pulled out the scotch and two paper cups. "Close the door."

The adjutant sank into a chair across from his boss.

Haywood lifted the bottle and offered to pour Wiggins a hit.

His adjutant nodded and took the cup. "How'd it go?"

He shrugged. "Same crap, different day." He swallowed a good slug from his cup and poured a little more. "Thanks for the info on Null and Void and the case they're handling."

"No problem. I'd asked them earlier in the day. They said a few other teams had previously worked the homicide. Nanako doesn't think they'll turn anything workable. Buckner seems more optimistic."

"Yeah? Well that's fine, but I want you to keep a close eye on what they're doing and any progress they make and notify me immediately." He threw the last bit of amber liquid down his throat, then wiped his mouth with the back of his hand. "Seems like the chief has a great interest in what they're doing, so if he's interested, I guess I'd better be interested too."

19

SUTTON

Sutton stood in the break room at Topanga Station with his buddies, Rudy and Fish. He was running through scenarios where he could have fun exposing his female partner to police work.

"I could take her over to that homeless encampment near Victory and Shoup and let her FI and search some of the ripest and most psychotic citizens."

"Nah," Fish said. "Pedroza got typhus over there last month. Buckner has a kid. You don't want her dragging that shit home."

"We could go over to Lanark Park, and try to have her control a couple of hardened gang members. If they get the jump on her, she'll have to fight her way out."

He laughed. "Or better yet, maybe a prank right here at the station so you can watch too."

Rudy chugged some of his energy drink, then wiped his mouth with his hand. "You need to be careful whatever you do. Don't forget there are cameras all over the station. The last thing you want to do is have her running to a sergeant. My impression is they're willing to let *Ms.* Buckner through probation at any cost. If you screw with her too much, the price tag might be you."

"Well, I know if I give her a rough time and she gets her panties in a twist, I can count on you to back my play. Right?"

Fish and Rudy exchanged a glance.

"Uh, yeah."

Rudy cleared his throat. "Sure."

20

———

ROY

Roy told Katie he had a doctor appointment and would have to cut out a little early. He asked her to cover for him if anyone got nosy about his whereabouts.

Her clenched jaw and narrowed eyes told him she didn't like it, but she'd nodded mutely...likely remembering he'd ignored her drinking on duty. He hated putting her in a position where she might have to lie for him, but he had something he needed to do.

Bugging out on his partner was just the warmup. Once in his car, and out of the parking structure, he dialed his in-laws.

"Hello," George said.

"Hi George. It's Roy. I really hate to do this, but I'm going to have to ask you to watch Gage until about seven thirty. We've got a lead on our case, and we need to track it down."

Silence and then a rustling noise came to his ear.

"Hello?"

Ceci.

Obviously, George was so pissed he didn't even want to talk to him.

"Uh, hi, Ceci. I've been detained at work and I won't be able to pick up Gage until about seven thirty."

"I see. So, I should fix his dinner?"

"It would be great if you could. Otherwise by the time I get him and get home, it would be eight before he gets to eat."

A dramatic sigh came through the line. "Alright. I'll see what I can find for a toddler. I doubt he'll want the artichoke-stuffed-chicken I've made." Another sigh. "See you at seven thrity—sharp," she said, then hung up.

Now I know where Amber gets her need to have the last word, he thought.

He sighed too. It had been a hell of a long day. About noon he'd snuck away from Katie to make an appointment with the department psychologist that he and Amber had been seeing since her ordeal two years ago.

Doctor Angela Stevens had expressed surprise he would be coming alone but agreed to stay late to see him.

At the doctor's office, he pulled into the valet lot and gave his keys to the lot attendant. He pocketed his receipt.

In the counselor's lobby, he walked to a light switch and flipped it. From previous visits he knew this alerted the doctor her next client had arrived.

Seconds later the doctor poked her head around a door leading to the rear of the space. "Come on in."

Roy followed her down a hallway past several offices,

which he assumed belonged to other department psychologists, but he wasn't sure because there never seemed to be anyone but Doctor Stevens in the facility.

Once inside, they took their usual positions—she in a large upholstered chair, him on the love seat, minus his wife by his side.

The doctor had a yellow legal pad on her lap.

He gave himself a few seconds to gather his thoughts, but he was distracted by the ticking of the antique clock on the doctor's desk.

"Doc, I feel like I'm losing control of my life. Everything is all about Amber these days. Gage's childcare responsibilities have fallen to me to arrange, and her parents backed out of their agreement to watch him during the week. Because of that, I'd asked her to go with me to look at preschools tomorrow, and she freaked out because she says she needed to sleep."

Stevens looked at him but said nothing.

"I finally got her to agree to go look at schools, but then she dropped the bomb that she doesn't think we can come here together anymore."

"Did she say why?"

"She doesn't think she'll have the time." He bit his lip. "Kinda tells you how important our marriage is to her."

"Is that what you're afraid of? That your marriage isn't important to her?"

"I'm not afraid but more hurt. Everything is all about her and her getting through probation."

"In our previous sessions, we've all talked about Amber's need to feel she is in control of what happens to her. Those feelings are a direct result of her kidnapping and sexual assault."

"I see that, Doc. I do. I've been supportive of her joining the department, although I don't think it's a wise move. I've changed assignments and taken over all the household and childcare duties. But sometimes I want to matter too."

"Well, she got out of the academy, what...last week?"

He nodded.

"Maybe you should give her a chance to get her feet on the ground and see what happens."

He scrubbed his face with his hands while shaking his head. He looked up. "I can try. I'll do my best."

The doctor leaned forward. "Tell me about your assignment at RHD."

He shrugged. "It's definitely different. They've pretty much left me and Katie, my partner, to ourselves. We're working on a cold case of a cop who was murdered."

"How do you like Katie?"

He sighed. "She comes with some pretty serious baggage." He grinned. "But then I do too. In fact, I'm pretty sure that's why they paired us up."

"Go on."

"Well, she's Japanese. Her husband and little boy were killed by a deuce in a car accident. She was driving, but not at fault."

The doctor nodded. "I see."

There seemed to a recognition, and Roy wondered if maybe Katie had seen Doctor Stevens too.

"Do you work well with her?"

"Yeah. I guess so. She's a detective and doesn't make me feel *less than* because I'm a street cop." He rubbed his hands together. "We seem to think along the same lines as to how our investigation should go, and I like that. The murder victim was one of my probationers. He was a nice kid and with a few years on the job would have been a great asset to the department." He fixed his gaze on the psychologist. "I mean to find out why that didn't happen."

PART III

21

AMBER

At the station, before changing into her uniform, Amber spotted Sutton with his flunkies, Fish and Rudy. A conspiratorial vibe permeated the threesome as they watched her head to the ladies' locker room.

After roll call, her stomach gurgled as she made her way to pick up the gear for her and her partner. There was something about his gaze that made her wary.

She gathered their equipment and hauled it to the black and white.

As usual, he stood jaw-jacking with his buddies rather than helping her do the vehicle inspection and gas their ride.

He sauntered over as she tightened the gas cap. "I think we'll run this baby through the wash rack before we clear."

She nodded and climbed into the passenger seat.

He opened the door and settled in behind the wheel and

swung the SUV into the mini car wash tucked in a corner of the station's parking lot.

As the police vehicle rolled through the soap, water, and whirling brushes, she started their Daily Field Activity Report while her partner softly whistled to himself.

With the outside of their ride clean, Sutton drove next to the vacuum. "You handle the suction, and I'll wipe down the interior."

She tensed at his verbiage but exited and grabbed the vacuum hose. She started with her side of the car, sliding the nozzle into the depths of the seat cushion. The rattling of something solid being sucked up the tube made her look closer. A cache of sunflower seed shells were wedged into the seat cushion, and there were more on the floor between the driver and passenger seats.

"Disgusting," she muttered to herself as she leaned forward, reaching beneath the driver's seat to extract more of the wayward seeds.

Suddenly, she was pushed against the passenger seat. Her partner ground his groin against her butt. "Did Farley do this to you?" His voice was a raspy whisper. "Did you like it?"

She bucked him off her backside, spun around, and jabbed the vacuum hose wand into his nuts with the force she'd been taught to wield her baton.

He doubled over gasping for air.

"Touch me again like that, and I'll kill you," she hissed.

"What did you say to me?" His words were strained—his body still hunched.

"Touch me again, and it'll be the last thing you do."

He looked at her sideways as he slowly eased himself

upright. "Physically attacking your TO is gonna get you fired," he said, panting.

"You'd really report that after what *you* did?" Her voice was saturated with incredulity.

Regaining some composure, he squared his shoulders. "Who do you think they're going to believe? Me, the seasoned professional, or you—the nut job who's damaged goods?"

As soon as his words were out of his mouth, she knew it was true. His behavior was so appalling no one would believe he'd be so dumb to pull such a stunt in the station parking lot.

Reporting the incident would poison her forever in the department. Coworkers would be leery of her. For the time being, it would be best to keep this to herself—and work out an appropriate redress.

"I'm not going to say this again, keep your hands off me or be prepared to pay."

He smirked victoriously while walking gingerly to the driver's side of the SUV. He grinned. "What other fun things can we do tonight?"

22

———

KATIE

Katie was back at her desk, making a list of tasks she and Roy needed to do when they returned to work on Thursday.

Wiggins sauntered over to their cubicle. "Where's Buckner?"

"He went to the head, and then was going down to talk to some of the Gang and Narcotics officers about a couple of gangsters we're looking at on the Lowe case."

She was pissed her partner had left her to make excuses for his absence. She figured they were even now.

"How are things coming? Do you think the gang angle has any legs?"

"It seems the best place to start. But we plan on re-interviewing everyone we can."

"Okay, keep me posted on your progress. Haywood said the chief is interested in how you guys are doing."

F-ing great.

"We'll do our best."

"Okay. I'm outta here. You and Buckner should take off soon too."

"Yeah, and remember we're taking tomorrow off. We'll be back on Thursday."

"Fine with me. Most everyone else takes Fridays and Mondays so it's a bonus to have you as extra bodies on those days." He turned to go. "See you Thursday."

Katie waited five minutes after Wiggins left before she rammed her arms through her jacket, flung the strap of her purse over her shoulder, and headed home. She resented lying about Roy's whereabouts and hoped he didn't make a habit of leaving early.

As she slogged along the freeway, her thoughts turned from annoyance at Roy to the unsettling feelings she had about him.

She liked him—a lot. He had a quiet controlled quality, and he didn't seem like one to fly off in a rage—unlike her dead husband. The fact her deceased husband was a hothead was her dirty little secret.

Guilt washed over her. Hiroki would be here if it wasn't for her, and here she was defaming his memory.

But she couldn't ignore the fact her partner had stirred feelings in her she hadn't experienced in a long time. Roy hadn't noticed, but she'd actually taken more care with her appearance today. She was thinking that maybe tomorrow she should visit the nail salon and maybe try a different haircut.

She pulled into her garage and climbed the stairs that led to the back door of her condo. She dumped her purse and jacket on top of the washer and dryer, beelined to the cabinet, grabbed a glass, and seized the opened bottle of red wine on the counter and poured.

She downed that, and then poured another.

23

AMBER

Amber came into the house through the door connecting to the garage, making sure it didn't slam closed. It was 6:30 a.m., and she didn't want to wake Gage or Roy if they were still sleeping.

Entering the kitchen, she found her husband adding creamer to his coffee.

He looked up and smiled.

"Wow. I haven't seen you in days." He walked over to her and took her into his arms.

She closed her eyes and forced herself to not tense.

She felt him place a kiss on the top of her head.

"How was your night?"

She eased from his arms. "Terrible and long."

He sat down at the kitchen table. "You want something to eat? You can tell me about it."

She shook her head. "No, I'm not hungry. But I do need a drink." She grabbed the orange juice from the refrigerator and then shuffled to the pantry, where they stored their few bottles of alcohol. Grabbing the vodka, she quickly made a weak screwdriver.

He watched her every move.

What does he think you are? An alky?

"How come you're so late?"

"We arrested a couple of hypes who had a bunch of stolen property, including credit cards and ID. It was a nightmare to book."

"Sounds like a good caper. How'd you find them?"

"Radio call about a suspicious vehicle." She sipped her cocktail.

"And?"

She'd debated all night whether she should tell Roy about the attack from Sutton. Truth was, she wasn't sure keeping quiet was the right move. She could trust him to give her solid advice.

"I need to talk to you about something."

He frowned. "Okay," he said, caution in his tone.

"Last night at the start of shift, my partner told me he wanted to wash the black and white. We went through the wash rack. He pointed to the vacuum and told me, 'you handle the suction.'"

His frown deepened.

"I was vacuuming the passenger seat and some idiot had spit sunflower shells all over the floor. I leaned over to reach near the driver's seat and all of a sudden Sutton was behind me grinding his dick against my ass, asking me..." she took a deep breath, "asking me if Farley had done that—and if I liked it."

She was relieved when his jaw dropped open. His expression hardened, and his face and ears turned red. "What did you do?"

"I jabbed him in the nuts with the end of the vacuum hose and told him if he ever touched me again, I'd kill him."

Roy's outrage turned to a wince.

"What's wrong?"

"Remember your law class in the academy? You committed a felony threat. You said you'd kill him, *and* you had the means to do so with the gun on your hip."

"Oh, so I'm supposed to just accept it when my training officer sexually assaults me?"

"I didn't say that. Did you report it?"

She bit her lip. "No," she murmured.

"Why the hell not?"

"Because I wasn't sure what to do. This was my third day on the job. I didn't want to be labeled as someone who can't work well with others. I just want to do my job and get off probation." She threw back a healthy slug from her glass. "Besides, he said it was his word against mine, and who would supervision believe?"

Roy ran a hand through his hair. "What a screwed-up mess. I'm inclined to go beat the crap out of him, but on the other hand, you're the one who wanted to be a cop and handle things—"

"I did handle it," she snapped. "I won't allow that kind of treatment from him or anyone else. And if he tries it again, I *will* kill him."

"Stop saying that!" He sighed. "Are there video cameras in the wash rack?"

"I looked later and didn't see any. Before I left this morning, I casually questioned one of the mechanics who works in the garage. He told me neither the car wash nor the garage has cameras."

"That's great. It really would be a he-said, she-said." He sighed again. "I hate it that he did that to you. But since you didn't notify anyone right away…"

She could tell he was thinking things through.

"How did he treat you the rest of the shift?"

"About nine thirty we met with two of his cronies at a 7-Eleven. Neville Bass and Rudy Gomez. I'm sure he told them. He had me stay in the car"—she made a quotation gesture with her hands—"*working on the log* while he got out and talked with them for about ten minutes. The other two guys kept looking over at me and smirking. Fish and Rudy got a Code 3 call and took off. We started to back them but got a hot shot of our own and had to go there."

"Those guys are tight with Sutton?"

She nodded.

"I think you're screwed. He was probably setting up an alibi with his buddies. However, if he does anything else like that again, don't shoot him. Deck him and report it."

"Da-Da!"

Gage's cry rang down the hallway.

"Ah, our little champion is awake," he said.

It hurt her that her son wasn't calling for his mommy, but she reasoned he'd seen more of his father for the past few days, so it was natural for him to call his daddy. She finished off her screwdriver. "I'm tired. I'm going to pop in and see our tadpole, then go to bed."

She freshened her drink, then sauntered to her boy's crib. Roy followed.

"Good morning, honey. It's Mommy."

Her heart swelled at the look of joy on her son's face. "Ma-ma-ma-ma-ma." He stretched his arms out toward her.

She snatched him out of his crib and placed him on the changing table. "Let's get your diaper changed, and then daddy can make you some breakfast."

She made short work of changing him, then gave him a tight hug and smothered him with kisses before handing him over to Roy.

"Mommy will see you before she goes to her job. Okay?"

"Come on, champ. Time to find you some breakfast," said Roy.

"Nana."

"You want a banana? Or would you rather go to the donut shop?"

"Do-na!"

He held out his hand, but the toddler ran ahead.

"I wish you luck once he's hyped up on sugar." She smiled. "I'll see you when I wake up." She padded down to her bedroom and turned on the TV to the morning news.

Even over the false joviality of the news anchors, the sounds of Roy cajoling Gage into his outfit reached her ears. Not long after, she heard them leave.

She turned off the TV and tried to sleep, but her husband's words kept her from drifting off. *You're the one who wanted to be a cop...you committed a felony threat.* Three days in, and she was already FUBAR—F'd up beyond all repair.

Tears slid down her cheeks as she got out of bed and retrieved her phone.

24

———————

KATIE

Katie sat up in bed and analyzed her physical condition. Was she heavily hung over, or functional?

With relief she realized she was functional. It would be a terrible waste of a day off if she was too sick to do anything. *But what is it you have to do? Nothing. It's your day off.*

She had some coffee, then showered. As usual, the shower connection leaked more water than the head dispersed.

Afterward, feeling that her stomach could handle food, she made herself a breakfast burrito. Then, as she put her dishes into the dishwasher, her phone chimed with a text message.

It was from Roy. *Call me when you get this.*

What did he want?

She thought about it a few seconds, then called him.

"What's up?" There was a lot of background noise.

"Are you doing anything special today?"

Her heartbeat increased. "Why? What did you have in mind?"

"I'm out of the house this morning with my son. My wife needs to sleep. If you're not busy, I thought we could meet up to discuss our next moves on the case. I could take you to brunch."

What did he mean? Like a date...or work with a kid?

"Uh, I guess that would be okay, although I've eaten. Why don't you come over to my place? I've got a table where we can spread things out."

"Okay, Gage is finishing his donut. What's your address?"

After giving him directions to her condo, she ran to the bathroom to put on some makeup and do something with her hair. She also ditched her baggy jeans for some colorful leggings with a coordinating top.

Once she looked decent, she spruced up the guest bathroom, and ran a quick dust rag over the furniture.

Minutes after she finished, there was a knock at the door.

25

———————

ROY

Roy held his son in his arms while he waited for his knock to be answered.

The toddler's eyes were wide and staring, waiting to see what would happen.

Katie opened the door and smiled. "Well, hello there. Who's this cutie?" She motioned them to come inside.

"This is Gage." He looked at his little boy. "Can you say hi? This is Daddy's partner, Katie."

The boy buried his face into his father's neck.

Roy laughed. "I guess not." He tried to put his son down, but he clung to him. "We've already been to the park playground and visited the donut shop."

She motioned for him to follow. "Come in and sit down."

He stepped inside and surveyed her home. It wasn't a large condo, but she'd made the most of the space, with a small sofa and a sleek recliner anchoring the living room. The butter yellow sofa faced the large window that overlooked the street below. The dining table sat in a nook between the couch and the kitchen.

"This is a nice place." He moved to the couch, sat down, positioning Gage next to him. He slipped the canvas backpack off his shoulder and down onto the floor.

"Can I get you anything? I have milk or orange juice if he's thirsty."

He patted the diaper bag he'd set by his feet. "All stocked up. Plenty of diapers and plenty of snacks. The one thing I forgot was something for him to play with. I'll give him my phone and he can watch cartoons."

"I have a few things he can play with." Katie's face softened. "Give me a minute."

She went down the hall, and he realized she must be getting toys that belonged to her late son.

Gage slid off the couch and began to explore.

Katie returned, carrying a plastic red fire truck, a net bag filled with building blocks, and a small wooden train.

"Hey." She knelt beside the boy. "Would you like to play with some toys?"

The boy's eyes lit up, and he ran to grab the fire truck. "Mine."

Roy laughed and shook his head. "The one word he's learned to say correctly is *mine*." He stood. "That truck is *not* yours. It belongs to Katie." He pointed to his partner. "She's letting you use it for now. You'll give it back when it's time for us to go home. Do you understand?"

The toddler nodded. "Mine."

Katie chuckled and stood. "Let's go over to the kitchen table. We can keep our eye on him from there."

He took a few minutes to show his son the building blocks and train. "Daddy will be sitting right over there at that table if you need me. Okay?"

The little boy knelt, then pushed the fire truck around on the floor.

She sat on one side of the table where her laptop was set up.

He sat next to her. As they put their heads together, fruity soft scents wafted from her hair. He discreetly inhaled deeper.

"I've been doing a bit of homework on our case. I found something you might find interesting," she said.

"What's that?"

"Adam Lowe's wife, Brandi, married his best friend a little more than a year after her husband's murder. She married another cop."

He scoffed. "Who'd she marry?"

"Brent McGee, a sergeant at Hollywood Division."

"I think I've heard of him, but I don't know him. Do you?"

Katie shook her head. "No. But before he married Adam's widow, he was married to a Hollywood casting director, Robyn McGee."

"How'd you get all this background info?"

Katie grinned at him. "I took pics of the chrono log, FI's, and crime reports in the murder book and emailed them to myself here. I started doing research online. Gotta tell ya, it's pretty scary what's available online about everyone through open sourcing."

They both startled when Gage yelled and slammed the

fire truck into a tower of building blocks he'd built.

"Use your inside voice and don't throw toys," Roy said.

"Mine," the toddler declared.

"No. Those are not your toys."

"Mine!" The boy picked up a block and threw it in the direction of the table.

Roy hustled to him, lifted him to his feet, and gave him a light swat on his fanny.

"These toys do not belong to you and you're going on a time-out." He lifted his son and walked him to an empty corner of the front room and sat Gage facing the wall.

The toddler wailed in protest.

"You'll sit here for three minutes—which starts when you stop crying. The sooner you stop crying the sooner you can play again."

He came back to where Katie sat at the table with an amused smile on her face.

"Oh, the joy of toddlers."

"Hmph. He's really stepped up his game at testing us."

"Trust me. It only gets worse." She looked at her laptop screen. "Why don't we interview Brandi Lowe McGee tomorrow and see if we can chat with her husband tomorrow as well?"

Gage's wails had turned to whimpers.

He set the timer on his watch. "Son, your timeout is starting now. Three minutes."

The boy started crying quietly.

"Stop crying or your time will start all over."

The boy pulled up his knees and buried his face in them.

"He's killing me," Roy mouthed silently.

"And he knows it," she mouthed back.

26

———

AMBER

Amber couldn't believe her luck at getting a morning appointment with Dr. Stevens, the shrink she and Roy had been seeing since her kidnapping.

She parked her car with the valet and dashed up the steps to the office building.

Once inside the doctor's lobby, she flipped the light switch to let the therapist know she was waiting, then sank into a chair. Two minutes to eleven. *I'm sure not going to get much sleep today. It's gonna make for a long night.*

The door between the lobby and offices opened. The doctor motioned to her. "Come on back. Good to see you."

She flopped onto the loveseat that she usually shared with Roy. "Thank you for seeing me on such short notice."

"You're in luck today. I have training downtown this afternoon, so I had kept my morning open." The doctor made a notation on the legal pad on her lap. "What's up?"

She'd already decided she'd tell the doctor a watered-down version of the incident with her partner. She didn't trust that what she revealed to the shrink wouldn't be passed along to her captain. While she hadn't initiated a personnel complaint against Sutton, she needed to talk about what happened.

"My training officer and I were washing our black and white. He kind of invaded my personal space and then made some inappropriate comments."

The doctor pressed her lips together. "What did he say?"

She bit her lip. "He asked me if I liked it when Farley had attacked me."

"What did you say?"

"I told him he was an ass and not to ask me about it again or I'd deck him."

"You said he invaded your space. What did you mean?"

Amber blew out a breath. "He was standing close behind me."

"Then what happened?"

"We got in our car and went on patrol."

"He didn't apologize?"

"No."

"Did you report the incident to anyone?"

"No, not at work. I told Roy."

"Why didn't you tell a supervisor what happened?"

"Because it was only a rude question. If I can't deal with crap from my TO, how am I supposed to make it on the street?"

"How did your husband react when you told him?"

Tears began to roll down her cheeks. "I think he was mad, but he told me I'm the one who chose to be a cop." She wiped away her tears. "I told him I could and *would* handle it." She gave a weak smile. "He wanted to go and kick Sutton's ass. I could see he was trying to decide what to do."

"And what did he decide?"

"He didn't. I did. I made sure he understood I had it under control."

27

ROY

After Gage was relieved from his punishment, he sat on the floor quietly playing with the toys Katie had provided.

While his son played, he and Katie constructed questions to ask Brandi and Brent McGee when they interviewed them the next day.

When he looked at his watch, he was surprised to see that it was lunchtime. "Hey, I'm getting hungry. Why don't we go grab a bite?"

Katie smiled at him. "Yeah, sounds like a plan. I'm ready to eat."

They went to a local cafe and had a pleasant lunch.

The toddler was a good boy, happy to have been given some crayons and a placemat he could color.

After lunch, they returned to Katie's condo. When he parked at the curb, Katie twisted in her seat.

"Looks like your little soldier is down for the count."

He turned off the engine and looked. Gage was slumped in his car seat, his head at an awkward angle.

"Why don't you bring him inside? He can sleep in my spare bedroom, and we'll be able to continue to work," Katie suggested.

"Oh, we shouldn't hijack your entire day."

"Don't be silly. I'd probably be working on the case with or without you here."

A few minutes later, his son was sleeping in the bed belonging to Katie's deceased son.

It broke Roy's heart to see that it appeared she hadn't changed a thing since the boy's death.

They returned to the kitchen table.

"You want a soda or something?"

"No thanks." Throughout the day he'd thought about Amber's attack by Sutton. Sure, he knew there were a few officers on the job—both male and female—who had the reputation of bestowing unwelcome advances, but they usually got suspended or fired.

She popped the tab on a soda for herself and sat next to him.

"Hey, did any of your TOs say or do anything to you on probation that seemed inappropriate?"

She grinned at him. "It depends on what you consider inappropriate."

"Well…maybe come on to you, or say something to shame you?"

"You mean like calling me geisha girl, or making jokes about not letting me drive the patrol car because 'we all know Asians can't drive'?"

He made a face. "Yeah, I guess you've been there. Did you report any of that?"

"Is stuff like that happening with your wife?"

She was quick on the uptake. He shrugged.

"In my day it was pretty common for stuff like that to happen. It was also common for it to go unreported. Nothing positive came from being a probationer and a whiner." She took a sip of her drink. "It was easier to laugh it off for the few months it occurred. It didn't last long. The guys wanted to know they could trust that I wouldn't go running to make a complaint if they told a dirty joke or something." She swallowed another sip of soda. "Actually, the women were as bad, if not worse."

"Hmm." His partner was elegant and gentle, but she had to have a spine of steel to suffer what she'd been through and still be standing. Katie and Amber weren't all that different.

But Sutton's behavior was way beyond racial stereotypes and tasteless humor. The question was, what could he do about it that wouldn't reflect badly on his wife?

Katie's phone rang. "I'm sorry. I have to answer this. I'll be just a minute."

He tried to pretend he wasn't listening, but she was sitting right next to him.

"Yeah, it's something with the shower head. More water comes out of the joint in the wall than the nozzle." She listened. "Yes. I've tried to tighten it myself." She sighed. "No, I didn't over tighten it."

Katie looked at him and shook her head. "When can someone come out to look at it?" She listened. "Monday? That's the earliest?"

He grabbed a note pad by the computer, did some scribbling, and held it up to her.

Her gaze skimmed the paper. "I've got a friend who's offered to help. If we can't fix it, I'll call you back." She hung up. "You know about plumbing?"

"Not a lot." He grinned. "Enough to be dangerous. But maybe I can figure it out." He rose from his chair. "Let's go have a look."

"I'll grab some tools and supplies I've got." She scurried to the kitchen sink and opened the cabinet below, then yanked out a small red metal toolbox.

On their way to her bathroom, they looked in on Gage who slept, snoring softly.

He tried to shake off the provocative feeling of being alone with a single woman in her bedroom.

"Right in here," she directed, pointing toward the adjoining bathroom.

He slid past her, avoiding looking at the bed, where he knew he'd imagine her naked. Instead he focused on the spotless bathroom. "Here, you can be my supervisor," he said, handing her the pliers and the sealant tape. "Do you have a cloth or rag?"

She grabbed a hand towel from a shelf above the toilet.

He placed the cloth over the shower head connection and used the pliers to remove the head.

Within a few minutes, he had the old sealant removed. Once the new tape was in place, he reattached the shower head.

"All done," he said, looking down at her.

Her face was lifted toward his.

Several seconds passed.

Her gaze dropped to his lips and then anxiously back to his eyes.

He knew what she wanted.

No. Don't do it. Nothing good will come from it, and you're married. But it had been so long since he'd seen desire in a woman's gaze. She wanted it, and he did too.

He lowered his head and kissed her.

28

AMBER

After almost four hours of sleep, Amber stomped through the house, slamming drawers and growling with frustration while trying to get dressed.

"Where the hell are Roy and Gage? I've got to leave in a half hour."

She thought back to her session with Dr. Stevens earlier in the morning. *She thinks I need to keep in mind that he is having a hard time with my change of career, and I should care about his needs too.*

Driven by anger, she pulled her hair into a French braid in record speed.

Finally, she heard the garage door and the voices of her husband and son.

She marched to the kitchen to greet them. She took a deep breath to expel her anger and draw in some compassion. The second she saw them, she was flooded with uneasiness. Not about Gage—he toddled over to her to be held. But Roy. Something was way off with her husband.

"Where've you been? I was getting worried."

He made himself busy reaching into the refrigerator, grabbing a beer, and opening it. He took a long steady swig before he answered.

"I was working. I met with my partner, and we did some prelim on the case we're handling."

"You were able to concentrate with Gage around?"

"Yeah, well he had a nap after lunch, and Katie had some toys left over from after her boy died."

Alarm bells and red flags exploded in Amber's mind. His partner was a *woman?* How did she not know that?

He'd worked with dozens of females during the course of their marriage, and she'd never given it a second thought. But there was something odd about his demeanor.

"Her son died? What happened?"

He explained about the car accident. "Her husband was killed too."

"How come this is the first I'm hearing about...what's her name?"

"Katie. Katie Nanako."

"Why haven't you mentioned her before?"

"When? I never see you. And when we are together, the conversation is all about your needs and your job. You seem to have lost interest in Gage and me."

Deep down she knew he was right, but now she was scared of what she sensed and what she was feeling. She was ready for a fight. "I haven't lost interest. I can only spread myself so thin." She moved over to the counter to stand next to him and look him in the eyes.

"What?"

"You're acting weird." Her gaze fixed on his face. She thought she caught the scent of orange blossoms.

He turned away from her. "What do you mean? I'm not acting any different."

No need to put him on the defensive. She'd have to keep alert for anything suspicious. "Okay. Maybe it's me. I've got to go." She gathered her purse and a fleece jacket.

"After what happened last night, you going to be okay with your partner?"

She lifted her chin and shrugged. "That all depends upon him."

29

KATIE

Katie sat on her sofa, staring at the television and sipping on her second glass of Chardonnay. The TV droned in the background of the thoughts swirling in her head.

What had she done? Since the beginning of time, women conveyed an invitation of interest with their eyes and soft lips. What had she been thinking giving her partner the signal she wanted to be kissed?

And to her elation, Roy had accepted the stimulus and kissed her—long and hard. But as their hands started to roam, he'd pushed himself away.

Her face warmed at the memory. Worse yet, he'd felt the need to apologize.

"Katie, I'm sorry. I don't know what made me do that. I shouldn't have." He had motioned they should get out of the shower.

Of course, she'd played her part well. "No, need to apologize. I should have stopped us sooner, but I was caught up in the moment. It's been so long." Her voice had trailed off as they gathered up the plumbing supplies and made their way back to the front of the condo.

"We can't let this affect our work on the case," he'd said.

She'd looked him dead in the eye. "Of course not. It was a weird moment in time. One that meant nothing."

"Then we'll never mention this again. Agreed?"

"Absolutely."

He hadn't wasted a second gathering Gage and scurrying out of her house. He was clearly shaken by their encounter.

Katie realized her glass was empty once again. She sighed and headed to the kitchen. She filled her wine glass again. *Was this the second or third time?* She shrugged and gulped about half of the light-colored contents.

"So now, Katie, what's your next move going to be?"

30

SUTTON

Sutton sat in the empty roll call room and downed his second energy drink in as many hours. He hadn't slept well and was paying the price. He'd had a couple of dreams where IA was arresting him.

He blamed the powers that be who'd assigned him to work with that unstable bitch Buckner. His balls still hurt where she'd whacked him with the vacuum hose. He crumpled the aluminum can from his drink and pitched it toward a large plastic trash bin against the back wall. He missed.

"You won't make the Lakers if you can't make a ten-foot shot from a chair."

He turned to see Fish and Gomez entering.

"Fuck you, Rudy. You can't even make your way into your old ladies snatch, much less leave anything in there."

Fish retrieved the can and made a show of slam-dunking

it into the trash. "Whoosh, Fish shoots and scores. The crowd goes wild." He raised his arms in victory and took imaginary bows and trotted to a seat in the back row.

Fish leaned toward him. "So, what are you going do to her tonight?"

Sutton rubbed his hand over his lips. "I was thinking we could go to the barrio across from Lanark Park." He grinned. "You know those gangsters aren't going to put up with some little girlie playin' cop."

"Yeah, but then if things do go sideways, we're in the middle of it too," Fish complained.

Rudy turned to his partner. "What's the matter, Neville? You scared?"

"I don't want to be dinged for poor tactics just to screw with Buckner."

"That's the beauty of it," Sutton said. "With the three of us there, if things go south, we can lay it all on her."

Other officers filed in for roll call, soon followed by the watch commander and sergeants.

He told his buddies, "I'll get ahold of you guys later, and we'll get it set up."

PART IV

31

ROY

After Amber left for work, Roy sat on the floor and played with his son, although his heart wasn't in it. He was too distracted by what had happened with Katie.

What the hell were you thinking? You haven't even worked with Katie for a week, and you crossed a line you've never crossed before. What's the matter with you?

"How about you haven't had sex in almost two years," he muttered to himself. "Anyone else wouldn't have stopped with only a kiss."

"Da-da, mine." Gage grabbed a wooden train engine and toddled off.

Breaking away from kissing Katie had taken every ounce of self-discipline he possessed.

She'd seemed as sexually needy as he was, and only the

thought of his child sleeping in the next room had given him the strength to stop...at least that time.

No! What happened today with Katie can never happen again —with her or anyone else. Instead of thinking about screwing your partner, maybe you'd better start thinking of ways to reconnect with your wife.

He thought about two years ago, the devastation and loss he experienced when she was kidnapped by a madman. He'd believed in her then, and he believed in her now. But he wasn't acting like it. He was unsupportive of her desire to feel secure—thinking only of himself—not taking into account how much she had been through and how much stronger she was now. But no matter how courageous she was, she was still scared and damaged by the horror she'd lived through. She needed to be a cop to feel safe.

They needed to figure out a way to make their marriage work. *But sex is a part of a marriage, and even years after her trauma, she can't stand to have you touch her.*

He rose from the floor and stepped to a large mirror that hung in the foyer near the front door. He stared, then whispered to himself, "What we've been doing for the past two years hasn't worked. Maybe it's time for us to try something else. I just wish I knew what the something else was."

32

AMBER

One thing Amber was determined to do was to make connections with the people she worked with. Not only with the officers, but the civilian employees too. Her conversation with Nacho in the garage made her realize that civilians were on guard with those in uniform. She'd noticed right away that civilians rarely spoke to cops unless spoken to. She didn't like that and didn't believe in it. They were all supposed to be on the same team.

After roll call and getting the car prepped, Sutton was jaw-jacking with his buddies Fish and Rudy outside the kit room, so she explored the records unit. She could still keep her partner in view, but she also had the time to make conversation with one of the civilian clerks, Debbie Bailey.

"Debbie, what exactly do you do here in Records?"

"Our main function is to process the crime reports and

duplicate them for detectives and send the originals to R&I downtown. A simple burglary report requires twelve copies. Arrest reports even more. We also store hard copies of the officer's Daily Field Activity Reports, Sergeants' Logs, as well as send out crime alerts to other agencies."

"I'm surprised that most of this isn't digital now."

Debbie laughed. "When you've been around a bit longer, you'll realize how poorly managed and strapped for cash the city is."

Amber looked up and saw her TO and his buddies were gone. "Gotta run. Thanks for the info."

She hurried outside to the rear of the station to see her partner clustered with a group of male officers near their patrol vehicle. *Darn it!*

As he saw her approaching, he called out to her. "Where you been? Is it that time of the month? Things taking a little longer?"

Asshole. "Yes, sir! And imagine that—we've only worked together a few days and our cycles have already synced."

The group of brawny cops burst out in unrestrained laughter and guffaws. A beefy P-2 punched Sutton in the arm. "She's got you pegged, Duane."

Triumphant satisfaction filled her as she watched her partner's features change from pasty pink to florid red.

"Let's go." He pushed his way through the chortling cops.

One they settled into their seats, he turned to her. "Don't you *ever* pull a stunt like that again."

"Don't try to humiliate me in front of my co-workers, and it won't be a problem."

Neither of them spoke as he drove stone-faced to a couple minor radio calls—a business dispute and a drug overdose.

After making the proper notifications and getting the information they'd need for their log on the teenage boy who almost died from using Fentanyl, Sutton finally spoke as they exited the ER.

"Jeez, look at the fog rolling in. Gonna be a cold and damp one."

They got in their vehicle and drove slowly down the murky streets.

She was writing in their log when her phone vibrated. She slipped her cell phone from her pocket and saw it was a text from Roy.

Hey, wanted to tell you that I love you, and I hope you're having a good night. Gage and I miss you.

"Put your phone away," her partner snapped. "Didn't they tell you in the academy to keep your phone in your pocket?" He shook his head. "You're salty as hell. Mouthin' off to me in front of other officers, and now using your phone while on patrol. I'm gonna write you up for the phone incident. Maybe that will adjust your attitude."

She sighed. "Fine. Can you take me back to the station? I need to use the head."

He wordlessly turned east toward the station. Once they arrived, he pulled into a parking space. "I'll wait for you here. Make it snappy."

As she dashed from the car, she wondered if he'd stayed put to avoid any more kidding from anyone who'd seen or heard about their earlier exchange in the parking lot.

As soon as she was in the locker room, she grabbed her phone and called her husband.

He picked up on the first ring.

"Why in the hell did you text me? I'm going to get written up for looking at my phone."

"Your partner is that petty?"

"Yes!"

"That's idiotic. I just wanted you to know that I was thinking about you. I was worried he might be giving you a hard time."

"He has been. But I told you I would handle it, and I am. Please don't call me when I'm working unless it's an emergency. I've got things under control. I've got to go. I'll see you in the morning." She hung up.

It wasn't until she was jogging back to the black and white she remembered Roy's female partner and the scent of orange blossoms clinging to his clothes.

I bet Katie Nanako wouldn't yell at him if he texted her a message. Damn it.

33

———

HAYWOOD

On his way to PAB, Haywood sent his adjutant, Wiggins, a text. He advised that he wanted a meeting with the cold case teams at eleven, and they should be prepared to discuss their cases.

At the appointed hour, he marched into the conference room and faced his three teams of detectives.

"Thanks for adjusting your schedules to make this meeting. When I assumed command as the commanding officer of RHD, one of the things I vowed to do was stay abreast of what my people were doing. The CCU is an area where there isn't a lot of pressure, but it can have a huge impact on our clearance numbers for COMPSTAT. With three full teams, I'm hoping you guys will boost our clearance rate. That's why every Thursday morning, we'll be meeting to see where you're at on your cases."

He looked around the table. "Let's start with our newest team, Buckner and Nanako. What are you working on, and what have you got so far?"

Nanako spoke. "The murder of Officer Adam Lowe. We've only had the case a couple of days, and we've reviewed the reports and made a list of witnesses we'd like to re-interview."

Haywood made a note on his pad. "What made you choose that one?"

Buckner leaned forward. "Adam Lowe was my probationary officer. He was a good kid and would have made an outstanding cop."

"Do you have any leads?"

Buckner shook his head.

"We're going to start re-interviewing some of the witnesses," Nanako chimed in.

"Who are the witnesses?"

"The victim's wife and her husband."

"Why the husband? Is he involved?"

Buckner spoke up. "He was Adam Lowe's best friend."

Haywood raised his eyebrows. "Really," he said, drawing out the word. "The best friend stepped right up to comfort the widow and now they're married." He looked at Buckner. "Who's the new husband?"

"A sergeant in Hollywood."

He poised his pencil ready to write. "And does this supervisor have a name?"

Nanako looked at her notes. "Brent McGee."

"Assuming McGee and the widow aren't involved in Lowe's death, do you have any other leads?"

"There were a couple of South Side Slayers mentioned in

the chrono log, but nothing panned out during the previous investigations. We'll take another look."

"Okay. At our next meeting, I'll expect a full report on what you've found."

He turned to the other detectives who'd been working the unit for years. Each team ran through their cases and what they'd accomplished.

Haywood rose from his chair. "Buckner and Nanako, you guys get in high gear and move forward." He looked at the other two sets of detectives. "I want you to open at least one more case each. And the first team to close a homicide gets a four-day weekend."

34

ROY

Roy took the 101 freeway to Studio City to Art's Deli. There was sexual tension between he and Katie, but he was determined to ignore it. It didn't help when his mind drifted to Amber yelling at him the night before for sending her a text to say he loved her.

As always, Art's was packed, but they got a table and were able to eat. They kept the conversation to safe subjects like the weather and sports.

Afterward, Katie rubbed her stomach. "Oh, I ate too much." They made their way to the sidewalk of Ventura Boulevard. "Why didn't you tell me the sandwiches were the size of a house?"

He laughed. "The pictures on the wall weren't enough of a clue...*detective?*"

"I thought like all menus, the picture was bigger and better than the actual meal. The menu photos didn't lie."

I'm just glad you didn't order wine with lunch. He pointed down the street. "Brandi McGee's yoga studio is three blocks down. Walking would be easier than trying to find a parking spot, and you can walk off some of that pastrami you inhaled."

"Lead on, partner."

A few minutes later, they stood in front of Rx Yoga. He held the glass door open for Katie.

Once inside, he stood for a moment to give his eyes time to adjust to the dim interior. The front windows were covered with baby blue light-blocking draperies. The walls were painted a matte fawn brown. Yoga mats of various vibrant shades formed an asterisk on the bleached wood floor. The studio was empty.

Katie sniffed the air. "Sandalwood essential oils. Smells relaxing."

He shrugged. "If you say so."

A shapely blonde with long curls approached them from a back area. Her lavender leggings and matching cropped tank top made it plain she hit the beach or a tanning studio. "Hello. May I help you?"

"We're looking for Brandi McGee," he said.

"You found her." The woman extended a toned arm that certified Mrs. McGee not only practiced yoga, but also worked out with weights.

Katie shook Brandi's hand and introduced herself and Roy.

The woman frowned. "Buckner? How do I know that name? What's this about?"

He explained why they were there. "We want to talk to you again because maybe you've thought of something that didn't seem important at the time. I have a personal interest in the case. I was Adam's training officer."

She nodded and smiled. "I remember now. Adam really looked up to you." She motioned for them to follow. "I appreciate that you're willing to look into Adam's murder, but I don't understand how I could be of any help."

She led them to an area filled with several opulent overstuffed couches and chairs. "Please have a seat. Would you like some blueberry infused water, or Chai tea?" She glanced at the clock. "I have a class starting in twenty minutes."

"We'll be brief," said Katie as she sank into a plush chair. "Can you tell us what happened the morning your husband was killed?"

A melancholy expression filled the blonde's face. "I didn't know anything was wrong until I was awakened by the sirens. I answered the front door in my pajamas, and they were loading Adam into the ambulance. An officer told me to go back inside and I did. I needed to put some clothes on." She covered her eyes with her hand. "It wasn't long afterward a detective told me that Adam had been shot." She lowered her hand. "They drove me to the hospital where they told me he'd died. I asked to see the body so I could say goodbye."

He kept his voice low to match hers. "When I worked with Adam, you guys hadn't been married long. Was everything okay at home? I know being a police officer's wife can be difficult."

"I was fine with it. Adam and I were high school sweethearts. I'd known from our first Sadie Hawkins dance that he wanted to join the LAPD."

"What about on the job? Was Adam having any problems with anyone?"

Brandi shook her head. "No. He loved his job and was doing very well." She smiled. "He excelled at everything he did. His supervisors loved him."

Roy leaned forward. "Sometimes being good at what you do will cause problems. If you've got a slug officer who does as little as possible, they don't like being shown up by some new kid."

She shrugged. "If my husband was having any problems at work, he didn't mention them to me."

He rubbed his chin. "If I remember correctly, didn't Adam have a brother on job?"

Brandi nodded. "Justin."

"Did the brothers have a positive relationship?"

She held her hands up and wobbled them in uncertainty. "I think Adam felt guilty that being in the academy, and then on probation, kept him from helping Justin with their mother's care. She had dementia, and Justin, after his divorce, lived in her house in Reseda as her care giver."

Katie spoke. "Do you think Justin was put out by being the only one taking care of his mom?"

Brandi shook her head, causing her springy curls to jump. "He wasn't the only caregiver. They hired people to care for Linda while Justin was working. Adam did what he could. Mostly maintaining the yard and helping with doctor visits and such. Well, until he was murdered. We never told his mother."

He nodded. "Understandable. How did you and Justin get along?"

The blonde smiled back and shrugged. "Fine. It's not like

we socialized much. Not long before Adam's death, Justin got hurt at work. He was hit by a drunk driver. Then his mother died. Because of his injuries, he had to quit being a policeman. Eventually, he got a boat-load of money." She blushed. "Of course, that doesn't make up for the pain and suffering he went through."

He looked at his partner. "Do you remember anything in the chrono log about him being interviewed?"

Katie shook her head. "No, but that doesn't mean he's not in there."

"I'd like to touch base with him." He turned his attention back to Brandi. "Do you have contact information for Justin?"

She nodded. "He lives up on Mulholland off of Laurel Canyon. Let me go find his address and phone number."

The hard-bodied blonde bustled from the room.

Katie drummed her fingernails on the arm of her chair. "You think Adam's brother might have information?"

Roy shrugged. "Probably not, but if the brothers were close, and something was bothering Adam, maybe he discussed it with his brother. It's a long shot."

Brandi returned with a blue piece of note paper with Justin's name, address, and phone number. She handed it to him with a smile.

He could tell she was ready for them to go.

Katie must have sensed it too, but she wasn't ready to leave. "We have a few more questions. The man who found the body, did you know him?"

Brandi sighed and shook her head. "No. We hadn't met many of our neighbors. We kept to ourselves—not because we were anti-social, but with Adam's schedule, and I was starting this studio, we didn't have a lot of time for socializing."

"What about your current husband, Brent? Did he know Adam?" He knew the answer, but he wanted to see what she'd say.

She smiled. "They were best friends. They'd gone through the academy together. When we did do any socializing, it was with Brent and his wife, Robyn."

"This may sound insensitive," he said, "but how did you and Brent wind up together?"

Brandi waved a hand. "You're not the first one to ask that question. It wasn't anything weird, but Brent and Robyn had been having marital troubles throughout their marriage."

Katie raised her eyebrows.

The blonde shook her head. "She's a big-wig casting director in Hollywood, and most of those folks didn't think much of cops. It caused friction."

Katie leaned forward. "Exactly how long after Adam's death did you and Brent get together?"

Brandi lifted her chin and shot her a dirty look.

She held up her hands. "I'm not suggesting anything—but I have to ask."

"Gosh, who knows. At least a year. There was so much to take care of... Brent helped me so much." She smiled.

"One last question, Mrs. McGee," Katie said. "Can you think of anyone who would want Adam dead?"

Tears formed in Brandi's eyes, and she slowly shook her head. "No. He was the perfect husband. I never met anyone who didn't like him. He was the love of my life."

35

KATIE

Walking along the sidewalk on Ventura Boulevard, Katie dodged stepping on a piece of gum as she and Roy walked back to where they'd parked their car.

He offered her a mint. "What did you think of Brandi McGee?"

She popped the lozenge in her mouth and rolled her eyes. "Typical Southern California blonde bimbo. The highlighted hair extensions, spray tan, and substantial silicone boobs."

He grinned. "Tell me what you really think. Did you believe her story about how she became a widow?"

"I think so. She didn't seem to know much, but at the end of the interview when she said Adam was the love of her life, it rang true to me."

"It's kind of strange that the best friend swooped in within a year. Especially when he was having trouble at home with the wife."

There was an awkward silence and she wondered if Roy's mind had gone to their kiss from the day before. She gave him a sidelong glance. "You think McGee offed his best friend to steal his wife?"

"I wouldn't rule it out. We should talk to McGee's casting director ex-wife. What was her name?"

"Robyn. We can get her info from Brent. He works at Hollywood Division."

"So, we're heading over the hill," he said. "Damn. We should have called to see if he's working."

She rolled her eyes at him. "I did, and he is." Then she smiled. "But don't you think it would make sense to take Laurel Canyon and see what Justin Lowe has to say on our way to interview McGee? It's right on the way."

He grinned at her. "No wonder they made you a detective, and I'm still just a street cop." He pulled out his cell phone and the blue paper Brandi had given him.

Forty minutes later they'd parked their plain-wrap detective sedan two doors away from Justin Lowe's home.

Katie scrolled through her phone. "Looking in the murder book, I see that about five years ago, Adam's brother, Justin Lowe, was interviewed by a couple of detectives who looked at this case." She scanned her screen. "I think this going to be a waste of time. Their notes say he didn't have anything of value to add to the investigation."

"Would have been nice if they'd been more specific." He opened his car door. "Let's get this over with so we can go talk to Brett McGee."

Katie exited her side of the vehicle and gave a soft whistle.

"He must have received a sizable settlement to have digs up here. These places run in the millions."

He nodded and began to walk up the driveway. "Hit by a deuce and had to leave the job. I wonder what kind of shape he's in."

On the front porch, they rang the bell, resulting in formal Westminster chimes announcing their arrival.

They heard movement and after a minute or so, the carved wooden entry was opened by a pudgy man in cargo pants and a polo shirt.

"Hi, I'm Roy Buckner from the LAPD, and this is my partner, Katie Nanako." He smiled. "Are you Justin Lowe?"

The man gave a quick jerk of his head, known in the LAPD as a Metro nod, and opened the door wider. "Yeah. Come on in."

After they'd entered, Justin led them past an open space of white leather furniture, contemporary glass tables, and gray walls.

Katie noticed a pronounced limp in his gait.

He brought them to the rear of the house to the family room. The attached kitchen was restaurant-worthy equipped with professional appliances.

"Whoa! What a great view," Katie said, awe in her voice as she looked out the huge glass windows.

Justin stood a little straighter and smiled. "Yeah, I had to have this place when I saw the panoramic view of the city."

Roy glanced around. "It's a beautiful home. How long have you lived here?"

Justin's smile evaporated and he sighed. "Ten years." He motioned they should sit on a contemporary sofa. "You wanted to talk about Adam's murder?"

"Yes, we work the Cold Case Unit, and we're taking another look at the homicide of your brother."

Justin sighed. "I won't be much help. I was recovering from getting hit by a drunk driver. The next thing I know my doorbell is ringing." He shook his head. "My caregiver hadn't arrived for the day, but I saw the department car, so I hobbled to the door—which was no easy trip. It was my captain and a department Chaplin. They told me Adam had been murdered." He lowered his head.

Roy leaned forward. "Do you have any idea who would want your brother dead?"

"None at all," he said, lifting his gaze and massaging his thigh. "Adam was a good kid. He'd become a cop, got married to a beautiful woman, and they'd bought their first home..." He sighed. "My brother was living the American dream."

Katie nodded. "We're the two of you close?"

Justin nodded. "As we grew up, he was my little buddy. He wanted to be like me and do everything I did." He smiled. "Of course, there was a three-year age difference, so he never could."

Roy shifted in his seat. "Did you go to the scene?"

"No. I wasn't in any shape to do that. The chief called me later in the day and told me to call RHD at any time, and they'd give me an update on the case." He scoffed. "Here we are eleven years later, and the killer still hasn't been caught."

Katie looked him in the eye. "Yeah. Well, we're gonna try and take care of that."

36

ROY

"So, I want to know how a P-3 cop can afford a mini-mansion in such an affluent neighborhood," Katie said.

Roy laughed as he maneuvered their car along Hollywood Boulevard. "The same way everyone else does. Credit cards, and probably a side hustle."

"The guy is totally screwed up. Did you see the limp and how he was rubbing his leg?"

"Better that he rubs his leg than having him stroking something else."

She sighed and rolled her eyes.

Twenty minutes later they sat in the lunchroom at Hollywood station, sitting across a table from Brent McGee.

The sergeant was the perfect Ken to his wife's Barbie. All-American good looks combined with a lean body.

After they'd introduced themselves, Katie let Roy explain why they were there and start their questioning.

"We chatted with your wife, Brandi, a little while ago. We're hoping that as Adam's best friend, maybe he told you some things that he wouldn't have shared with her."

"Like what?"

"Maybe any trouble he was having with anyone on the job. Your wife said Adam was a hard charger—maybe a co-worker who wasn't so ambitious didn't like it."

Brent stared at him. "Come on. You can't seriously think that a police officer would kill another cop over work ethic."

Roy shrugged.

"Geez. As a sergeant, I've got worker bees, and I've got slugs. I lean on the slugs, but no one would consider killing anybody over it."

Katie tilted her head. "Okay. Then what other reason could there be? According to Brandi, they were soulmates." She righted her head. "Unless you know something she didn't."

McGee narrowed his eyes. "What. Are you saying you think Adam was having an affair?"

"We're looking for answers. Was Adam a player?"

"Of course not."

Roy shifted in his seat. "What about Brandi?"

McGee sat straighter in his seat. "Absolutely not. I'm sure it looks kind of funny that I was Adam's best friend and wound up marrying his widow, but we didn't fall in love until after his murder."

Katie leaned forward. "How long?"

The sergeant frowned. "I don't know. A year? Maybe longer."

"It's kind of strange. Neither you nor your wife remember when you started dating."

"It was a long time ago—a decade."

Roy nodded. "What about anything he was working on prior to his death. Any suspects he'd been hassling? Dopers, gang members?"

McGee shook his head. "Nothing he told me."

"Okay." He looked at his partner. "Can you think of anything I've missed?"

She slid her business card across the table. "If you think of something that might be useful, give us a call."

"Yeah, fine." He rose. "I've gotta get back to work."

She stood, and so did Roy.

"One more thing," he said. "We'd like to talk to your ex-wife, Robyn. Do you have her contact information?"

"Why would you need to interview her? She doesn't know anything about Adam's murder."

"Maybe she'll remember when you and Brandi started dating," Katie jabbed, flashing him an engaging smile.

McGee frowned but pulled a field interview card from his pocket and scratched out a phone number. He tossed it on the table and marched out of the room.

37

AMBER

Amber had picked up her gear as well as her partner's when Sergeant Dunkley stopped her.

"Hey, Buckner, I'd like to have a chat with you after your car is set up. I'll be in the sergeant's office."

"Yes, sir."

Each supervisor on the watch had a cadre of officers assigned to him or her. She and Sutton were part of Dunkley's "den".

Great. My jerk training officer must have written me up for Roy's text last night, and Dunkley wants to chew me out.

She flew through the vehicle check to prepare to hit the streets. There was no sign of her partner, so she hurried into the station.

Feeling on display as she walked past the watch commander to the supervisor's office, she moved with purpose. The door was open, and Dunkley sat behind a computer typing at a frantic pace. The monitor and keyboard rested on a long stainless-steel counter attached to the wall.

She knocked lightly.

"Come on in, Buckner. I'm almost done here."

She sank into a rolling chair behind a computer next to Dunkley's. She glanced around the area, noticing at least a dozen war bags belonging to supervisors tucked into cubbies built into the far wall.

Above the countertop various notices, orders, and phone directories were taped to the wall. While the space was neater than where the officers wrote their reports, this office was an example of organized chaos.

Dunkley finished his report and got up and shut the door. Returning to his seat, he swiveled to face her. He smiled. "Don't look so worried."

She tried to smile back, but her stomach was in knots.

"I like to meet with each of the probationary officers in my den to see how they're doing and if they have any questions or concerns."

He leaned back in his chair and blew out a breath. "You're working with Duane Sutton." He smiled again. "Not always the easiest fella to work with. Have you had any difficulties with him?"

Her mind flashed to the incident in the station car wash, then her partner's smart-assed comment in the parking lot, and lastly on his threat to write her up. *Does the sergeant know about the text message incident? Is this a trap or a test of some kind?*

She shook her head. "No. We're getting along fine." She hesitated. "I can see how some probationers might have difficulty with following his rules, but they're rules for a reason. Safety." She smiled, hoping she'd given validation to his worries, but also reassuring him that she had no problems with Sutton.

Dunkley nodded and gave her a measured look. "Okay. But if anything changes, don't hesitate to get ahold of me."

She rose. "I won't. But I doubt it will be necessary."

"All right. Be safe out there."

"Roger that, sir."

She opened the door leading to the watch commander's office, and the first people she saw were Sutton's buddies, Fish and Rudy. They stood at the watch commander's desk, waiting for the lieutenant to approve a report.

They looked startled to see her and narrowed their eyes when they saw she'd been inside talking to her den sergeant.

Great. I wonder how long it will take for them to tell Sutton I was meeting with Dunkley.

38

ROY

"Man, I don't want to fight all the traffic going home. We're right in the middle of rush hour," Roy said as he and Katie pulled out of the Hollywood station parking lot.

"There is no rush *hour*. The freeways are a mess twenty-four seven. It's too bad we had such a big lunch at Art's Deli. We could grab a bite to eat."

He gave her a sidelong glance. "We could stop for a drink until the roads die down a little." *What are you thinking? Alone with Katie drinking?* He returned his attention to the road. Out of the corner of his eye, he saw her turn to look at him.

"I think that's an excellent idea, and I know where we should go."

"Where?"

"A place called Death & Company. It's at Hewitt and 3rd."

"Never heard of it."

"They've got the best cocktails. My favorite is the Tradewinds—tequila, apple brandy... I don't remember what else, but the drink is sensational."

He shrugged. "Okay. I'm game. We'll take our department ride back to PAB and then we can drive over."

Once they returned to the Police Administrative Building, Katie hustled to their cubicle to type up some quick notes so they could update their file in the morning.

Filled with guilt, he slunk past empty desks to the more private area containing the cold-case murder books. Taking a deep breath, he called his mother-in-law.

"Hello, Roy."

"Hi, Ceci. I'm afra—"

"Let me guess. You're going to be late."

"Yes. I'm sorry. I shouldn't be too long. I have to type up some interviews we conducted today."

"Have you and Amber found someone else to watch the boy?" Her tone was sharp.

"We're working on it."

"You need to find someone. We won't be able to watch him next week."

"I understand."

"Good. Try not to be too late."

"I won't." His words weren't necessary. She'd hung up. *What in the hell are you doing? Lying to your mother-in-law so you can go drinking with your female partner. Are you nuts?*

He rose and sighed. Maybe he should tell Katie that Gage was sick and he had to leave. She'd been a mother. She'd understand.

But the fact she's not a mother is why you feel the need to spend time with her. You feel sorry for her.

And you're full of shit. You're lonely for a woman's companionship. A gentle smile, a soft touch, a soulful kiss... Stop! Follow through with what you started. Have one drink—then go home.

As he approached their cubicle, Katie swiveled in her chair. "Got the childcare taken care of?" Her eyes sparkled with glee.

He gave her a small smile. "Yep. My mother-in-law wasn't happy. I won't be able to stay long."

The merriment in her gaze dimmed. "Oh, okay." Then she smiled. "Still better than sitting in traffic on the 5 Freeway."

"You've got that right."

She stood and slung her purse over her shoulder. "You ready?"

A little later they descended a set of stairs to a bar area called the Standing Room. Dozens of people—young and old—sipped cocktails.

"Geez, it's dark in here," he said.

"It's a *bar*. It's supposed to be dark."

Katie walked through the area while Roy trailed behind her. She forged her way to another larger area, the main bar. She looked back at him. "Follow me."

He had to walk fast as she weaved through tables to a small nook equipped with a banquette in a rich violet hue.

She slid onto the upholstered, curved seat.

With no other chairs at the table, he sat next to her. "This is a happenin' place. We're lucky to find a table."

"You don't get out much, do you?" She laughed. "I called ahead. They know me here and saved this for us."

They were served quickly, surprising for such a busy lounge.

"So, tell me about your wife," Katie said, then sipped her favorite cocktail.

Danger! Keep it light and not personal. He took a sip of his Sour Soul, a drink he'd chosen for his state of mind.

"She's a fighter. She's been through hell and back, and yet she's put that behind her and is starting a new career. It's amazing how she does it."

Katie cocked her head and smiled. "She's got you for support." She shrugged. "You have a solid but quiet strength. It has a calming effect on people. I've certainly noticed it, and I've seen others respond to it too."

He ducked his head as his cheeks warmed. "Oh, I don't know about that."

She placed her hand on his. "Well, I do."

He raised his head and signaled for their server to bring another round.

39

AMBER

Amber found Sutton in the driver's seat of their SUV in the station parking lot. He was looking at his phone. He quickly closed the porn he'd been looking at and scowled at her as she climbed into the passenger seat.

"Where the hell you been?"

"Sergeant Dunkley wanted to talk to me."

He frowned. "About what?"

"I *thought* he might ream me about getting a text on my phone last night." She paused to let that scenario sink in. "But as it turned out, he just wanted to know if I was doing okay."

"Nosy ass. What'd you tell him?" He edged out onto the street.

"That I was doing fine."

He didn't say anything but nodded. He turned onto Roscoe Boulevard. "Go ahead and clear."

She punched the Clear button on their car computer, alerting the dispatcher they were available to be assigned radio calls.

A few minutes later they got a message over the radio. "21A1, call the watch commander."

"Jesus! How do they expect us to get any work done?" He glanced at her. "Phone the station and find out what he wants. You've got the number for the inside line, right?"

"Yes." She pulled out her phone and found the number. "This is Officer Buckner on 21A1. You wanted us to call."

"Buckner, Captain Vega wants to talk to you. Tell Sutton to haul your ass back here Code 2."

"Yes, sir." She disconnected and relayed the watch commander's message.

"What the hell did you tell Dunkley? You must have said something that has them worried."

"I didn't. I told them everything was fine."

"Then why are they calling you in for all these little chat sessions?"

"I have no idea. If I knew, I'd tell you."

He made a U-turn in front of a speeding Hyundai, causing the driver to brake hard.

"Send 21A43 a message to meet us at the station."

Wordlessly, she did as she was told. They hadn't even handled a call and her night was already screwed.

40

SUTTON

As soon as his partner was out of the car and on her way to the captain's office, Sutton pulled out his cell phone and called Rudy.

"Where are you guys? I need to talk to you."

"We're finishing up a ticket."

"Meet me at the station behind the garage...by those metal sheds where they keep old files."

"What's going on? We heard the request to call the WC and then saw you were out to the station."

"I think that bitch I'm working with is bad-mouthing me. We got called back to the station so she could meet with the captain."

"Oh, that doesn't sound good. Fish and I saw her coming out of the sergeant's office after roll call. She was having a pow wow with Dunkley."

"Yeah. She told me. She swears she didn't complain about me, but with Vega wanting to talk to her, I think she's lying."

"Okay. Give us about ten minutes. Fish is almost done with this moron. Looked right at us and waved as he was talking on his phone."

"Sign his ass up," Sutton bellowed and hung up.

He exited the patrol vehicle and sauntered toward two rusted outbuildings situated against the cinderblock fence. The steel storage sheds sat positioned facing each other and spaced so each could be opened, only one at a time.

Duane eyed the setup and realized the odd arrangement was used to save space. Grabbing a door handle, he was surprised when it was unlocked. He grabbed his flashlight from his sap pocket and shined it in the shed.

The container was stacked with storage boxes marked from the previous decade. Some boxes were marked *Detectives*, others were marked *Admin*, and several were marked *Sgt Logs & DFARs—Daily Field Activity Reports*.

"Nothin' to see here," he grumbled.

The sound of the automatic electric gate opening and a car entering the police facility had him glance toward the parking entrance.

"Finally."

The black and white SUV flew through the parking lot and came to a hard stop next to him.

Fish was driving and Rudy was the passenger officer.

As he walked over, Rudy rolled down his window. "What are you doin' back here?"

"Killing time until Buckner finishes having tea with the captain." His gaze scanned his surroundings. "Listen, last night we didn't get a chance to drive over to the projects. I want to do that tonight. Same plan."

Fish glanced at Rudy. "Do you really think that's a smart move with her already having chats with supervision?"

"That's exactly *why* I need to do it. The sooner she quits or get fired, the less I'll have to worry."

Rudy scratched his ear. "What exactly do you have against this chick?"

He narrowed his eyes. "She's a flippin' nut case. She was captured, raped, and God only knows what else. I'm not comfortable riding in a patrol car with her for twelve hours. She could go whacko at any time."

He didn't miss the look exchanged between the partners. "Listen, you pussies, if you're too scared to go and tangle with some gangsters—"

"It's not that," Fish said. "We don't want to take any suspension days over a dame."

Sutton leaned back and frowned. "What century do you think you're in, the nineteen forties?" He eyed his buddies. "Dame," he scoffed. "Okay, if you won't go in with us, can you at least be in the area?"

"Sure," said Rudy. "Just send me a text...and be sure we aren't on a call or something."

"You two having a radio call is highly unlikely—you haven't handled one in at least six months."

"Screw you." Rudy grinned and flipped him the bird.

Fish stomped the accelerator, and they sped away with pieces of gravel pelting Duane's lower legs.

PART V

41

ROY

Well into his second drink, Roy knew he needed to eat to combat the effects of the alcohol. He ordered several appetizers for the both of them.

She ordered another Tradewind and leaned toward him, this time her hand moved to his thigh. "I know how screwed up I am since the death of my husband and son. After what she's been through, how is your wife holding it together?"

He shook his head, trying to ignore her hand as she slowly massaged his leg. "She's not. Well, that's not really fair. She made this career change so she could feel safe and in control."

Katie blew out a breath. "That must be a hit to your marriage—that she doesn't feel safe."

He noticed his partner's eyelids were heavy, and he was beginning to hear her slur a little.

"I'm not gonna lie. It does hurt. Of course, I understand it. She suffered unspeakable things because of my inability to protect her."

The leg massage stopped. Katie brought both hands to the side of his head and turned his face toward her. "Amber was kidnapped. There was nothing you could have done."

He looked into her dark brown eyes and wanted to believe her words were true—but he knew better.

She dropped her hands from his face, placing one hand back on his thigh. She inched her hand higher on his thigh. "*I* feel safe with you." She took another hit from her cocktail and swallowed. "Will you let me make you feel better, Roy?"

42

AMBER

No one was in the administrative section when Amber returned to the station. However, light spilled from the captain's open office door.

She walked carefully to where she could poke her head around to look into the room to see if Marnie Vega was in or not.

The captain must have seen movement in her peripheral vision because she looked up from the paperwork she'd been reading.

"Buckner, come on in, close the door, and take a seat."

Once she was seated, Vega smiled at her. "Officer Buckner, I wanted to check on you and how things are going."

Amber smiled back. "Everything's fine."

"Do you feel comfortable with your training officer?"

"He seems very knowledgeable about the job. I'm learning a lot."

Her commanding officer smiled again. "Yes, but that wasn't the question."

She paused not sure of the best way to answer. But having two supervisors ask about her relationship with her TO in less than an hour...maybe someone had seen the incident in the car wash or heard about it.

"It depends on what you mean by being comfortable. I trust his knowledge of police work and how things should be done."

The captain pursed her lips. "But..."

Again, Amber hesitated. "I think he enjoys being the person in control."

Vega displayed a poker face. "I think as police officers we're all trained to maintain control. Our lives depend on it."

"True," Amber replied. "It's imperative when dealing with the public." She let her statement hang.

The captain was no dummy. Vega had to know she was implying Sutton was not only controlling with the public, but he was controlling to her as well.

"You come from a nursing career, so you're used to hierarchy. It's no different in the LAPD."

"Of course. As long as it doesn't over-step policy and procedure." She smiled.

"What are you trying to say, Officer Buckner?"

"I think you'd better be selective about who you assign to be trained by my current TO. I can take care of myself, but a lot of younger officers won't have the life experience or fortitude to stand up to him if necessary."

"What I'd tell those workers, and *all* probationary

employees is that they remember they're still in the learning phase of their employment." Vega smiled. "After all, you don't know what you don't know."

The captain rose and held out her hand. "Be careful out there, Buckner. Being low woman in the car is tough, but you'll get through it—most of us have."

43

———

HAYWOOD

Haywood sat across the table from Marnie Vega at a Mexican restaurant not far from where she lived.

"Glen, I've got a bad feeling about Amber Buckner." She recounted the meeting she'd had with the probationary officer.

Marnie popped a chip stacked with salsa into her mouth. "The problem is she's not some twenty-something kid who's intimidated by her TO."

"Do you think Sutton's bullying her?"

"He's an asshole. None of his probationer's like him." She brought her Margarita to her lips and sipped. "But"—she swallowed—"no one has come right out and accused him of misconduct. I'm worried that Buckner might be the one to do it. With her background, the press would be all over that story."

"You could meet up with her again and keep it light. Ask her about her home life, and how her husband likes working cold cases, and if he's making any progress. Ask about their kid."

"What's that going to do except make her feel more comfortable with me and feel that she can open up about whatever the hell Sutton does to his P-1s."

"Bring the prick in for a chat too. Remind him Buckner's been through a lot and that she's not some arrogant kid who's unable take care of herself—after all, she's already dumped a guy. Something *he* probably hasn't done."

"Easy for you to say, Glen. She's not in your command. I haven't dumped anyone either. I can't speak for Sutton, but the fact that *civilian* Amber Buckner literally blew up someone intimidates the hell out of me."

44

AMBER

As soon as Amber left the captain's office, she retreated to the locker room, which thankfully was empty, and used her phone to punch in Roy's number. Her call went to voicemail.

Next she called her parents.

"Are you all right?" Fear filled her mother's voice.

"I'm fine, Mom. Is Roy there?"

"No, dear, he called earlier and said he had to work late—something about typing up interviews."

She sighed. "Gage is still there with you? It's almost his bedtime."

"I know it, dear. This whole thing is bad for the baby. Maybe you should reconsider this idea of being a policeman —for the sake of your son."

"Mom, I'm a police *officer,* and we've been over this a

hundred times. I won't quit. I've got to go. Thanks for babysitting. I'm sure Roy will be there soon."

As soon as she hung up, she was filled with dread. *If Roy is just typing up interviews, why didn't he answer? Do I dare contact him at RHD?*

She searched her phone, found the work number he'd given her, and called. That number also went to voicemail. *Understandable. It's after office hours, so citizens wouldn't expect anyone to answer. That's why there's no answer.*

But something was off. She felt it in her bones. She used her phone to go to the LAPD website and found the number for RHD but didn't hold out much hope her call would be answered. *Probably no one mans the phone after hours.*

The phone rang and she was surprised when it was answered.

"Detective Hogan, RHD. Can I help you?"

"Hi. I'm trying to get ahold of Roy Buckner. Is he there?"

"No ma'am. He went home for the day."

"Oh. He'd asked me for some information regarding a case he's working on. He indicated it was urgent."

"Did you leave a message on his voicemail?"

"No. I don't have his direct number," she lied. "Can you give it to me? How long ago did he leave?"

Amber could hear the detective shuffling through some papers—probably looking for an internal phone list.

"He and his partner left a couple hours ago. Okay, here I've got his number."

Detective Hogan recited the number she already had for Roy's work number.

"Got it. Thank you very much."

After she'd hung up, tears came to her eyes. *He and his*

partner left a couple hours ago. That doesn't mean that they left together, she told herself.

Then she remembered how yesterday he came home from Katie's house smelling of orange blossoms. Would that be the case tonight?

45

____

ROY

There was no doubt about it. Katie was hammered. He wasn't much better. There was no way either of them was in any shape to drive. What was he going to do?

They needed to get out of the bar for one thing.

"Katie, listen to me. We need to leave the bar."

She gave him a blissful smile. "I think that's a magnificent idea." She started to slide sideways to leave the table and stand.

"Wait! Let me help you." He rose and he was happy to see he didn't sway. He moved to help her up. "Wait. We need to pay for our drinks." He retrieved his wallet and grabbed some bills and threw them on the table. He was pretty sure he'd left a better-than-decent tip.

Next he grabbed her arm and helped her to stand. He was relieved to see she was pretty steady on her feet.

"You're doing great. We have a bunch of stairs to climb, but you can use the handrail. I'll be right behind you."

She giggled as they mounted the stairs. "No pinching my ass."

"We need some cool, fresh air."

They topped the stairs and burst out of the bar and into the night.

They swayed a few steps, and then he stopped and leaned against the brick wall.

She followed suit.

"Katie, neither of us can drive like this."

"I'm fine to drive. You want me to take you home?"

"No. Neither of us are getting behind the wheel." His tone was brusque.

"You don't have to get all cranky." She ran a hand through her black, shoulder- length hair, then swiveled to stand in front of him. She leaned into him. "What do you suggest?" Her tone was evocative.

He looked down at her upturned face. She was giving him that look again. The one where yesterday he'd lost control and kissed her.

He wasn't Superman. His body reacted. "Uber or cab," he said tensely.

She put her index finger to her lips. "How would we arrive at work tomorrow? How would you get your little boy?" She lowered her arm and smiled. "I think we should walk over to that hotel across the street, rent a room, have sex, shower and head home. If we get the sex part right, by the time we're done we should be sober enough to drive."

"I can't do that. My son is at my in-laws. I have to leave now."

"It will be easier to call them again and tell them you have to stay late than explain why you're in an Uber to pick up your son." She pushed her pelvis against his erection. "Besides we both want this. We both need it. We'll be helping each other." She stood on her tiptoes and kissed him.

He lost it and kissed her back. All he could think about was sinking into her...and if he wasn't careful, it would all be over before they'd made it to the hotel. It had been a long two years.

"I can't put the hotel charge on my credit card. My wife..."

"Shhh," she murmured, her lips still on his. "I'll take care of it. Come on." She took his hand and led him across the street.

46

AMBER

The mood was tense in the patrol car. Her partner hadn't asked her about her meeting with the captain, and she didn't offer anything.

When they cleared, they got hit with a bunch of radio calls, but nothing that resulted in a report or an arrest.

"I think we should head over to Lanark Park. Let's see if you can make a dope arrest."

"Sounds good." She intentionally slowed her breathing in an effort calm her nerves.

"I gotta take a leak first." He pulled into a convenience store that allowed cops to use the facilities.

While he was gone, she checked for a text or call from Roy then scrolled through her email. She kept her eye out for Sutton's return but was pretty sure he saw her putting her phone back into her shirt pocket. If he did see the phone, he didn't say anything.

"The dope dealers, they always run. You a decent runner?"

"I'm not as fast as when I was in my twenties, but I'll give it all I've got."

He grunted and swung their SUV around the corner, heading to the park. "If someone takes off running, you go in foot pursuit, I'll head him off with the car."

"In the academy, we were trained not to separate. They told us about an officer who was killed when he and his partner separated."

"Yeah, they told our class that too. That was a long time ago. When you're on the street for a while, you'll learn that things are done much different on the street than the way they're taught in the academy."

Sutton turned down Lanark Street. The area was a hotbed of gang activity with crowded apartments on the north and east side of the park. "What they like to do is hang out in front of the apartments and if we stop to shake them down, they'll rabbit across the street into the park. Most cops won't chase them into the park—and they know that." He turned and grinned at her. "But I've got you."

Swell, asswipe. I'll run into the park if it will make you happy.

"Up ahead on the right about fifty yards out. See them?"

"Yeah." She grabbed the mic. "21A1, show us Code 6 on Lanark east of Topanga Canyon."

Sutton gunned the engine and sped up to the group of Hispanic males gathered in front of an apartment building.

The group bolted—in all different directions.

Several males sprinted into the park, but there was a

cholo running north between the buildings who was a lot closer.

Amber ignored those running to the park and gave chase to the guy closest to her.

As the man ran, he tossed an object into an apartment patio.

"21A1, I'm in foot pursuit north through the buildings 21805 Lanark. Male Hispanic, Kings jersey and black pants."

As she ran, over her radio she heard an air unit say they were responding, and several ground units were also rolling her way.

She keyed her mic again. "Suspect threw something onto a patio with a yellow umbrella."

The man ran to the rear of the building into an open parking lot. He dived under one of the cars.

If his jersey had been all black, she would have missed him, but the white on the jersey caught her attention as he lunged beneath a red Ford Explorer.

Positioning herself behind the front end of a nearby Honda and using the engine block for cover, she drew her gun. She keyed her mic as the air ship flew overhead using their light to search the area. "21A1, I've got the suspect in sight under a red Explorer behind 21805 Lanark.

"You. Under the Ford, come out with your hands up." Her heart pounded in her chest, and she wondered where in the hell her partner was.

The air unit had picked her up with their night sun and directed other units to her.

Before any of them could get to her, Sutton appeared behind her. "Where is he?"

"Under the Explorer."

Her TO unholstered his gun. "Hey, dipshit, crawl out from under there with your hands up. I've got the gun you tossed, and you're going to jail."

Other officers began to arrive and surround the Explorer.

"You—under the car," Amber called. "Don't make this any worse. We've got you. Give it up."

"Okay. I'm coming out. Don't shoot."

Her partner kept his eyes and gun on the Ford. "When he gets clear, have him prone out. I'll cover you while you cuff him."

She nodded. She was laser-focused on the male beneath the Ford.

Soon two hands appeared. "I'm unarmed. Don't shoot." The suspect wriggled his body from beneath the car.

She commanded him to turn onto his stomach and spread his arms and legs. She then moved in and handcuffed him.

Once she had him secured, she helped him to his feet and patted him down for additional weapons. His arms, and even his neck sported gang tattoos.

Sutton swaggered over and dangled a black semi-auto by the trigger guard on his pen. "Lose this, buddy? I bet we're gonna find your fingerprints all over this."

The suspect stared at him, looked at his name tag, and then his expression turned to fury.

Sutton faced him. "What's the matter with you?"

The Hispanic, who looked to be in his late twenties, looked at her. "You arresting me, or not?"

She shot a glance at her partner.

"Yeah. Get him out of here. Search him before you put him in the car, get an FI, and run him for warrants."

She grabbed the suspect's bicep tightly and propelled him back between the buildings.

Residents who'd heard the commotion came outside to watch her walking the gangster to the black and white. Most had their cell phones trained on her.

"What's your name?"

"Antonio Lima."

"Okay, Antonio. Don't do anything stupid, and we'll get along just fine."

When they reached the patrol car, she searched him again for additional weapons or other contraband, then opened the rear door of their police vehicle and assisted him into the back seat. "Watch your head."

He glanced at her name tag. "Officer Buckner, I need to tell you something."

Oh shit. He's got another gun or knife on him and you missed it. Her muscles tensed. "Yeah, what's wrong?"

"Your partner. He raped my sister."

47

———

ROY

The sound of a door slamming jarred Roy from a deep sleep.

He opened his eyes, not recognizing where he was. Then he saw Katie and it all came back to him—a bar—a hotel—hot, frenzied sex. *What the hell have you done?* He glanced at his partner: pretty and sleeping without a care in the world.

He grabbed his cell from the nightstand and saw that it was a few minutes before eleven. He groaned. Then he saw that his mother-in-law, Ceci, had called him every hour on the hour for the past three hours. Amber had called him about 7:30 p.m.

He vaguely remembered letting his phone go to voicemail several times. *I've got to get out of here and go pick up Gage. I need a story. What's it gonna be?*

His phone vibrated and rang in his hand. Ceci. He answered.

"Buckner," he intentionally sounded crisp and official.

"Roy? Where are you?" In the background he could hear his son wailing.

Katie stirred by his side.

"I'm still at work. Is Gage okay?"

"He won't go to sleep. George and I have done everything we know to get him to go to bed. Nothing's working."

"I'm so sorry." *And I mean it. I'm sorry about everything.*

"When are you coming for him? I've been calling you for hours. Why are you there so late?"

"My partner and I were involved in a small traffic accident. We're both okay."

Katie sat up and gave him a questioning look.

He held his index finger to his lips. "As a precaution, they made us go to the hospital to be checked out. We should be out of here shortly."

Ceci sighed heavily into the phone. "I'm glad you're okay, but I hope you'll be here soon. George has an early tee time tomorrow, and I've got my bowling league early. I know I'm going to bowl horribly. I'm just so stressed and tired."

"Ceci, I'll get there as soon as I can. I think I see the doctor coming now. I should be there in less than an hour."

"I hope so." She hung up.

He lowered his phone and closed his eyes. *You can't undo this. It will hang over you for the rest of your life.*

Katie reached over and placed her hand on his arm. "Trouble?"

He used all of his resolve not to pull away. He inhaled, then blew the air out. "I've got to head home." He searched the floor to find his clothes. He started dressing.

"Are you angry?"

Yes. Yes! Angry at myself. How could I do such a dumb thing. "No." He zipped his slacks and sat on the bed next to her. He took her hand. "I'm not mad, but this can never happen again."

He agonized as her expression changed from sexual afterglow to confusion. *Look what you've done to her.*

"It wasn't good for you, was it?"

"What? No. It was great, but...I have a wife. I shouldn't have...succumbed to your many charms," he finished lamely.

She bowed her head. "Okay." She rose from the bed and slowly began to dress.

"Katie—"

"I *understand*. Pretend it didn't happen. We'll go to work tomorrow, and everything will be fine."

He knew it wouldn't be all right, but he couldn't worry about that now. He had to go pick up his little boy.

The drunken vivacious couple who'd entered the room the night before were gone, replaced by remorseful adulterers. Riding in the elevator, they avoided looking at each other.

When they got to their cars, he pulled her into an awkward hug. "I'll see you tomorrow."

"Yep. I'll be there."

"Go ahead and jump in. I'll wait until your car starts."

She did as he suggested, and as soon as the engine turned over, she gave a brief wave and drove away.

When he got into his car, his phone lit up with a text from Amber.

Are you okay? Mom said you were in a T/C. What happened? Don't call me, I'll get written up. I'll be home early. My partner and I got a gun tonight. W/C is giving us an early out as soon as we we're done with the paperwork. Just let me know you're okay from the T/C.

"Damn watch commander," he muttered as he texted her. "The last thing I want to do is see my wife any sooner than I have to."

48

KATIE

The next morning the stares of her RHD coworkers seared through Katie as she walked through the office toward her desk.

She'd curled her hair. Big deal. Yeah, she'd put on a little makeup, and horror of all horrors—she was wearing a dress.

She approached Darnell Wiggins who stood smearing cream cheese on a bagel in the cubicle that served as a small kitchenette.

He looked at her. "Good morning, Katie. You have a promotional interview or something?"

She smiled. "Nope, just tired of wearing the same old thing." She stepped into the cubicle and poured coffee into a Styrofoam cup.

Seeing Haywood coming her way, she exited the cubicle and passed him on the way to her desk. "Morning, boss."

"Morning, Katie. Pretty outfit."

"Thank you."

She sat down at her desk and wondered what time Roy would arrive. It was going to be disconcerting to see her partner after their tryst the night before.

Too bad. We did the deed, and I liked it. He might be married, but something is wrong with his marriage if he can make love to me the way he did.

Thinking back on their evening, he'd been starved for contact—and she was too. It was fate that had them partnered, and she was going to tempt fate every chance she got.

49

ROY

The night before, when he'd picked up Gage at his in-laws, they were furious. They hadn't appeared to notice his blood-shot eyes, and his rumpled appearance as they led him to the couch, where the toddler had finally fallen asleep.

Seeing his son was a dagger to his heart. What kind of an example was he being for his boy?

He'd taken the little one home, put him in his crib, and then showered. Afterward, he fell into his own bed, and immediately fallen asleep. The next thing he knew, Amber was in his bedroom tiptoeing toward him.

He sprang to a sitting position. "What are you doing in here?"

"I was checking to see if you were okay from the traffic collision."

He sighed. "I'm fine. What time is it?"

"Five."

He swung his legs off the bed. "Since you're here, I want to go in early and workout."

"Workout? What about the accident. What happened?"

"It was no big deal. We were rear-ended by someone yakking on their phone."

His room was dark, but he could tell she wanted to know more.

"Roy? Are you okay?

"I *told* you I'm fine. It was a nothing T/C."

"I'm not talking about the accident. You've been acting weird the last few days."

"You're not the only one who started a new job. I'm tired."

"Are...are *we* okay?"

"Yeah. Everything's fine."

"Okay." She watched him pulling on gym clothes. "I guess I'll hit the sack before Gage wakes up."

"Since he was up late, he'll probably sleep in." He hustled to his closet and picked out a suit, tie, and shirt.

She walked over and placed her hand on his shoulder. "Have a nice day, honey." She rose onto her toes and gently kissed him.

He remembered hours earlier Katie doing the same thing.

"I'll see you tonight." He rubbed her back as he walked past her and out to the garage.

After his workout and shower at the gym at PAB, Roy finished buttoning his shirt, and then draped his tie around his neck. He'd fled from the house to sweat out the booze from the night before, but he also wanted to avoid Amber.

She had sensed something was different with him and it was...he was filled with guilt.

How had he lost control and slept with Katie? *Because you haven't been laid in fucking forever.*

He finished dressing and headed up stairs.

As he walked past the cubicles filled with detectives, he felt as though all eyes were on him. *Cheater! Cheater!*

He imagined his coworkers were watching him, judging him, knowing his unfaithfulness to his wife.

He got to his cubicle.

Katie was already there. She swiveled around to greet him.

Aw shit.

Her gaze was filled with passion.

50

———————

AMBER

Amber knew she was pushing the limit of her mother's patience when she called Ceci at the bowling alley.

"I'm bowling a one sixty game. Do *not* ruin this for me."

"Mom, will you call me when you're done bowling?"

"Please don't tell me you want me to watch that little boy."

"Just do as I ask, Mom. Please."

Two hours later, after leaving Gage with her mother, she pulled into the burger joint at Corbin and Nordhoff in Northridge.

She entered the restaurant and saw him sitting in a booth by the window. She slid into the seat opposite him.

"I'm surprised you came."

"Me too." She smiled. "I guess you're part of the trend to let arrestees out of jail. So, what have you got for me?"

"You said you'd buy me lunch."

"Not a problem. What do you know?"

"Lunch first."

After Antonio Lima had put away an All-American Burger and some onion rings, he was ready to talk.

"Antonio. You told me my partner raped your sister. I need details."

"You're not going to believe me."

"Try me."

He fixed his gaze on hers. "It's been over ten years. My parents saw what happened to me, and how I'd been sucked into the gang. They didn't want that for my sister."

He gulped half his soda. "They signed her up for the cadet program." He shook his head. "Araceli got through the leadership program fine. Then she was assigned to the Topanga Cadet post."

She dipped a French fry in ketchup and popped it into her mouth. "Okay, then what happened?"

"It was during summer vacation. The cadets had a campout at Zuma beach."

"Go on."

Beads of perspiration popped out on his forehead. "I don't know what happened the other days, but on the last day, there were three girl cadets who were asked to stay behind and help the officers who ran the cadet program to clean up."

"Okay."

"My sister was one of those who stayed behind."

"So, what happened?"

"She got home on Sunday afternoon, and we all knew something was wrong. She was as white as you are, and she was shaking." Antonio shook his head. "We all tried to find out what was wrong, but she insisted she was fine." He sucked the remainder of his soda through the straw.

"Late that night, after everyone was asleep, she came to me. We snuck out onto the front porch, and she told me that her police advisor, Officer Sutton, got her drunk and raped her."

PART VI

51

HAYWOOD

Haywood had been with the LAPD long enough to recognize when two co-workers were having an affair.

Clue one had been when Nanako had shown up all dolled up in makeup and a skirt.

Clue two was when Buckner showed up ten minutes later, acting nervous as a nun at a penguin shoot.

He had to give Buckner credit. Less than a week, and he'd nailed his partner. As their captain, he wanted to know more.

He hit the button on the side of his desk to summons Wiggins. Had his adjutant picked up on the vibe he was getting?

Darnell thumped the door once and entered.

"Morning, sir."

Haywood motioned for his adjutant to take a seat. "What's going on with Nanako and Buckner?"

The sergeant shifted in his chair. "They're typing up the interviews they did yesterday. They talked to Adam Lowe's wife, Brandi, her *new* husband, Brent McGee, and Justin Lowe. He's Adam's brother."

"That's not what I'm talking about. What happened with Katie's transformation, and Buckner acting like he got caught looking up Barbie's skirt?"

Wiggins shrugged. "Who knows?"

Haywood grinned. "They're screwing." He grinned. "I didn't think either of them had it in them. Imagine that, Null and Void doing the nasty." He chuckled. "Send them in to brief me on their case."

52

ROY

Roy was finishing typing up the interview they'd done with Justin Lowe when Amber called. Guilt had him jumping to answer.

"What's up?"

"I don't want to bother you at work, but I have a situation and I need advice."

The last thing he had time for was another problem, but she needed him. His guilt over his infidelity pushed away anything else. "Tell me what's wrong."

He listened as his wife described going to Lanark Park, the foot pursuit, and the arrest of a gang member.

She told him of the accusations he'd had made when she was putting him in the car.

He silently fumed hearing she'd met an arrestee at a restaurant. Eyeing Katie at the desk next to him, he lowered his voice. "What the hell are you thinking? The guy is an asshole gang member."

"Roy, I believe him. He says my partner raped his sister."

He thought of all the things he could say—he *should* say—and bit them back. *He* was the one who'd acted irresponsibly. *Cheater! Cheater!*

"Okay. I can't talk about this now. Do not meet with him again. Write down all the information you have, and we'll discuss it once I'm home."

Wiggins appeared and motioned that their boss wanted to talk to him.

"I've got to go," he said, disconnecting the call. Under his breath, he muttered, "Damn Sutton. He needs to be tuned up."

The adjutant still stood there. "Hey, you two. Haywood wants to meet with you to see where you're at with your case."

Could this day get any worse?

53

KATIE

During their meeting with Haywood, Katie couldn't help but think the whole thing was a colossal waste of time.

He asked many of the same questions he'd inquired about days before. The only difference was they were able to provide a little information from witness statements. And even then, her captain didn't seem all that interested. He listened to the gist of their interview but didn't have anything helpful to offer.

Afterward, she and Roy sauntered back to their cubicle and looked at each other.

"What the hell was that all about?" Katie nervously smoothed her skirt.

He shook his head. "I'm not sure. Maybe he wanted an update before the weekend."

She shrugged and looked at her partner. "Did you bring your lunch?"

He gave her a wary look. "No. I left too early to make anything."

"Want to have lunch with me?"

"Where?"

"The Rendezvous across the street?"

"How about somewhere else?"

"What? You're afraid to go to a restaurant with me?"

"It's a restaurant inside a hotel."

She rolled her eyes at him. "They're used to cops coming in and getting us in and out. I thought you'd like that since we've got Robyn McGee to interview today."

She saw the mistrust in his gaze. *He blames me for what happened last night.*

"Come on," she urged. "Haywood screwed up our morning. Let's have lunch, and from there we can go talk to Robyn McGee."

He squared his shoulders. "Fine."

A half our later, they were in the Rendezvous lounge, which was located in a hotel across from the police headquarters.

He'd ordered a chicken sandwich with a soda.

She'd ordered a Caesar salad with a chicken breast on top...and a glass of wine.

When the server brought their drinks, he frowned as she walked away.

"What?"

"I think you have a drinking problem."

Katie's lips formed a thin line. "I think you need to mind your own business."

"Look, you drink on duty on a regular basis. I'm not willing to ride a complaint because you like your liquor."

"I need to take the edge off. In case you've forgotten, things have gotten complicated between us." She liked it that his facial features hardened.

"I thought we weren't going to talk about it." He made a motion with his hands. "We were going to push it behind us."

Katie pushed one of her ebony curls behind her ear. "Maybe *you* can forget what happened last night but I'm not there yet."

He looked at her, and she saw sincerity in his eyes. "I haven't forgotten or regretted what happened between us, but I won't throw away my marriage either."

"You're a liar. You regret sleeping with me."

The server brought their food.

He waited until the waitress left. "No Katie. There's no regrets for having sex with you." Sadness filled his face. "I've been sexually dead for a long time. You brought me to life and made me realize that I need to fix my problems at home."

She scoffed. "That's great for you, but what about me?"

"I didn't mean to make things harder for you."

She took a big swig of her Chardonnay. "Well, you did." Tears filled her eyes. "While you make up with your wife, I've got no one."

"I'm sorry. I don't know what to say, or how to fix things for you."

She leveled her gaze on his. "Love me again."

He threw his head back and looked at the ceiling. "I can't."

"You can't, or you won't?"

He lowered his head and looked her in the eye. "Why are you doing this? What is it that you want from me?"

"The same thing you want—to feel loved."

Twenty minutes later, she and Roy left the lounge, rode the elevator upstairs and locked themselves into a hotel room.

54

AMBER

Dreading facing her parents, Amber parked in their driveway.

She used her key to enter through the front door. She could hear cartoons on the television at the back of the house, and Gage playing with his favorite musical toy.

"Mama," he yelled catching sight of her.

Ceci looked up from her tablet where she played some kind of video game. "Have a seat. Did you find a babysitter?"

As she sank onto the sofa, she remembered the lie she'd told her mother about looking for a pre-school.

"Yes, I did. It's a great place." In actuality, the night before, she'd luckily seen a flier on a bulletin board at the station. She'd called, and prior to meeting with Antonio Lima, had inspected the location and paid the first month's tuition.

"I'm glad that's settled," Ceci said. "Your father and I have reached our limit."

"I know, Mom. Taking care of him has been hard for you."

"How is Roy?" her mother asked. "We were so haggard from our day with the baby that we barely talked to him."

Amber shrugged. "He's fine. In fact, he went in early to the gym at PAB before he started his day."

Her mother looked up at her and frowned. "After a traffic accident last night, he drove to the gym?" Her voice carried her incredulity.

She nodded.

"Did he tell you about the accident?"

"They got rear-ended. The other guy was at fault."

Relief washed over her mother's features. "I'm glad to hear that. I was worried. I'm not sure, but I think Roy had been drinking."

55

ROY

This time after crazed sex there was no post coital cuddling or satisfaction induced sleep.

They took turns using the shower and getting dressed.

As the minutes clicked by, Roy's lunch threatened to make a second appearance. He stood before the bathroom sink, glaring with hatred at himself in the mirror while adjusting his tie.

Katie came behind him and wrapped her arms around his torso. "That was heavenly."

He turned to face her and gently grabbed each of her upper arms. "Katie, we can't do this anymore. I *won't* do it anymore. I shouldn't have let you talk me into doing it again."

"You didn't need a lot of convincing."

She was right, and he knew it. "Okay, that's true. But this isn't me. I'm not a cheater, and I won't do it again."

She looked at him evenly, then gave a quick nod.

He released her arms and moved past her. "Come on. We need to go interview Robyn McGee."

They rode silently on the 10 Freeway toward West Los Angeles and Bel Air.

Katie used her phone to navigate. "She's north of Sunset —in Bel Air proper. She must do well as a casting director."

Relieved his partner didn't rehash their recent romp or the future, he nodded. "Look her up and see if we know any of the movies or shows she's cast."

Katie punched buttons on her phone then gave a small whistle. "She's cast two of the last five Oscar-winning films. Looks like she moved from staffing television shows probably about the same time as when she and Brent McGee split."

They parked two doors down from a green, cape cod style home surrounded by a white picket fence.

"Cute house," Katie gushed, exiting the car.

"Seems big for one person."

"We don't know that she lives here alone." Katie's heel caught on a brick in the walkway. "She may have remarried… or maybe she's shacking up with a cabana boy."

Roy scoffed and rang the bell.

They heard footsteps before the door opened. A petite redhead, wearing a cobalt blue blouse over black slacks stood before them.

"I'm Officer Buckner, and this is Detective Nanako. We're here to see Robyn McGee."

"That's me," she said, smiling. She opened the door wider and looked him up and down. "Please, come in."

She led them across honey-colored wood floors past the formal parlor, and into a homey den. The coffered walls and ceiling were painted a rich creme color. The sofa and club chairs positioned in front of the stone fireplace were also ecru.

The only pop of color in the room was a red patterned area rug, and some throw pillows on the couch.

Obviously, this woman doesn't have any kids, he thought.

"Please have a seat. Can I get you something to drink?"

"We're fine, thank you," Katie said as she settled into an expensive chair. "This is a beautiful house. Very chic."

"Thank you. It works for me." Robyn looked at Roy, her blue eyes wide. "What's this all about?"

He explained they were re-examining the Adam Lowe case.

"I don't know how I can help you."

Katie leaned forward. "We have a few questions. We couldn't help but notice your ex-husband is now married to Adam's wife, Brandi. How did that come about?"

Robyn chuckled. "You mean did Brandi murder Adam in order to seduce my husband?"

Katie shrugged. "I wouldn't put it quite so blunt, but...yeah."

"I married Brent about a year before he decided to go into the police academy. He was a construction worker trying to get some gigs as an actor."

She smiled. "He had the looks, but he couldn't act. I tried to throw him work and managed to score him a few commercials, but I knew that acting wasn't a viable career for him.

"He was at an audition, and some cop trying to break into films told Brent the LAPD was hiring." She brushed imaginary lint from her slacks. "That weekend he took the written test, and a couple of months later, he was in the academy. He and Adam Lowe were in the academy together and became best friends."

"How did it come about that you and Brent divorced, and he and Brandi married?"

She inhaled, then blew the air out. "Brent and Adam were best friends. As they got further through the academy, they felt they could relax a little. The boys decided they wanted the four of us to double date and go out to dinner."

Robyn's expression turned wistful. "From the moment they met, I knew Brent was attracted to Brandi."

"How so?" The question came from Katie.

"He couldn't take his eyes off of her. He told all his best jokes in about an hour." Robyn shook her head. "It was like Adam and I didn't exist. My hussband had this goofy grin as bright as Glitter Gulch in Vegas."

Roy leaned forward. "How did Adam react to Brent's obvious interest in his wife?"

"You know, Adam was a mellow guy. He seemed more amused than upset. Brandi is a looker, and I'm sure he was used to it."

"And what about you? How did you react to your husband's infatuation with another woman?"

Robyn laughed. "Brent and I had a big fight that night. I told him he'd made an ass of himself, and I wouldn't be surprised if Adam distanced himself *and* his wife from us."

Katie nodded. "How did Brandi react to Brent's attention?"

The redhead scoffed. "That Brandi, she's a smooth one. She plays all innocent, but I spotted her a number of times catching Brent's eye and giving him a smile—a smile meant only for him."

Roy shifted in his chair. "Did they have an affair? Is that why you and Brent got divorced?"

Robyn smiled and shook her head. "No on both counts. Our marriage was doomed almost from the start. Brent is pretty conservative. Most of Hollywood isn't."

"You're saying that you and Brent divorced over political differences?" Katie's tone held a hint of disbelief.

"It wasn't politics so much as the fact that he'd bring up controversial subjects at any gathering of my industry friends." She sighed. "I told him to stop because I was losing the opportunity to work on exceptional projects. He couldn't control himself, so I booted him out. Oh, and I think he was seeing other women by that time too."

Roy shot a look at Katie, then focused on Robyn. "Do you think the other woman was Brandi?"

Robyn threw her head back and laughed. "You'd think so, wouldn't you? No. They had some kind of sick game going. They'd flirt and lust after each other, but never do the deed."

Katie tilted her head. "How can you be so sure?"

"Because like any rich bitch Hollywood wife, I hired a detective and had my husband followed."

56

———

SUTTON

Sutton twisted the top off his beer and took a healthy slug. He'd been irritable since last night after Buckner went in foot pursuit and actually caught the guy.

That hadn't been the plan at all. His intention was to have some gangsters rough her up a little, then he, Rudy, and Fish would come bail her out.

Instead, she'd captured a gangster and got a gun out of it too.

But that wasn't why he was peeved. He couldn't put his finger on it, but there was something hinky going on between his probationer and the suspect, Antonio Lima. It was like they had information he didn't.

He moved over to stand in front of his kitchen sink and look outside. "Damn squirrels. They run across the side fence and make the dog next door go nuts." *I'm not sure who I'd pop first, the squirrel or the dog.* Finally, the neighbor called in her dog.

He reconstructed the previous night and nailed down the moment when he felt things were off between the Lima and his partner.

She'd put him in the rear seat of the car, and when she'd turned around, she had that deer-in-the-headlights look—like he might have overheard something he shouldn't have. But what would a hardened gangster have to say to a boot cop?

Then he got a crazy idea. What if she'd somehow hired Lima to run from her and *let* her catch him? Then to *really* make herself look good, what if she'd given him a gun to toss?

The more he thought it about it, the more plausible it seemed. He'd told her they were going to Lanark Park, and when he got back to their black and white after taking a piss, she'd been on her phone. She could have been texting Lima.

He slid his phone out of his pocket and dialed.

"What do you want asshole?"

That was Rudy's standard way to answer his phone calls. "You and Fish are working tonight, right?"

"Yeah."

"Listen, you know that gangster Antonio Lima we bagged last night?"

"Yeah."

"See if you can find him and shake him down again tonight. I got a funny feelin' about him."

"What are you looking for?"

"I'm not sure. He just seemed too relaxed with Buckner."

"What do you mean?"

"It was almost as if they were plotting against me."

Rudy sighed. "Look, Duane, I didn't want to say anything in front of Fish, but this crusade you've got against your partner is gonna get you in trouble. She's not unsafe or whacky like you thought. She's done well for somebody who only has a few days out of the academy."

"Are you done?"

"Yeah. I don't think you're listening."

"You're right. I'm not. Try to find the *cholo* and mention Buckner. See how he reacts. Can you do that?"

"Yeah, I'll do it. But he may be holed up since you pinched him last night."

"Try. That's all I ask."

57

KATIE

"This is certainly an interesting turn of affairs," Katie said. She punched the address of Enigma Investigations into her phone. "We're headed to little Santa Monica Boulevard just west of Overland."

Roy nodded. "At least she didn't hire someone in Hollywood or the Valley. This place isn't all that far away."

Katie scoffed. "Yeah, but it will probably still take us the better part of an hour to get there."

Enigma Investigations was located in a small strip mall. Luckily, they were able to find parking in a small lot behind the building. While most businesses had a rear entrance, the PI's did not.

He held the door open for her, and a motion detector caused a melodic chime to sound to announce their arrival.

A lanky white guy, carrying a manila folder and wearing

tan cargo pants with a short-sleeved, button-down shirt appeared from the back office area and stepped to the front counter. He appeared to be in his forties.

"May I help you?" He focused on Katie. "You must be Detective Nanako." He extended his hand. "Ernest Exacto, owner of Enigma Investigations."

"Guilty as charged." She shook his hand. She nodded toward Roy. "This is my partner, Roy Buckner."

The PI offered his hand. "Detective, pleasure to meet you. On the phone, you indicated you needed information from an investigation I conducted some years back. I don't suppose you have a warrant, do you?"

Roy frowned. "Do we really need to go that route? We came from your client's home, and she stated she had no problem if you provided us information from the case."

The man nodded. "Yes, Robyn called me right after *you* called." He smiled. "I'm such a stickler for procedure that I always like to have a warrant if I can get one." He smirked. "With a name like Exacto, I do like to be precise."

"Uh huh," Roy intoned.

"Since Robyn gave me permission to talk to you, I will. In fact, while I was waiting for you to arrive, I located the file."

"Good," Katie said. "Do you remember the case?"

Exacto smiled. "Most of my business is following cheating spouses; most of them are run of the mill." He tapped the manila file folder. "But this one was memorable because the suspected cheating spouse was a police officer, and he obviously had the hots for his friend's wife."

"And?" Roy motioned Exacto should move on to the point.

"And Brent McGee often met for coffee with Brandi Lowe,

had lunch with her, and even occasionally met for walks in Chatsworth Park with her. But as far as I could tell, he never had sex with her."

Katie was taking notes. "When was that?"

Exacto opened the file and read from his report.

"It was almost twelve years ago in June, when I took the case."

"Two months before the Lowe murder," Roy murmured.

The PI continued reading aloud. "Subject McGee on three occasions drove to the Castaway Lounge in Marina Del Rey. On each of those occasions he met and drank with a different woman, then left the location with her following in his own vehicle to her residence. He'd enter, stay for several hours, and then go home."

"So, McGee was a cheater, but not with Brandi Lowe?" Katie turned the file on the counter so she could read the investigator's notes.

"Yep. That's right."

"What did Robyn say when you divulged the results of your investigation?"

Exacto twisted the file to face him. "I make notes about the client's reaction to the results of my report in the back of the file." He flipped to a page toward the bottom of the stack.

"I wrote she was calm and collected. She paid with a check, thanked me, and that was the last I've seen or heard from her until she called me a little while ago."

Katie nodded toward the file on the counter. "We're going to need the information on the ladies McGee picked up in the bar."

Exacto grimaced.

"We may not even talk to them," she continued. "It's been

a long time, and they probably won't remember him. We won't have to mention you at all."

"I don't like it," Exacto complained. "But Robyn paid for the info, and she said I could give it to you."

Katie gave him a big smile. "Excellent. Could you make me a copy of your file?"

58

ROY

For the first time ever, Roy was grateful for the traffic on the freeway—and Friday night traffic was the worst.

He needed to figure out what the hell was going on with him. He'd never been a player. Not with his ex-wife, and certainly not with Amber.

You're a cheater now. Once might be an impulse or bad judgement. Twice in two days was reckless. Are you trying to end your marriage? That's where this is going if Amber finds out.

He sighed and stared at the taillights of the car in front of him, not really paying attention, letting the driver in front of him lead him on the slow crawl north on the 101 Freeway.

"*Do* you want to end your marriage?" He shook his head. "Great. Now you're talking to yourself."

His phone rang. He looked at the screen. His friend,

Speakeasy. Roy pressed the button on his steering wheel, allowing him to talk hands-free. "Hey, brother."

"Padre. I haven't heard from you in ages. How are ya? How are things at RHD?"

He immediately thought of Katie. "They're going."

"I thought you'd sound more excited. You walk and work with the elite."

"Yeah, well it's not what it's cracked up to be."

"What's wrong? I've never heard you talk this way. You're the guy who gets along with everyone and everyone loves you."

"Yeah, maybe a little too much," he muttered.

"What'd you say?"

"I need advice. But you have to keep my business to yourself. Can you do that?"

"Padre, you're scaring me. Yes, I can keep a secret."

He was so ashamed. He didn't even want to say the words.

"Padre, what's wrong? Are you sick? Is it Amber or your boy? Are they sick?"

"No, no. It's nothing like that." He was sorry he'd brought it up.

"Stop jerking me around. What the hell is wrong?"

"I cheated on Amber."

There was silence on the line.

"Did you hear me?"

"Yes. I need to process what you just told me." Another bit of silence. "Why?"

"Because I'm an idiot, that's why."

"Roy, I've known you for almost twenty years. You're not the type who cheats. What's going on?"

He quickly related that the physical side of his marriage

was non-existent since his wife had been kidnapped. "I miss being close."

"I'm sorry, man. That was a long time ago. How terrible… for both of you. I know you guys were getting counseling. Isn't that helping?"

"Speakeasy, we don't even sleep together."

"You said you *cheated*. E-D. Does that mean the affair is over?"

He sighed. "Sort of."

"It either is or it isn't."

"I work with her. It's my partner."

"Oh hell."

"Yeah. It sucks."

"Padre, you've been around long enough to know better."

"I thought so too. It just kind of happened. She's a widow. She lost her husband and son in a car accident. She's lonely, I was lonely, and…"

"You need to stay away from her. Otherwise you're gonna keep screwing her." He paused. "Maybe that's what you want. Are you looking for a way out of your marriage?"

"No. I love Amber. She can never find out about this."

"She's out of the academy, right? How's she doing?"

"Her TO is some asswipe named Duane Sutton. He's been giving her a hard time. Last night, they popped a gangster and got a gun out of it. Sounds like she did well."

"Good for her." Speakeasy paused. "Go home and talk to your wife. But for God's sake, you can't tell her you slept with your partner. Explain what you've been doing hasn't worked, and maybe you should do something new. Then the two of you figure out what that entails."

"Easier said than done, my friend."

"I hear ya. But I know what I'm talking about. I screwed up three different marriages because I couldn't keep my pants zipped. Every one of my wives were honorable women who didn't deserve that kind of treatment. Now I'm older, broke from being divorced so many times, and the only women who are interested in me are either alcoholics, crazy, or have a passel of kids, cats, or both."

"Thanks, pal. You always put things in perspective for me."

"You're welcome. And either transfer or get a different partner asap. I'll check in with you soon."

"Later."

The rest of the way home he thought about his buddy's words.

He's right. What Amber and I have done for the past few years isn't working. We need to shake things up.

When he got home and walked into the house, soft music played, a roast was in the oven, and freshly baked cookies cooled on the counter.

"I thought I heard you come in."

He turned.

Amber walked into the kitchen, holding Gage's hand. She looked fantastic. Her long hair framed her face, and she'd put on makeup. Skinny jeans and a form- hugging sweater showed off her figure—trim and toned from the physical training in the academy.

"Daddy!" Gage broke from his mother's grasp and ran to him.

"What's the occasion? You look...fantastic."

"There's no occasion, and thanks. It's been a while since we've had dinner together." She smiled.

"Daddy, play."

"Give me a second, Son. I want to kiss Mommy hello."

The boy watched with curiosity as his parents embraced.

Roy knew to go slow. And kissed her chastely. But he didn't mind because he experienced something he hadn't felt in a very long time. Hope.

59

KATIE

Saturday morning, and Katie didn't know what to do with herself. She'd already gone to the market and had completed two loads of laundry. Now what? The day loomed before her.

She'd cleaned her condo the night before while consoling herself with a bottle of a Sauvignon Blanc. She'd been mad at Roy. He seemed to blame her for their lunchtime tryst, and he'd wanted it as much as she did.

She was glad her parents weren't alive to see their daughter the past few days. They'd be horrified to learn she'd slept with a married man.

But no one understood her loss. Her husband was not her soulmate. He'd been demanding and critical. He'd pressed her to quit her job because he thought it was sordid. She'd have been rich if she had a dollar every time he'd lectured her: *"I'm a pharmacist, I help people. You wear men's pants, carry a gun, and consort with criminals."*

But Hiroki had given her Koji. After her son was born, she had a reason to get up in the morning and a reason to live. Until a drunk driver shattered her heart.

That fateful night, prior to the accident, Hiroki had chastised her in front of the people at the airport, shouting at her in Japanese. There wasn't a big crowd in the wee hours of the morning, but it was still humiliating.

The onlookers hadn't understood the language, but they'd translated her husband's scowl and the fist he shook at her.

If they'd known Japanese, they would have heard him say she was a moron to bring their child out into the cold. He didn't know why she was so headstrong and why she couldn't be more like his friends' wives. And then the final blow. He wanted a divorce.

Was it wrong that she didn't feel the loss of her husband? Oh, she'd pretended and lied to family, friends, and co-workers after the accident. She couldn't control her tears at the funeral, but her distress was due to the death of her son, who was buried next to his father during the same service.

Now, she was alone. Totally alone.

She really should go visit Koji. She liked going to the cemetery. It was so peaceful and quiet. That's what she'd do.

60

AMBER

Amber woke up disoriented. She wasn't in *her* bedroom. She was in Roy's...the master bedroom they hadn't shared in almost two years.

She smiled to herself, remembering the night before when they'd finally had some physical contact. After the initial sweet kiss, he didn't push her, and they'd merely held each other until they were both asleep.

She was alone in bed, and she could hear Gage and her husband talking, probably from the kitchen.

A little later she was showered, dressed, and ready to discuss with Roy what the gangster Antonio Lima had told her when she was putting him in the police car.

Going into the kitchen, she found the toddler sitting at the kitchen table avidly watching *Paw Patrol* on television.

Roy was pouring cereal into a plastic bowl. He smiled

when he saw her and went to her and gave her a kiss on the cheek.

She tried not to cringe. *Let him touch you. Otherwise, he'll find someone who will.* She hadn't forgotten the scent of orange blossoms he'd carried two nights ago.

She made herself a cup of coffee. "We need to talk about the guy I arrested the other night."

"What guy?"

"The gangbanger I arrested in the foot pursuit."

"Oh, jeez, I forgot all about that." He sighed and held up the egg carton.

She nodded. "I think he's telling the truth." While he scrambled eggs, she retold the gangster's story.

"You have to promise me you won't meet with him alone again."

"I understand. In fact, I was hoping you'd go with me and have him tell you the story. I didn't really know what to ask him. You would."

He set his fork down and locked his gaze with hers. "You realize this guy is alleging major misconduct. You should have immediately called for a supervisor or at the very least *told* a supervisor—that night. Now you've dragged me into it."

He is never satisfied with what I do.

"But because you're right out of the academy, they won't come down too hard on you. Maybe a comment card in your personnel package—and those are removed after six months if you don't screw up again." He swallowed the last of his eggs. "You've got a number to contact this dude? What's his name?"

She nodded. "Antonio Lima."

Roy's head snapped up. "Did you say Antonio Lima?"

"Yeah. What's the big deal?"

"Is he a South Side Slayer?"

She cocked head. "Yes. How did you know that?"

Roy quickly told her about the Adam Lowe case. "Antonio Lima is a potential suspect in the cold case I'm handling." He grinned at her. "Okay. Set up a meeting. We'll both go. Have him meet us at Orcutt Park on Roscoe. Set the time and the place, without letting on I'm your husband. Keep it short and if he has questions, tell him you'll answer them when you meet."

She grabbed her phone and started texting.

After a few minutes, her phone chimed. She looked at the screen. "He says one o'clock."

"Perfect. That gives us about three hours. We've got to find someone to watch Gage. While it would be more convenient to go to your station to run his rap sheet, I think we should drive downtown to my office. No one at PAB will bat an eye at me showing up. At your division, they'd wonder why you were at the station, and why I was on a Topanga computer."

"What are we going to do with our boy? I can't ask my parents again."

"What about that teenage girl down the street? She might be looking to make some money."

"I'm not comfortable leaving him with a stranger."

Roy's cell phone rang. He grabbed it up and answered.

Amber had seen the caller's name. *Katie.*

PART VII

61

ROY

"Hey there," Roy said, into the phone praying Katie wouldn't bring up their dalliances, making for awkward conversation in front of his wife.

"Listen, I happened to be in the area of Justin Lowe's home and guess who's visiting?"

"Adam's brother? What are you doing up there?"

"I visited my kid at the cemetery. Afterward I thought I'd take a drive up Mulholland. I cruised by Justin's house on a lark. But guess who's there?"

"Who?"

"Either Brandi or Brent McGee—or both. There's a pickup truck in Justin's driveway registered to the McGees. I called into work and got the on-call detective to run the plate."

"Well that's weird. I didn't get the impression they were all that close."

"I got a photo of the truck in the driveway. We'll store that away in case we need it down the road."

He glanced at Amber. She was watching him closely.

"Hey, Katie, if you're not doing anything, I need a favor."

"Name it."

"Could you watch Gage for me for a couple of hours?"

Amber gasped.

"Your son? I...I guess so. Is everything all right?"

"Everything is fine, but my wife and I have an appointment, and there is no way we can take him along. We'd ask her parents, but after our accident the other night, I think they're kind of burned out on babysitting. I wouldn't ask you if it wasn't important."

"Okay. Should I come there?"

"No. I'll drop him off. Can I bring him in about forty minutes? I'll bring his lunch, and he should go down for a nap shortly after that. With any luck he'll sleep the entire time you've got him."

"Will your wife be with you?"

He glanced at Amber whose expression was dour. "Uh, yeah."

"All right. See you then."

He hung up.

"How could you do that without asking me?"

"It came to me while I was talking to her. She and Gage got along fine the other day when I was over there."

"I know *you* feel comfortable with her watching him, but *I* have no clue about her at all."

He ran a hand through his hair. "Well, it's your parents or Katie. There aren't a lot of choices."

He could tell she was weighing their options. "Okay. I should probably meet her anyway."

Later he, Amber, and Gage stood in front of Katie's door. He knocked.

She welcomed them with a smile. "Hello. Please come in."

The three of them shuffled inside.

Katie offered her hand to his wife. "Hi. I'm Katie. Roy's partner."

"Amber," his wife said, displaying her polite social smile and giving Katie's hand a firm shake. "Roy's wife. Gage's mom."

He inwardly winced. He was probably imagining it, but both women seemed to be reciting their résumé in relation to him.

"We really appreciate you helping us out, Katie. Especially on such short notice."

Katie waved her hand, "It's no big deal." She stooped down to look Gage in the eye. "Do you remember where the fire truck is? Can you go find it?"

The toddler ran off to where he'd taken his nap earlier in the week.

"This is really nice of you, Katie." Amber smiled. "He's a good boy, but he can be a handful if he gets out of sight."

Katie laughed. "Oh, I know little boys." She motioned to her sofa. "Would you like to sit down? Or something to drink?"

Roy shook his head. "No. We have to go. Thanks for doing this Katie. We should be back no later than three."

"No worries. I'm sure we'll be fine."

Gage returned, carrying the red fire truck. "Mine."

His wife handed the diaper bag to Katie. "Everything he needs is in here. There's two sets of extra clothes."

"Don't worry. I'll take good care of him."

Roy looked down at his son. "You're going to stay here with Miss Katie. You do what she says." He grabbed Amber's hand. "Come on. We've got to go."

62

ANTONIO

Antonio paced the gravel parking lot at the Orcutt Horticultural Center. He'd stolen and ridden a bike from his apartment. The exercise had taken some of the edge off what he was doing.

Years of carrying his sister's rape inside led him to despise the police. Over the years he'd tried to get his sister to report the piece of crap cop who'd defiled her.

Araceli had told him to forget she'd ever told him. "Nothing will happen to him, and he may come after you." It killed him to think his sister was carrying her burden to protect him.

After learning of his sister's rape, he'd put a green light on Sutton, but the *puta* had disappeared. Antonio made the assumption the douche bag had transferred or quit.

But the other night when pinched by the cops, he about

shit a brick recognizing Araceli's attacker and confirming it by his name tag.

As for why he'd told the chick cop who'd cornered him under the car, he couldn't say. It was the first time he'd been arrested where the officer didn't seem to judge him. She seemed to be pretty green, so maybe she hadn't turned into a bitch yet.

"Speak of the devil," he whispered as a nondescript sedan pulled into the lot. The woman officer was riding shotgun. Some dude was driving.

They got out of their ride and approached him. The chick smiled.

"Antonio, this is my partner, Roy."

He sized up the other man. The detective was all business and clearly had been around for a while.

"Let's have a seat," the cop said, bobbing his head toward a picnic table and benches.

The cops sat on one side.

He sat on the other.

Roy pulled out a tape recorder and set it on the table. "I'm going to record your statement."

Antonio shook his head. "No. I ain't gonna talk if what I say is recorded."

"Look, pal, you're looking at going back to the joint on the felon with a gun charge you picked up two nights ago. If you can give me solid info, I'll tell the DA you helped me out."

Antonio smirked. "Geez, I'm not afraid of gettin' locked up. Nobody stays inside for very long anymore."

To his credit, the man cop nodded. "True enough, but it never hurts to have it on the record you cooperated when we asked. I want to record what you tell me. You've made some serious accusations about a police officer. I need to know everything about it. I don't want to miss something important because I'm taking notes. You can either do this my way or Officer Buckner and I take off. Your choice."

Antonio looked at the woman. She gave a slight nod. "Fine. Let's go."

He turned on the recorder, and after some introductory information about the date, time, and who was there, he told Antonio to tell him what he'd told Officer Buckner on Wednesday night.

Antonio related the story again.

"Do you remember when this happened? The closer you can get to a date, the better."

"Yeah, it was near the end of August, eleven years ago."

"How do you know that?" It was Buckner who asked the question.

"Because it was right around my birthday." He could feel heat creeping up his cheeks. "I was kind of sorry I wasn't part of the group to go to the beach. It would have been cool for my birthday."

"Okay, so you said two other girls were with your sister at the campout. Did they see your sister's assault?"

"No, but that's because they got raped too." He saw the woman shoot a look at the man detective.

"You're saying all three girls got raped?"

Antonio nodded. "Yes. Yes. There were three cops and three girls. The cops got the girls drunk and then had sex with them. My sister was fourteen."

"Who were the other girls?"

"My sister's friends. Maria Gonzales and Teresa Pineda."

"What are the names of the other two officers?"

He shook his head. "I'm sure my sister knew. She may have told me then, but that was a long time ago."

"Where did the assaults happen?"

"At the beach. The rest of the kids were driven back to the police station on a police bus. The cops and the girls had stayed behind to clean up and pack a van."

"Where did they get the booze?"

"The cops gave it to them."

"I mean, where did the cops obtain the booze? Was it in the van or did someone go buy some?"

Antonio shrugged. "Look, I wasn't there, and it's not like my sister told me every little thing they did."

The man turned off the recorder. "We're going to need to talk to the girls."

Antonio scoffed. "Good luck with that."

"Why?" It was Officer Buckner. "What do you mean?"

He sighed. "Maria killed herself about three months after it happened. Rumor was she got knocked up." He shrugged. "Was it from the rape? Who knows? Teresa Pineda was killed in a drive-by about a year after it happened."

"Well then, we'll speak with your sister. What's her name?" Buckner said.

"Araceli. Araceli Espinosa. I don't even know where she is. After the beach campout, she dropped from the cadet program. She started using drugs, then started whoring to pay for them." He squeezed his eyes tight. "She may be dead. I wouldn't be surprised."

63

———

KATIE

After Roy and his wife left, Katie played with Gage for about an hour. She'd given him a snack, and then put him down for a nap.

Amber Buckner was just as she'd imagined. A little taller than average with long brown hair and wide eyes that were a striking green. She was pretty, and Katie could see why her partner would be attracted to her.

Katie sat on the couch and started checking social media to see what she could find out about Brandi and Brent McGee as well as Justin Lowe. She was hoping to find out how close the McGees were to Justin. It certainly seemed odd that one or both of the McGees would visit Lowe the day after the cops were there.

She hadn't been at it long when Roy and Amber returned. She was dying to know where they'd been and what they'd been doing, but she would never ask in front of his wife. Katie was fairly certain she could glean the information form Roy on Monday.

They didn't stay long. Her partner headed to the bedroom to gather up the boy, and Amber offered her an envelope. From the weight and feel, she knew it was probably a thank you card containing a gift card inside.

"We really appreciate you taking care of Gage. I hope he wasn't any trouble."

"No, we played, he snacked, he napped. We had a great time together."

Roy appeared with his son sleeping in his arms.

"I'll see you on Monday, Katie. Thanks again."

After they left, her condo seemed barren. She sat down and reviewed the photos she'd taken of the Adam Lowe murder book. "Damn. I don't have any of the witness statements."

Some detective you are. I wonder if there is anything in the official files to indicate how tight Justin was with his brother and Brandi?

She wandered into the kitchen to pour herself a glass of wine. The walls of her home were closing in. She needed to get out. *It's late Saturday afternoon. Traffic won't be bad. You could go to the office and take a look at the murder book. You've got nothing else to do.*

She changed her clothes, put on makeup, and curled her hair. She looked at herself in the mirror. *Who are you kidding? You're making an excuse to go out. After you go downtown, you'll head to a bar and maybe, just maybe, you'll meet someone nice.*

She drove to PAB, but inside she knew she was stalling until the bars started to get crowded.

After a discouraging review of the witness statements in the murder book, Katie pushed herself away from her desk. "What a waste," she muttered. "I hope this isn't an indication what the rest of my night is going to be like." She grabbed her purse.

The main dinner hour was well over when she walked into a restaurant near her home that had a bar large enough to accommodate those who wanted to socialize before dinner, and the lonely.

She slid onto a chair at the bar and gave the bartender her drink order. While she waited for her wine, she scrolled through her phone. She was halfway through her drink when a lone male came in and sat at the bar leaving an empty stool between them.

He ordered a beer and watched the Dodger game on the television over the bar. During the commercial he turned to her and bobbed his head toward the television.

"You like the Dodgers?"

She smiled. "I live in LA. They're the home team. I like them better than the rest of the teams."

"I take it you're not a big baseball fan."

She shrugged. "Not really. I keep up on how they're doing so I can talk to my co-workers, but I don't pay a lot of attention." She shook her head. "I'm not truly invested."

"What do you do?"

Ah, he understands the language of being single in a bar...I threw out the work hook, and he bit.

"I'm a doctor." It was her standard bar reply.

His eyebrows shot up. "Impressive."

"It's not nearly as glamorous as it sounds."

He extended his hand. "Brad Cooper."

She sat back in her chair and gave him what she called her BS face.

He laughed and withdrew his hand. "No. I'm not pretending to be an actor—although people think that all the time. Mama named me after my grandpa."

She smiled. "What do you do...Brad Cooper?"

"I'm a fireman."

"Really?" Her tone held surprise. It wasn't often you'd find a hose jockey out by himself on the prowl. "Where do you work?"

"Station eighty-nine, in North Hollywood. What's your name?"

She extended her hand. "Autumn Fawn, and I am *not* named after my grandmother."

He shook her hand. "It's a very pretty name." He nodded at her glass. "Let me buy you another. You can tell me all about saving lives."

She laughed. "I'll tell you my stories but trust me, they aren't worth the price of a glass of wine."

64

AMBER

Early Sunday morning, Amber found Roy sitting at the kitchen table, making notes on a yellow legal pad.

"What are you doing?"

"That gangster is alleging some serious crimes. I want evidence to back it up. I'm making up a list of things we can do on our own to confirm the story Lima told us."

"What about investigating him for your case? What are you going to do?"

"Right now, nothing. We'll see how the rape investigation goes and get whatever information we need from him. Once he's helped us, we'll take a look at his involvement the Lowe murder."

"Do you think it's worthwhile to try to find Antonio's sister, Araceli?"

"I think we should make the effort. If she's as strung out

as he says she is, she won't be a very credible witness. But I'd like to talk to her anyway."

"Do you find it strange that the other two girls are both dead?"

"Yeah, it seems odd. I'd like to check it out. I can probably inquire about the Teresa Pineda drive-by without raising any red flags."

"What should I do?"

"There are documents at your station I need. The bad thing is that the documents are a decade old and probably stashed away somewhere."

She remembered the record clerk, Debbie Bailey. *She'd* probably know where those reports were. She told him about the clerk.

"It's going to be tricky. You need to find out from her where the documents might be stored, but you can't tell her why you need them."

"Why not?"

He made a face. "Because there are no secrets in police stations. Cops are the biggest gossips in the world. You have to trust me on that."

She shrugged.

"Not only that, it will seem very odd for a P-1 to be looking for such old DFARs and logs." He gazed off into space. "I've got to come up with a plausible reason for you to be looking for them."

He set down his pen and looked her right in the eye. "Amber, if these allegations are true, and Sutton gets wind of what you're doing, you could be in danger."

"What? You think my partner is going to try to kill me?" She grinned at him and shook her head.

"Desperate men do stupid things. He's getting close to retirement. If the story is true, he thinks he's gotten away with it all these years. He could do anything to make sure the story doesn't come out."

A wave of fear washed over her as she realized what was at stake.

He turned to a new page on the legal pad. "Okay, I'm going to make a list of what documents I need you to find."

65

ROY

Roy's original thought was that Amber should snap photos of the documents he wanted to review with her phone. Then he'd changed his mind. There'd be way too many documents to photograph.

"Listen, I want you find all the DFARs and Sergeant Logs from that year in August...especially the ones that are labeled *Admin* or *CRO*."

"What's CRO?"

"Community Relations Office. The CRO office includes the senior lead officers and the cops who work the youth programs. The logs from the CRO unit probably won't look like your Daily Field Activity Report. Their logs will look like a supervisor's log."

"Why wouldn't I just grab the folder containing CRO

logs? If Sutton was working in the CRO section that should be enough. Why do I need all the logs?"

He smiled at her. "Good question, hon. Remember, there were two other victims. That would indicate two more cops may have been involved. Once we have the date of the campout nailed down, I'll look at what *everyone* was doing that weekend. When you get to the station, log onto the computer and search the Forms folder for *Sergeant Log*. A blank form will come up—you'll know what you're looking for. We need to confirm what the CRO sergeant was doing that weekend too."

She nodded.

"Find the folders for August and bring them home. The DFARs will probably be divided by watch, days, nights, etcetera. Sergeant Logs will probably be divided that way too. There will probably be a number of folders. Find an empty paper box in Records. Put the folders in the box and load them into your car. Here's the tricky part. You need to try to avoid the station cameras."

She made a face. "You're not asking for much are you?"

"Remember it's more important for you to stay safe than to snatch these documents immediately. There is no statute of limitation for rape in California, so we've got time on our side. If you can't get them tonight, you'll try tomorrow."

"I guess so. But if Sutton did rape a cadet all those years ago, how can we be sure he's not currently sexually assaulting arrestees or probationary partners—other than me, now?"

66

SUTTON

There was nothing that Sutton liked better than holding court in the station parking lot at change of watch.

The day watch officers came in wrung out and looking to go home. He and his posse were fresh, drinking coffee, and ready to take on whatever the shift would throw their way.

As the most senior officer at the division, he only abided by the rules he felt were necessary—and immediately clearing after roll call wasn't a mandate he chose to follow. And for good reason.

Fish was telling one of his best stories in months.

"The bar was nearly empty so the pickin's were slim. I see this gal at the bar alone and sit next to her but leave a seat between us. Close enough to talk, but not so close she feels I'm invading her space."

Rudy grinned at him. "Yeah, I bet the invading her space came later. What'd she look like?"

Fish smirked at him. "I had me some mighty fine sushi last night."

Sutton affected a falsetto. "Oh, Neville baby, I gonna love you long long time."

Fish shook his head. "No. It wasn't like that. She was actually pretty cute, and damn, the girl could drink."

"So, what happened?" Rudy motioned with his hands for Fish to continue. "Were you a fireman or a doctor?"

"Fireman, and I'm glad that's what I said. *She* was a doctor —although that could have been a lie." He started laughing and snorted. "She told me her name was Autumn Fawn!"

The three men laughed hysterically.

"Was the sex good? Did she have any kink in her?"

Fish got more serious. "I'll get to it; I'll get to it. Gotta tell ya, she could really pack the booze away. I suggested we go to her place, but she wasn't having that."

Sutton punched Fish in the arm. "Yeah, she probably thought you were some kind of whacko serial killer."

"Well, she was kind of weird herself. Started crying about someone named Koji. I certainly didn't want to take some crying female to my place. She might be one of those weirdos who think because I banged her, we we're soulmates or some BS."

"So, what'd you do?"

"Well, you know I carry a lot of my camping gear in my truck—including my sleeping bag."

Sutton burst out laughing. "You screwed her in a sleeping bag? Let me guess. You were in the bed of your pickup. How old are you? Seventeen? Geez!"

Rudy tried to help his partner. "Did you at least find a place away from the bar?"

Fish nodded. "We weren't too far from that hole near the railroad tracks. I figured if that spot behind the blue spruce was good enough for Rudy and me to catch a nap on duty, it was suitable enough for Autumn Fawn and I to fornicate." He let loose with another peal of laughter.

"Did she give you her number?"

A look of amazement came over Fish's face. "You know, I don't think I even asked."

The trio broke out in more laughter.

67

———

AMBER

After Amber put on her uniform, she hustled down to the officers' report writing room and logged on to a computer.

As the system came to life, she saw her partner stop at the coffee maker in a small alcove across the hall from where she was sitting. *He can't see me on the computer before roll call—he'll want to know what I'm doing.*

"Buckner. What are you doing in there?" He sauntered over while sipping his coffee. He came behind her to see what she had on the screen. Luckily, the system was slow, so she didn't have time to pull up the forms section.

"I was checking to see if I had any e-learning videos to watch."

"There's no time for that crap before roll call. Log off and get your ass up there. Of all the things you should be worrying about e-learning isn't one of them."

She signed off the computer and followed him upstairs.

Hours later, she considered the fabled phenomenon of strange things happening during a full moon. She hadn't anticipated that would include her training officer acting oddly. He'd been in a jovial mood from the moment she'd climbed into their car and nothing she did during their shift seemed to break him from his spell. They handled a few radio calls, the most exciting responding to pick up found property.

As they drove into the station parking lot for their Code 7 lunch break, she wondered what was up with her partner. *Does he know I'm conducting my own investigation of him?* She shuddered.

It was almost four in the morning, and the "June gloom" fog had rolled into the San Fernando Valley, giving the station parking lot a graveyard ambience. The yellow-lenses from the pole lights tinted the thick vapor golden—when you could see them.

Her stomach grumbled in anticipation of gathering the list of documents Roy had written for her to find.

Sutton maneuvered into a parking stall at the station and killed the engine. "I'm going to the cot room and try to snag a little shuteye. Go ahead and request. After our forty-five minutes are up, come out to the car and use the computer to put us out to the station. Don't do it over the air. No need to alert supervision we're takin' an extra-long break."

"Yes, sir."

He started to exit and then looked at her. "What are you gonna do?"

"Maybe talk to the Records clerk. Learn how things work. They always seem pretty busy in there."

He sighed. "What a friggin' waste of time." He shook his head as he exited the vehicle.

As she watched him stroll toward the station, she picked up the mic. "21A1 requesting 7 at the station."

"21A1, okay 7."

Sutton was already inside the station when she reached the back door. *Good thinking to tell him you'd be talking to the Record clerk. If my partner or any of his minions see me looking at paperwork, he won't give it a second thought.*

Entering the Records Unit, she saw her pal Debbie in front of a large table that held rows and rows of open-ended boxes. She had a pile of crime and arrest reports at least a foot high. She was counting out copies and distributing the reports into various boxes.

The woman was obviously busy, but Amber only had forty-five minutes to find the reports she needed.

"Hi, Debbie. Would you be able to help me with something?"

"I'd like to, but I have to get all these arrest reports distributed before the court detail officer comes for them, and he should be here in a few minutes. What do you need?"

She moved closer and lowered her voice. "My partner has court on a case that's eleven years old. He asked me to find the arrest report and his DFAR and make a copy so he could take them to court with him."

Debbie stopped her distribution. "That's ridiculous. Why is he making *you* do that? *He* should be doing it. I have half a mind to go to the Watch Commander."

Amber shook her head. "No, no. no. I don't mind. It's important for me to learn how to do these things. But where would I find such old reports?"

The clerk started doling out the paperwork again. "Eleven years? They're going to be out in the parking lot. There are two metal storage sheds behind the garage. They're full of old reports."

"Is there a key somewhere?"

Debbie laughed. "No. They aren't locked. Heck, I think one shed is missing a door. The boxes are stacked in there. They used to be in order, but as the years go by, people need something, go back there and find it, and leave the boxes all a mess. I hate going there."

"Well, it will be good for me. Maybe I'll get inspired and organize things a little."

The other woman grinned. "Trust me when you see what you're dealing with, you'll want to get in and out."

"Thanks a lot." She started to walk away, then returned to Debbie. "Hey, do me a favor. Keep it to yourself about Sutton having me look for his reports. It's really not a big deal."

"He's an asshat, but your secret is safe with me."

Walking out into the fog, she couldn't believe her luck. Not only were the reports in a secluded place where she was unlikely to be disturbed, but the fog would shroud her from station cameras. Win-win.

When she reached the sheds, she realized Debbie wasn't kidding. The rusty structures looked like they could collapse any second. She crept to the closest one and opened the door. She grabbed her flashlight off her duty belt and turned it on.

Cardboard boxes lined the walls and were piled on top of each other, causing the boxes on the bottom to buckle with the weight of those on top. *How can anyone think this is the proper way to store files?*

It didn't take her long to figure out the boxes were in

order from the left wrapping around the interior with newer dates on the right near the shed's front.

Unfortunately, this structure's contents only contained about seven years of documents.

She turned off her light and slunk to the second shed. This building appeared to be the older of the two, and true to Debbie's description, one door was merely propped against the front opening.

She made quick time of entering and beginning her search. She found the needed year but there were so many boxes containing different documents. Finally, she found a carton labeled Sergeants Logs. She found the August folder and yanked it out of the box and set it on the ground. Below that box was one marked DFARs. She found those August logs quickly.

She whispered to herself. "Where is the box of CRO paperwork?" She finally spotted a crushed box marked Admin/CRO and reached for it.

"Police! Let me see your hands!"

Bathed in the glare of an officer's flashlight, she raised her hands in the air.

68

ROY

Roy hadn't slept. If he wasn't worrying about Amber trying to locate evidence against her training officer, he was worried about her finding out about what he and Katie had done.

Katie. A whole different problem. He'd decided he was going to have to sit down with her and have a long talk. Last night while staring into the dark of his bedroom he rehearsed different lines. Of course, at 3:00 a.m. they'd sounded perfect and gentle. In the gray of the dawn, his speech sounded stilted and blaming. *Shit!*

Rising early, he got ready for work. He wanted to see whatever Amber brought home...assuming she was able to locate the documents he'd asked for.

He was pouring coffee when he heard the large garage door open.

A few minutes later, she came inside, but her arms were empty except for her purse and jacket.

"Good morning. How did it go?"

She set her belongings down and headed to the refrigerator, shaking her head.

"Does that mean you didn't get a chance to look, or you couldn't find the logs?"

She took out a beer and opened it. "I got caught."

He closed his eyes and threw his head back. "Oh crap. Tell me what happened."

They both sat at the kitchen table.

"I found the folders. I had the sergeant's logs and the DFAR folders on the ground. I'd just found the CRO box when a P-2 assigned as station security discovered me. He lit me up and damn near put me in cuffs."

"What do you mean he lit you up? Where were you?"

She quickly explained about talking to Debbie and the storage sheds.

"Once he realized I was a cop and let me put my hands down, I told him I was looking for a report because you'd gotten subpoenaed to court on an eleven-year-old case."

He nodded. "Quick thinking."

"Not really. That's the same thing I told Debbie the record clerk, but I told her it was for my partner. What if the P-2 and Debbie somehow compare notes?"

"Highly unlikely. I doubt some P-2 is going to spend a lot of time chatting with the record clerk—unless she's hot."

Amber smiled. "She's a grandmother, but she looks great for her age."

"Were you able to bring any of the files home?"

She grinned. "Yes. I got all of them. I grabbed them right

before I left work. They're in my car. I didn't have a box." She set her beer down. "Come with me and we can carry them all in one trip."

He was curious to see what the logs would reveal.

They brought the manila folders to the kitchen table.

"I'll take the CRO folder," he said. "You can go through the supervisor logs. We don't know who the CRO sergeant was, so you'll have to read the narrative and see if anyone is talking about a cadet campout."

"Lima thought the trip occurred near the end of August. Maybe we should start looking from the fifteenth on?"

He nodded. "That makes sense." He opened the CRO folder and started leafing through the pages. "Okay, I've got Sutton's log where he's talking about prepping for the camping trip."

She stopped going through the papers in front of her.

He flipped through more pages. "Got it. August twenty-fifth. That was a Friday, so if the girls were assaulted on the last day of the trip, we're looking at August twenty-seventh." He flipped through more pages. "I've got the twenty-seventh." He read for a few seconds. "Oh, shit."

"What is it."

Roy looked her in the eye. "Eleven years ago, the CRO sergeant who was in charge of the cadet campout is my current boss, Captain Glen Haywood."

69

HAYWOOD

Unlike most people, Haywood didn't mind Mondays. His detectives were rested and ready to work, there was always something to do, and the day flew by. Sitting at his desk, he was like a general, prioritizing things to be done and ordering the tasks to be completed. He liked being in charge and controlling things.

He sipped his coffee while reading the morning report... anything the chief thought was important and worthwhile for the department's commanding officers to know.

There was a quick knock at the door, and Wiggins poked his head into the office. "Morning, boss. You got a minute?"

He motioned for his adjutant to come in.

"I was looking at the security logs from over the weekend, and I saw something strange. Buckner and Nanako were both here on Saturday."

Haywood frowned. "What time were they here?"

"That's the weird thing. They weren't together. Buckner showed up in the late morning. Nanako in the early evening."

"Did you pull up their computer records to see what they were doing?"

Wiggins smiled at him. "Of course." He passed a computer printout to his boss. "Buckner ran the usual stuff, wants, warrants, rap sheet, FBI record, FI search on a gangster from the South Side Slayers."

Haywood nodded. "Yes, I think they said something about South Siders on Thursday. Wonder why he came in to run them on Saturday?"

"If you look at the rap sheet, you can see that one of the gangsters was popped in Topanga last week for an ex-con with a gun."

"Interesting."

"You know, boss, I think Buckner may be a bit of a hot head.

"What makes you say that?"

"The other day he was on a private phone call and after he hung up, he was talking about tuning up someone named Sutton."

"Sutton? You sure about that?"

"Yeah. Heard it clear as a bell."

"Hmm. I thought I heard that Buckner's wife's training officer is named Sutton." He shrugged and smiled. "What was Nanako doing here on Saturday?"

Wiggins passed another sheet of paper over to him. "She was looking at Brandi Lowe—Adam's wife. She also looked at Brandi's husband, Brett. Then she was looking at Justin Lowe —Adam's brother."

"When you say looking at, what do you mean?"

"She seemed to be searching addresses and phone numbers mostly, and she did citation and FI searches too."

Haywood grabbed his chin. "Hmm. Seems like they're looking pretty hard at Brandi and Brett McGee being involved. I wonder what the connection to the brother is?"

"Want me to ask?"

He sat silent, thinking. "Yeah, if you can do it without being obvious. We don't want to tip them off that we get those security notifications. But inquiring about where they're at on their case shouldn't seem out of line. Be careful not to be pushy."

"Relax, boss. I've got it." Wiggins rose. "Remember you've got that phone call with the guy from the ATF at ten."

"Thanks for the reminder."

As soon as the adjutant was out the door, he picked up his cell phone and called Marnie.

"Well, Glen, this is a surprise. Aren't you busy on Mondays? I'm busier than a mosquito at a nudist colony."

"Actually, I *am* busy, but this can't wait. I have to ask you for a favor."

"What is it?"

"On Thursday night, one of your units made an arrest of an ex-con with a gun." He looked down at the printout Wiggins had given him. "Arrestee was Antonio Lima. I need that paperwork." He heard her chuckle. "What's so funny?"

"That was Amber Buckner's arrest. She and her partner were over by Lanark Park, Lima took off running, tossed the gun, and Buckner caught him hiding under a car. Why do you need the info?"

Because I'm asking you for it, you stupid bitch. "It may be related to a case we're working on here."

"Okay I'll have the reports emailed to you."

"Wait. There's more."

"What?" Her tone carried annoyance.

"I won't ask you to send me the paperwork, but I need to look through all DFARs and Sergeant Logs, including specialized units, near the time Adam Lowe was murdered."

"The Topanga officer who was shot in his driveway years ago? You think this Lima dude is connected to the Lowe murder?"

"Maybe. Keep it to yourself, but we may be looking at the wife and her husband—a sergeant at Hollywood. If you get the files, I'll swing by for them, or meet you and grab them. I can't let it leak that we're potentially looking at another cop."

"Jesus. Files that old would be in storage. I'll have to ask Records to find them."

"Once you've got them, text me."

"I understand. I'll call you back."

He disconnected the call, reached into the bottom drawer of his desk, and brought out a plastic bottle of antacid tablets. He shook three into his palm and quickly chewed them.

70

ROY

For once, Roy didn't mind the traffic on his way to work. His mind was filled with questions, possibilities, concerns about what he and Amber had found in the logs about the cadet camping trip.

The logs themselves weren't that helpful in telling what happened on last day of the outing, but they were certainly helpful in telling who was involved.

As he drove, he decided to tell Katie. She might see things that he'd overlooked. But they couldn't talk about it at the office.

He sighed. It was going to be a busy day. He was glad he and Katie had set their personal boundaries and hoped they each could uphold them.

As luck would have it, Katie was waiting for the elevator

to whisk them up to the fifth floor. Like him, she too held a metal container of coffee.

"Good morning, Roy. You're looking pretty serious considering we aren't even at our desks."

"Yeah. I need to talk to you."

She frowned and glanced to be sure no one was within earshot. "This isn't going to be a *where do we go from here* conversation, is it?"

The elevator opened and they stepped inside. "We *do* need to talk. But not here. Let's go in, be seen, and then we need to get out of here. We'll bring the Lowe murder book with us."

"What's going on?"

The elevator door opened. "We can't talk here. Let's be sure we aren't needed and hit the field."

She shot him a sidelong glance and used her ID card to proceed through the locked entrance leading to their office.

When they got to their desks, he set down his coffee and briefcase. "I'm going to check in with Wiggins. Be sure to respond to any emails or calls that need an immediate answer. I think we're going to be very busy the rest of the day if not the rest of the week."

"I don't like surprises, Buckner," she called after him.

He intentionally stopped by the sergeant's desk. "Hey, Darnell, how was your weekend?"

"Good. Nice and relaxing. How was yours?"

"Pretty much the same. It's funny how a murder that happened so long ago can fill your mind. I thought about the Lowe homicide the whole weekend."

Wiggins smiled. "Yeah, a lot of the cold case guys say that. Some of them even held off retirement in order to try to make that one elusive arrest. They finally give up, retire, and die a few months later. Who wants to go out like that—over-invested?"

"Not me, brother. I've got a family to occupy my time."

"Glad to hear it."

Feeling like he'd made enough of an appearance, he returned to the cubicle he shared with Katie. "You all set?"

"Yeah, but what's this all about?"

"Let me check my emails and phone messages. Then we'll leave."

PART VIII

71

KATIE

Roy tossed the keys to their detective ride to Katie. "You drive. You need to take me to my pickup. I've got some files to grab, and then I think we should go to your place so we can figure out what the hell we're dealing with."

They got into the vehicle, but Katie didn't start the engine.

"Let's go." He motioned for her to move.

"I'm not turning the key until you tell me what the hell is going on."

"Drive me over to the erector set," he said, referencing a metal parking garage owned by the city. "I'll grab the files and tell you on the way to your house."

She didn't move.

He sighed. "We're working two cases now...and one involves our boss—Haywood."

"What? What kind of case?"

"*Please*, go and I'll tell you on the way. This is serious. It could mean jail time for the people involved."

She started the car and backed out of the parking stall, then drove like a NASCAR driver out of the garage and over to the parking structure where his truck was parked.

He removed a box out of his truck and stored it behind the passenger seat of their plain wrap ride. He got in and fastened his seat belt. "Let's go."

Katie hopped on the freeway. "So, tell me."

He quickly related the foot pursuit and arrest of Antonio Lima by Amber and her TO—but intentionally didn't tell his partner the gangster's name.

"That's a good catch. That should earn her some respect."

"Yeah...it's gonna earn her something, but I doubt it will turn into anything positive. The guy Amber arrested was Antonio Lima—a South Side Slayer."

Katie turned head to him, her eyes wide. "The same Anotonio Lima who was looked at in the Lowe murder?"

Roy nodded. He went on to explain about Lima's allegation about Sutton assaulting his sister.

"And she believed him?"

He nodded. "Yeah. Over the weekend we both met with him. I believe him too. That's why I asked you to watch Gage."

"Oh shit. How is Haywood involved?"

"He was the CRO sergeant at Topanga at the time of the cadet outing."

"You don't think he's involved, do you?"

"Let me go on. There's more."

Katie's eyes widened again.

"There were twenty-five kids on the trip and five officers. There were two female youth services officers. They took twenty-two of the kids back to the station on the bus. That left the three girls, Araceli Espinosa, she's Lima's sister, Teresa Pineda, and Maria Gonzales. They were left alone with Duane Sutton, Glen Haywood, and...Justin Lowe."

"Adam Lowe's brother? That Justin Lowe?"

"That's the one."

"What does it all mean?"

He sighed. "Nothing good, that's for sure. But we need to find out."

72

MARNIE

Marnie liked calling the shots at Topanga Division and liked having a whole section of the city her responsibility.

Sometimes the road got rocky with the community wanting certain things, requiring her to ask her troops to go the extra mile so the public could see that the LAPD cared.

She walked a narrow tightrope to maintain relative happiness from all parties. Knowing there was no way to make everyone happy, she did her best not to inconvenience someone unnecessarily.

That's why she was so annoyed with Glen wanting some extra paperwork. She wouldn't burden her staff who were busy with their own tasks to find the documents he wanted.

As she did on most Mondays, she got a fresh cup of coffee and did a lap through the station, showing her face.

When she got to the Records Unit, she talked to the Principal Record Clerk, Anita Greenfield.

"Good morning, Captain."

"Hey, Anita. How are things going? How is your mother?" *Thank God you remembered she and her mother share a house.*

"She's fine...and turning into a cranky old lady." Anita laughed.

"Everything good in paperwork central?"

The head clerk nodded. "Yeah, that new hire from Hollywood Division is working out well."

"Glad to hear it. Hey, if I were looking for DFARs and sergeant's logs from eleven years ago, where would I find them."

A look of puzzlement crossed Anita's face. "They're probably out in the aluminum sheds out back. What is it exactly you're looking for? I can go out and find them for you."

"No, no. I'll send my adjutant. No need to take you away from what you're doing."

"Well, that's where they'd be. If he has any problems finding what you need, have him come get me."

"Will do. Thanks a lot."

Marnie returned to her office and made herself a note to gather the files from the shed. *I'll go out and get them before I go home.*

She grabbed the paperwork from her inbox. Her adjutant had gone through the chief's daily log and supervisory logs, highlighting anything that he thought Marnie should know about.

She skimmed through the logs and about fell off her chair when she saw an entry by the night watch commander.

0520 Hours. I was notified by Beaker #64208 who was

working station security that he'd found Probationary Officer Buckner #64579 in the aluminum storage sheds in the parking lot. She was looking for a report for her husband who has a court case on an arrest he made when he worked Topanga ten years ago. Good obs skills by Beaker. Wrote him a comment card.

Marnie sat back in her chair. What were the chances that Glen was asking for ten-year-old files kept in sheds at her station, and Amber Buckner was snooping around the same spot, looking for old files?

Something was going on. Should she alert Glen? Should she call Buckner in and lean on her? *No. Obtain the files, go through them and see why all of a sudden, the files are of such interest.*

More curious than annoyed, she exited her office, telling her adjutant that she'd be gone for about twenty minutes.

As she walked to the sheds against the block wall, she noted the heavy fog was burning off, and it was turning into a nice day.

It didn't take her long to figure out which shed held the documents she wanted. She stepped inside and saw the dust had been disturbed on a number of boxes. *Buckner no doubt.*

She found the box holding the DFARs. The month of August was missing. She then looked at the box containing sergeant's logs. She saw a box marked Narco and Vice. She lifted that box down to the ground. *Hmm…DFARs and sergeant logs are here.*

Her gaze fell on the CRO box. The August files were missing. What did it all mean?

73

ROY

On the remainder of their drive to Katie's condo, Roy was glad his Haywood bombshell had overridden any uneasiness between them. They were all business now.

Once settled at Katie's kitchen table, he showed her the documents establishing that their boss, Sutton, and Justin Lowe worked in the CRO office and were on the camping trip in question.

Katie placed her fingers on the side of her head and massaged her temple. "What does this mean? Do we think there's a connection between Adam Lowe's murder and the alleged rape of the female cadets?"

"I'm not sure how they'd be linked, but it's quite a coincidence both events would happen near the same time."

She gave him a hard look. "We shouldn't investigate the

cadet issue at all. We need to alert someone, so it doesn't look like we're trying to cover up police misconduct."

"Cover up? Hell, if those guys did what Lima says they did, I want their asses to fry. Besides, who are we going to go to, Haywood?"

"Internal Affairs. They're the ones who should be investigating. We're already working on a case."

"Yes, but it *may* be connected to the cadet rapes."

Katie shook her head.

"Let's do this," he said. "Let's see if we can locate Lima's sister and see what she has to say. She's the only victim left alive."

"Didn't you say Lima told you he hadn't seen his sister in a long time—she was a working girl?"

He nodded.

"Did you run her record?"

"No. Our computer searches can be monitored. What if someone, say Haywood, put a flag on Espinosa's name. He'd be notified we were running her."

Katie smiled. "Smart thinking. But how are we going to find out about her?"

"I'll call a buddy I know who works Vice at Van Nuys and tell him I'm in the field on a case and ask him to run Espinosa's rap sheet. I'll ask him to send me a DMV photo of her too. If anyone does have an alert on Espinosa, they'll see it was a Vice officer doing the search and hopefully, won't find it out of the ordinary."

"Very resourceful, but that doesn't tell us where to find her. How do we do that?"

He smiled back at her. "I'll have my buddy send the whole DMV record."

Several hours later, armed with the printout of Araceli Espinosa's DMV photo and rap sheet, they parked at the curb of a nondescript business on Sepulveda Boulevard in Van Nuys.

The glass door was painted with the letters VOTS.

As they entered, Katie asked, "What is this place?"

"It's a shelter for working girls—Victims of the Streets. The director knows many prostitutes, male *and* female. If Araceli is tricking in the valley, Linda Tyler will know her."

Once they settled inside the director's office, Roy introduced Katie to Linda.

"Officer Buckner is one of VOTS biggest advocates. Whenever he comes across someone who might benefit from our services, he actually brings them here."

Katie glanced at him and smiled.

"But since it's unlikely Detective Nanako needs our shelter, how can I help you?"

He pulled out the photo of Araceli Espinosa, turned it toward Linda, and pushed it across the desk.

"Araceli. I haven't seen her in months—maybe even a year."

Roy sighed. "Damn. We really need to talk to her."

Linda pushed the photo back to him. "What's she done?"

"Nothing. She's the victim of a sexual assault," Katie said. "We have potential suspects. We need her to tell us what happened."

Linda twisted the knob on a Rolodex. "I'll have to check to see if I still have a cell number for her," she murmured. She flipped through a number of individual cards, then sighed. "I'm sorry her number isn't here."

"Maybe some of the other girls," Katie urged. "Is there anyone staying here who might be in touch with Araceli?"

"I doubt it. Araceli has been gone for close to a year. We only allow the girls to stay for six months. If they want to go home, we assist them in getting there. If they don't, we turn them over to social services."

Linda handed Katie a trifold brochure. "We have teachers who home school grades four through twelve. Counseling is a required class. We have a substance abuse program. For the adults, we help them with training so they can find jobs. Real jobs."

He shifted in his seat. "What were the circumstances of Araceli's departure?"

"Once we got her clean and sober, she was one of our best residents. She trained for a job in an office environment. She finished her six months here, got a job at an auto repair shop, and planned to move home."

He retrieved a pen from his pocket. "Do you know the name of the shop?"

Linda shook her head. "No. I'm sure it was somewhere here in the Valley. But we teach the residents to be as independent as possible. We want them to know they can take care of themselves and be in charge of their own lives, so we don't get too involved with their job selection, unless they ask for help."

Katie refolded the brochure. "Wow, you've got fifty beds. You're doing God's work here. Could Araceli have gone back to the life?"

The director shrugged. "Sure, it's possible. There's no rhyme or reason to those who go on successfully and those who return into the sex trade. I will say that if she returned to working the streets, I think I would have heard about it."

He leveled his gaze on Linda. "Will you ask around? See if anyone has contact info. I wouldn't ask if it wasn't important."

Linda nodded. "I'll do my best."

74

HAYWOOD

Haywood had to fight his every instinct to call Marnie to see if she'd found the files.

She did have the arrest report on Antonio Lima emailed to him. From what he'd read, it sounded like Buckner's wife had done a stand-up job.

Wiggins tapped on the office door and then poked his head inside. "Captain Vega from Topanga is on line two."

He nodded and his adjutant retreated. He snatched up his phone. "What do have for me, Marnie?"

"Glen, the August files are gone. All the sergeant's logs. All the DFARs.

"What do you mean they're gone?"

"The boxes that held the files are there, but the August folders are missing. The files are gone."

"Who the hell has them?"

There was a pause on the line. "I have no idea." She sighed. "Why do you need these files? How are they related to Amber Buckner's gun arrest the other night? And how does that arrest implicate Adam Lowe's wife and her new husband."

Shut up and let me think. "I doubt the two things *are* related. Lima was a potential suspect in Lowe's death. I wanted to see if there might be information that Roy Buckner and his partner can use as leverage to question him again."

"What about all the logs? Why did you need them?"

"I'd heard Lowe worked at Topanga. I thought there might be something in the logs that would help. Maybe he had contact with Lima prior to the murder."

"Hmm. What does it mean if the files are gone?"

"I figure Buckner and Nanako must have picked them up. We'd talked about all of this last week. Guess they finally got to it."

"You need to tell your people that they just can't come marching into my division and walk off with official records. I want all of those files returned, Glen. I'm going to put a note in the boxes that *you* have them. I'll give you until Friday to bring them back here."

"Or what, Marnie? You're going to tattle to the commander or the chief? Don't you dare indicate I have those records because I haven't got them. I'll check with Buckner and Nanako, but if they haven't got them, the loss of official files is on *you*." He hung up on her.

75

KATIE

After they'd left the VOTS office, Katie told Roy she was hungry. They drove through In-N-Out Burger and cruised onto a residential side street and parked to eat their food.

Katie popped a French fry into her mouth. "How are we going to find Araceli if Linda Tyler doesn't come through?"

He stared through the windshield while chewing. It was clear he hadn't heard her question.

"Earth to Roy," she teased. "Come—in—Roy."

He jerked from his thoughts. "Sorry. I was thinking."

"No kidding."

He shifted in his seat, and his expression turned serious. "We need to talk."

Katie sighed. She'd hoped they would avoid this awkward conversation. They'd gone all day without even touching on their previous liaisons, and she wasn't anxious to talk about them now.

"What do you want to discuss?"

"Us."

"Is there an us?"

"Five years ago, maybe. But not now. I have a wife. I have a family, and more than that, I'm happy."

"You're married and you have a family, but you aren't happy. If you were, nothing would have happened between us."

He kept his gaze on hers. "You may be right." He ran a hand through his hair. "But I am determined to make it work between Amber and me." He paused and swallowed. "What we've shared meant a lot to me, and I thank you. But the last time *was* the last time. I hope you understand."

"I *do* understand. For different reasons, we needed each other. For those brief interludes, it was kismet, and now it's not. We're done and over. Let's not talk about it ever again and move on."

She watched the muscles in his face relax.

"You're a class act, Katie Nanako." He reached over and squeezed her hand.

Yeah. You return to your family life like nothing happened, and I'll go back to my empty condo and alcohol-fueled hook-ups with fake firemen.

She gave him a big smile. "You're not so bad yourself, Roy Buckner."

She wadded up her napkin and threw it into the cardboard box that had held her hamburger. "The day is still young. Since we can't go any further with Araceli Espinosa, I think we should try to find out how close Brandi and Brent McGee are to Justin Lowe. I find it really odd that one or both of them were at his house on Saturday."

"Good point," he said. "Brandi hasn't been Justin's sister-in-law for at least ten years. And now that he's a possible suspect in the rape of a cadet, we need to know more about him. The bad thing is that we can't start snooping around Justin Lowe's personnel file without tipping off Haywood we're looking at the cadet trip."

Katie started the car. "Who do we hit up? Justin or Brandi?"

"Brandi. If he thinks we're on to him, Justin won't give us anything. Brandi might be more open unless she has something to hide about Adam's death."

"Brandi it is, *and* if we need to talk to Justin again, he isn't all that far from her yoga studio."

He called ahead to be sure the yoga instructor was working. Once he hung up, he made a face. "Mrs. McGee is clearly annoyed that we wanted to chat again."

"All the more reason for us to see her again," Katie fired. "Let's see if she admits to meeting with Justin Lowe over the weekend."

As soon as they entered the studio, Brandi McGee hurried toward them. "I'm not trying to be rude, but I have a class starting in fifteen minutes. How can I help you?"

"We were wondering if you could give us more background on the relationship between Adam and his brother, Justin."

The blonde frowned. "Justin? I gave you his contact info. Why don't you ask him yourself?"

Katie added an edge to her voice. "Because we're asking you."

Brandi blew a wisp of hair out of her face. "What do you want to know?"

He smiled at her. "How long have you known Justin?"

"Seems like all my life. I met Adam in high school, and Justin was his big brother."

"Were there any problems between the brothers?"

She shrugged. "No more than any other siblings."

Katie caught her eye. "Did Justin ever make you feel uncomfortable?"

Brandi frowned. "Why are you asking me all these weird questions about Justin?"

"We're trying to get a fresh perspective on Adam's life and those who were close to him. Justin was a cop. Maybe someone was targeting him, and somehow got Adam by mistake."

He cleared his throat. "You mentioned Justin was hit by a drunk driver, and he left the department on a medical pension."

"So?"

"Do you remember when that happened?"

Brandi shook her head. "Can't you guys look it up in his files?"

Katie removed the edge in her voice. "His files are downtown in storage."

Brandi averted her gaze to Roy. "Let me think. It wasn't too long before Adam was killed. It was a rough period for the family. Their mother's Alzheimer's had gotten worse, Justin gets hit by a drunk, and then Adam's death."

"That's a lot for any one family," he expressed. "When was the last time you saw Justin?"

The yoga instructor smiled. "Funny you would ask. He asked Brent and I over for brunch on Saturday. We talked about you guys working on Adam's murder."

AMBER

Unfortunately for Amber, Sutton hadn't maintained his jovial mood from their previous shift. He'd barely uttered a word since they'd gotten out of roll call.

Worse yet, the radio was really quiet. Every hour seemed three hours long.

"What was the deal with that arrestee the other night? The guy who tossed the gun, Lima."

Her heartbeat raced like a 3-2 favorite in the Kentucky Derby. "What do you mean? You were there."

"You've been weird ever since we made that arrest. Especially right after we popped him. He seemed to be pretty chatty with you. What was he sayin'?"

"Nothing. I told him we were taking him to the station where he'd be booked."

Sutton set his lips in a thin line. "Let's head over to Lanark

Park. Maybe we'll find him again. Maybe we can chap his ass and catch him with another gun."

She didn't know what had set her partner off, but the last thing she wanted to do was to go looking for Lima.

A couple of minutes later, she spotted a car ahead of them with a rear taillight out. She ran the license plate to be sure the vehicle wasn't stolen. "Hey, that Hyundai has a rear light out. I'd like to grab a ticket."

"Not right now. I want to go find Lima."

Amber bit her lip. She had to do something. "Do you really believe he'd be stupid enough to be caught with another gun so soon?"

"Listen to me, sweet cheeks. Gangsters aren't like everyone else. They don't think the law applies to them. They'd as soon kill you as go grab a burger."

She clenched her teeth to keep them from chattering from fear. *Oh my God. Somehow, he knows that I met with Lima at the burger joint.*

"Do you remember Lima's address?"

"No," she lied.

"Call Records. They can check the index cards and give you the address."

She didn't have much choice. She pulled her cell phone out of her pocket, lowered the volume, and dialed the Records Unit. Switching the phone to her other hand she discreetly disconnected the connection after one ring but held the phone to her ear a few seconds longer. "The clerk must be in the bathroom or on her lunch break. No one answered."

"Shit." He nervously tapped his fingers on the steering wheel. "Try running him for his driver's license on the computer. There may be too many results for them to list though—there's probably a million Antonio Lima's in Los Angeles."

He was right. There were over two hundred, and the in-car computer wouldn't list them all. Inwardly, she cheered. Outwardly, she forced regret into her voice when she told him.

"Okay. We'll keep trying Records until we get the address."

The next time she called, she let the call go through. The clerk provided Antonio's address. Amber considered transposing the numbers, but her partner was so edgy, she wasn't sure what he'd do if faced with another setback.

It didn't take them long to find the small stucco bungalow and park several doors away. The small home was most likely built right after World War II. The yard was surrounded by a white picket fence, now gray and in dire need of paint.

Overgrown shrubs blocked the view of the front porch. And what little grass there was in the front yard looked more like straw stepping stones surrounded by dirt.

"Be alert, and if anyone bails out of the house, let em run," Sutton ordered. "We're just here for a friendly hello and see what our boy Lima is up to."

"Okay."

"Knock on the door. Don't stand in front of it. I'll cover you from the side."

She bristled at his implication she didn't know basic tactics. She also didn't like the plan at all. What if Antonio answered and greeted her by saying something to tip off her TO she and the gangster had met after his arrest.

As her partner moved to the side of the porch and got in position, her heart raced.

As she'd been taught in the academy, she gave three loud raps.

She could hear someone coming to answer, and the sound of several locks being undone. The porch light turned on and the entry was opened by a woman.

Amber needed a few seconds to make the connection, but once she did, she fought to conceal her gasp. She was looking at none other than the stripper Jewel Jubilee.

77

SUTTON

From his position at the side of the porch, Sutton saw his partner's look of surprise.

He stepped up to stand next to Buckner. He immediately recognized the woman as the stripper from the Bounce House a few nights ago. Wait! *It couldn't be.*

"Hello again," Buckner greeted. "We're looking for Antonio Lima."

The woman looked at him, then back to Buckner. "He's not here." She started to shut the door.

"Wait," Buckner said.

The entry was closed, and the locks were engaged.

Buckner looked at him. "That's the stripper from the other night. What is she doing here?"

"I...I...don't know. Let's go."

"What? Aren't you curious? Why is she here where Lima lives?"

"Come on. We gotta go."

"Wait! There's something wrong here."

He ignored Buckner and stepped from the porch, marching to their patrol car, then got in and started the engine.

She'd hesitated but soon followed. As soon as she climbed inside, he sped away.

"I'm not feeling well," he said. "We're going back to the station. I have to go home. They'll probably send you to the front desk."

"Do you feel faint? You got pretty pale for a minute."

"No. I'm okay. I just need to get out of here."

Once they arrived at the station, he went to the watch commander and reported he wasn't feeling well and needed to leave. As he'd predicted the sergeant assigned Buckner to work at the front desk for any walk-in traffic at the station.

He hustled upstairs to change into his street clothes. His hands were shaking so badly he could hardly dress.

Once in his own car he clutched his cellphone and dialed.

78

HAYWOOD

Haywood nursed his second beer at his favorite neighborhood watering hole. He eyed a blonde at the end of the bar. She was only about a seven, and he wasn't sure she was worth his effort.

His phone, which sat on the bar next to his glass, vibrated and lit with the caller's name. *Sutton.*

"Haywood."

"The shit's gonna hit the fan. I know it. I saw the girl. Actually, I saw her the other night but didn't recognize her. She wouldn't talk to me. Then tonight, I went over to the gangster's house, and the fuckin' girl answered the door!"

"Duane. Get ahold of yourself. What the hell are you talking about?"

"Weren't you listening? That little cadet gal I banged at

the beach has turned up. I just saw her. She's somehow connected to the gangster I arrested the other night. My partner must know something because she's been acting weird since we made that arrest."

Haywood was beginning to understand and the more he put things together the more alarmed he became.

"What are we going to do, Glen? Not only that, the little bitch is also a witness at an ADW call Buckner and I handled at a titty bar on Sunday. After all these years, that broad is turning up everywhere. What the fuck are we going to do?"

"Shut up and let me think." He'd never be able to put together a plan with Sutton panicking in his ear. "Are you at work?"

"No. I told them I was sick. I was so freaked, I had to get the hell out of there. What are we going to do?"

Haywood took a deep breath. "Stay home. Don't panic. I need some time to figure this out. I'll contact you as soon as I have a plan."

"You know this could be really bad for all three of us."

"There's no need to tell me what's at stake." He motioned for the bartender to close out his tab. "Watch how much you drink tonight but try to relax. I'll figure out what to do and get back to you. I probably won't call you until tomorrow."

"How you can be so calm? I've been worrying about this for eleven years. Now it's all going to fall apart."

"I have no intention of having any of it coming back on us. Have some faith, okay?"

"I'll try. Let me know as soon as you've got a plan. What are we going to do about my partner? I'm sure she knows something."

Sutton's panic was beginning to set his own heart racing. "Duane, you've got to remain calm. Go home and relax."

He disconnected the call.

79

SUTTON

Sutton hadn't slept at all. He shuffled to the kitchen to make some coffee, and while he waited, he downed an energy drink. *Thank God Patricia was already at work and the kids were on their way to school.*

He had the news on but wasn't listening. All he could think about was seeing the cadet-turned-stripper the night before.

How had he not recognized her at the shooting at the Bounce House? She obviously knew his identity then—that's why she wanted nothing to do with him. He should have made the connection.

While tossing and turning in bed, he'd racked his memory to come up with her name. All he could remember was Espinosa. He couldn't put a first name to the only virgin he'd had.

The passage of time had faded his memory of the girl and what happened at the campout. The day of their *private* beach party, after she'd sobered up a little, he gave her a warning that she could never tell anyone what they'd done. And if she did blab, she'd be the reason her gangster brother got sent to prison whether he deserved it or not.

She and her two friends had quit the cadet program immediately after the camping trip. He'd transferred to Van Nuys Division, promoted to training officer, and then moved back to Topanga Division.

Someone rang the doorbell.

He looked at the clock over the kitchen sink. "Shit. It's not even eight o'clock." He started toward the front of the house, then stopped. *What if the stripper found out where I live? What if she'd told her brother, and he's decided to come kill me?*

Whoever was out front rang the bell again.

Sutton tiptoed to his bedroom and grabbed his Glock off the nightstand, then tread softly to the peephole in the front door. Relief washed over him when he saw Haywood positioned there, looking pissed.

He undid the locks. "Thank God it's you. I was afraid it was the girl's brother coming to take me out."

The captain stepped past him, giving him a dubious stare. Once he was inside, he began talking. "I'm not sure how this got all fucked up, but we've got to initiate major damage control."

"Like what?"

"We're going to have to eliminate some people."

Sutton felt the color drain from his face. "Are you out of your mind?" He raked his hand through his hair. "We can't do that. We'd get caught."

Haywood gave him a fixed stare. "Really?"

He shook his head. He needed to backpedal. "Maybe I panicked when I saw the girl last night. I knew her, but maybe *she* didn't recognize me." He grinned. "I mean, if she hasn't squealed after all these years, why would she stir up trouble now?"

"No clue," the other man said. "But we need to be prepared. You remember her address?"

He nodded.

"Call Records and get the girl's phone number off the report from the strip club."

He shook his head. "If we're going to dump the bitch, I shouldn't be asking for her contact info. I'll be number one on the suspect list."

"That's why I want you to go through Records. The skirts who work there are more interested in catching a husband than anything else. They won't even remembered you called. And *if* we dump the stripper, how is some dumb paper shuffler going to make the connection?"

"I don't know, but it seems risky to me."

"I'll tell you about risk, Duane. Roy Buckner was snooping around, trying to find the logs from the camping trip. He must have figured out something."

A wave of panic washed over him. "Why would he be investigating the camping trip? Isn't he supposed to be solving murders for you?"

"Somehow he got dialed in. I think he knows what happened at the beach. We can't afford to have him doing a full-blown investigation. I've destroyed the logs. Now we have to take care of him and his partner."

"Are you out of your mind? We can't off two cops. We should dump the girl."

"It's imperative we stop Buckner from poking around in what happened back then. We'll have to dispose of the stripper eventually, but we've got to remove the focus on us."

Duane ran a hand through his hair. "What does Justin say?"

"We can't involve Justin in this. He has us by the short hairs as it is."

"I don't want carry anymore secrets. I'm too close to retirement for this kind of shit."

"Then you'd better be prepared to spend your retirement in the prison where bubba and his buddies will be looking for opportunities to turn you into their girlfriend or shank your sorry ass."

Sutton fought off a bout of dizziness. "What did you have in mind?"

"Buckner takes Wednesday's off. We'll have him meet us at one of my rental properties. I'll tell him I know about the affair he's been having with his partner, Katie Nanako. We play it off like it was a counseling session gone wrong. I dump him, and you back me up that it was self-defense."

"Any detective with more than a year on the job is going to see right through that."

"Not if we have our story straight beforehand. Now this is how we'll say it went down..."

80

ROY

Roy met Katie at a coffee shop off the 5 Freeway. They asked for a table in a corner where they ordered breakfast and coffee.

"You know, partner, every morning I wake up and prepare for work. I have my day pretty much planned out. Then, before I even leave the house, you call me and throw me a curve ball. What is it this time?"

"I found Araceli Espinosa—actually, Amber found her."

Katie's jaw dropped. "How?"

He smiled and explained about Sutton's plan to increase pressure on Antonio Lima that was thwarted when the stripper from their shooting incident the other night answered the door. Amber's TO freaked out and went home sick. She called me to tell me about it."

"How did she know the stripper was Araceli?"

"She didn't, but I put two and two together."

"Let me guess. We're going to talk to Araceli this morning."

He nodded. "Exactly. Hopefully, she didn't skip out overnight. We should get over to her house asap."

"Were you planning to go to the office first and pick up a car?"

He shook his head. "No. We can take my truck."

"If Sutton was sick last night, wait until we tell him we're hooking him up for rape."

"Let's hear what Araceli has to say. If it's as bad as we think it is, we'll go to the commander who heads Internal Affairs"

"I agree, but we need to have the evidence to back up her story. If those three officers raped those young girls, we want to be sure we make it stick."

On their way to Araceli's house, Katie called the office and advised the adjutant they were following up a lead on the Lowe homicide.

"Wiggins told me not to sweat it—Haywood isn't in yet himself." She dropped her phone into her jacket pocket.

They parked a few houses down from Araceli's home. Dogs barked aggressively from behind chain link fences.

"If no one noticed the po-po was in the neighborhood, they know we're here now," he gibed.

They made their way to the porch, but before they could knock, the door opened. Antonio.

"I'm not surprised to see you," he said, looking at Roy.

"May we come in? This is my partner, Katie Nanako."

The gangster took a step aside and motioned them inside. The home was small but well kept. Religious pictures hung on the walls, and the sofa back was adorned with a white crocheted throw.

"Sit down if you want." Antonio motioned at the sofa.

They both settled onto the couch. Roy began.

"Antonio, why did you lie to Officer Buckner about knowing your sister's whereabouts?"

The younger man made a face. "Because of what happened at the strip club the other night. I pick up Araceli up after work—some of the customers have given her a hard time at the bus stop. That *baracho* dude was trying to force my sister to do something she didn't want. I saw what was happening and told him to knock it off. The next thing I know, the drunk pulls out a piece and caps a round at me. I shot back and then bounced outta there." He ran a hand through his hair. "That's why I took off running the other night and tried to dump the gun."

Roy could see into the kitchen where a middle-aged woman made breakfast burritos while a toddler clung to her thigh.

"Well, that's not why we're here. We'll pass that info on to the detectives investigating that case. Do yourself a favor and make yourself available. If it went down as you said, you have nothing to worry about."

"Okay. You *do* know that last night the cop who hurt her years ago came here last night, right? He was with that woman officer who arrested me. My sister thought he recognized her, and they left—fast."

Katie smiled. "Can you please get your sister for us?"

"Sure. I'll be right back."

A few minutes later, Antonio returned with a Latina in her mid-twenties wearing no makeup and a T-shirt and jeans.

Her thick dark hair was pulled into a ponytail. She sat in the only chair available, a faux leather recliner.

He introduced himself and Katie to Araceli and gave her business cards for each of them.

Antonio stood beside her, fidgeting.

Katie looked up at him. "We need to talk to your sister alone."

"Oh, yeah. Sure." His cheeks flushed. "Uh, I'll just go into the kitchen and have my breakfast." He shuffled toward the woman and toddler.

Roy looked at Araceli. "Is there some place we can talk privately?"

"Let's go outside. We have seating there."

In Spanish she told the woman and her brother where they were going. She led them through the kitchen and out a side door.

The backyard had a concrete patio with a wooden cover. Carved benches and chairs sporting bright-colored cushions formed a square. In one corner a three-tiered fountain offered the soothing sounds of cascading water.

He could easily imagine family gatherings in the tranquil setting.

The young woman motioned for them to sit at a wooden table and chairs.

Katie began. "Your brother didn't want to leave you alone with us."

Araceli smiled. "He's been protective of me since we were little."

Roy nodded. "He told me and another officer that something happened to you on a cadet camping trip at the beach. Can you please tell us what happened?"

"He shouldn't have told you. I want to forget about it."

"I understand. But you have to understand that we want to be sure he—or they—don't do the same thing to someone else." He leaned forward. "Araceli, I know it's hard to revisit that kind of trauma. But you were a victim, and we want you to have justice and gain some peace."

"I'll never have peace." She sighed and stared off into space as she talked. "It had been a great weekend. All of us cadets, swimming in the ocean, playing beach volleyball... having fun together.

"On Sunday, the group was kind of subdued because we didn't want to go home. They asked for volunteers to stay and help Sergeant Haywood, and Officers Lowe and Sutton pack up the last of the supplies. My girlfriends, Maria, Teresa, and I raised our hands and the sergeant chose us."

She looked at Katie. "We were so excited that we'd been assigned to stay behind."

"It was Haywood who did the picking?"

Araceli nodded.

"Then what happened?"

"The lady cops got the rest of the kids on the bus and drove them back to the station. There were five tents to take down. The six of us dismantled two of them and got them in their duffels. It was getting hot. Officer Lowe went to the van and brought out an ice chest. I was glad because I hoped had he some bottled water inside. Then he says, 'Who wants to have sex on the beach?' And then he laughed."

Araceli bit her lip. "Us girls all looked at each other because we didn't know what to say. Then the sergeant told us, 'Don't worry, he's talking about a fruit drink.'

"We were all relieved and kind of laughed. Then Officer

Lowe opened the chest and took out orange juice and cranberry juice along with some Schnapps and vodka. He made us each a drink, but said he'd just give us a taste of the alcohol."

Roy couldn't imagine the three tenured cops would be drinking fruity drinks. "Did they make themselves the same drinks?"

She shook her head. "No. Sergeant Haywood got a smaller chest from the van that had beer in it. They started pounding it down pretty hard."

"Then what happened?" Katie asked.

"Every time our plastic cups would get kind of low, they'd *freshen our drink*. That's what they called it. The cocktail tasted good, so we kept drinking. Pretty soon were all pretty wasted. None of us had ever been drunk before, and we thought it was funny to be staggering around in the sand."

"The men," Roy said. "What about them? Were they drunk too?"

"They may have been buzzed, but they weren't hammered like we were. Before too long we were kind of paired off. Teresa was with Sergeant Haywood, and Officer Lowe had Maria by the arm. That left me with Officer Sutton." Tears formed in her eyes.

"They *freshened our drinks* again, then Officer Lowe said he had something he wanted show Teresa and led her into a tent." Tears began to roll down her cheeks.

"Then the sergeant took Teresa into another tent. Officer Sutton looked at me." She deepened her tone. "I guess it's just you and me."

Araceli brushed the tears from her face. "Then he leaned

in and kissed me. I didn't know what to do. I was only four-teen and he was a police officer."

More tears spilled down her cheeks. She let them fall. "He had me go inside the last tent, and we laid down. He undressed me. Sometimes he'd stop and kiss me." She looked at Roy. "I knew what he was doing was wrong, but I was afraid."

"I understand, Araceli. Tell me what he did next."

She lowered her head. "He took off his clothes. It was the first time I'd ever seen a man's...thing. He got on top of me and stuck it inside of me." She was crying as she spoke. "He kept saying these disgusting things. I was so beautiful, so tight, so soft. Then he started moving really fast, and it was over."

"What happened next?"

"One of the men yelled we should get going, so we put on our clothes and joined the others."

Katie sighed. "Did Maria and Teresa tell you they'd been assaulted too?"

"They didn't have to. We all knew what had happened. They looked as ashamed as me."

"Do you know if they told any other friends or maybe someone in their family?"

The young woman shook her head. "None of us ever spoke of that trip again." She paused. "Well, I told my brother that night. I shouldn't have done that."

He spoke softly. "Is there anything else about what happened in the tent that you can remember?"

Araceli raised her head and looked at them. "When he saw blood on the towel we'd laid on, he laughed and said, 'I'll be damned. I got myself a virgin.'"

PART IX

81

AMBER

Amber had texted Roy to be sure he could retrieve their son from nursery school. She was dying to know what he found out from Jewel Jubilee. That's how she still thought of the stripper.

He confirmed he would pick up Gage and added he had an interesting day. He'd tell her about it in the morning.

She figured that since Sutton had called in sick again, she'd be relegated to working the desk. But that wasn't the case. They'd assigned her to another TO—Dave Wilson.

She'd seen Wilson in the station, and he and his trainee had backed her and Sutton on a couple of calls. He seemed relaxed and knowledgeable. She'd envied Wilson's probationer.

Being that she was with a new training officer, she found

her hands shaking as she performed the shotgun check. If Wilson had noticed her jitters, he didn't say anything.

Once they gassed up their SUV, he pulled to the side of the garage and talked about tactics and how he liked to do things.

He told her where he carried his backup weapon and asked where she carried hers.

Since she'd left the academy, it was the first time she felt like a real cop and not a liability. It was the best feeling in the world.

82

KATIE

Katie and Roy decided they should try to talk to the families of Maria Gonzales and Teresa Pineda in case they'd disclosed about being raped on the camping trip.

They asked Araceli for the addresses of her deceased friends. She balked. "Their families don't know what happened to them. Let my friends rest in peace."

"We'll be careful with our questioning," Katie said. We need to try to corroborate your story."

Araceli's eyes flashed in anger. "You think I'm not telling the truth?"

It was Roy who spoke. "What you're saying happened a long time ago. We need as much evidence as we can find to support your allegations."

In the end, she decided to cooperate. She hadn't memorized her friend's addresses, but she gave them descriptions of her friends' homes and directions of how to get there.

Later, Katie and Roy left the second house of Araceli's friends.

"That's an hour wasted," he complained. "We reopened the wounds of their daughters' deaths for nothing."

Katie looked over at her partner as he drove back to PAB. "We had to try. It would have been easier if we could have asked more pointed questions. It's not easy to hint around, inquiring if their daughter disclosed anything about being sexually assaulted...without actually saying the word rape." She sighed. "But neither family even remembered the camping trip. Or so they say."

"I hate what the three of them did to those girls," he said. "I want them to be prosecuted and put away for a long time. When this comes out, we'll all be tarnished by their crimes."

"I know and it sucks," she said. "What do we do next?"

"We need to make an appearance at the office. Let's put in a couple of hours on Adam Lowe's murder. We've been so distracted by the cadet assaults; we're ignoring our cold case. We'll work a couple of hours, then leave early, go to your place and type out our interviews of Araceli and the families of the other girls."

"That should kill the rest of the day."

He nodded. "We'll read over our reports tomorrow, and then we'll contact Internal Affairs."

"Tomorrow is Wednesday. We're off, or should we try to switch our day?"

He thought for a minute. "No. Haywood would want to know why we want the change. We don't have anything compelling enough in our case to warrant adjusting our schedule."

"Okay, we write our statements today and call IA on Thursday morning."

83

HAYWOOD

It was still dark out Wednesday morning when Haywood popped a couple of antacid tablets. He held his hand out in front of him to see if he had the shakes. Just a slight tremble.

What a mess. He didn't see a way out other than his plan. It would have been so much easier to have killed the stripper, but there were other loose ends needing his attention first. In his mind, he ran over the scheme over and over again and it seemed solid.

One dangling problem would be Katie Nanako, but he was confident he could take care of her fairly easily too. He'd arrange for her to commit suicide after her affair with Buckner became public.

How had it come to this? I'm a respected captain in the Los Angeles Police Department, and I'm planning to rack up a body count that would qualify me as a serial killer. Go big or go home— or in this case— prison. Stupid people wound up in prison. One thing you're not, Glen, is stupid.

Of course, the wild card in the whole arrangement was Sutton. They were going to meet at eleven at the rental. He hoped his partner in crime could pull off his part of the ruse. There were so many things that had to go right.

He sent a text to Wiggins that he wasn't feeling well and wouldn't be coming in to work. He also said that if something important came up, the sergeant should call or text him.

With a clear mission in mind, he drove over to the neighborhood where he had his rental property.

He parked on the next block in front of a home with a tall hedge. From there he walked a few doors down and then ducked into the side yard of the residence that backed to his rental property.

He knew an old lady with a Sheltie dog lived there. The old bat was pretty much deaf and never even heard when her dog was barking. That was one reason why it was so hard to keep renters in his house.

It would have been simpler to poison the dog, but he'd been an animal lover since he was a kid. It was easier to have the rental empty—and in this instance, a necessity to his plan. He climbed over the fence while the Sheltie eyed him and yapped.

He let himself into his house through the back door. He did a quick walkthrough to be sure no vagrants had forced their way inside.

The place was a one-story mid-century, and it had belonged to his parents. They'd bought it almost fifty years ago, and it had come to him paid off in his inheritance. After they'd died, he'd spruced it up and filled it with some cheap furniture. The little bungalow was the start of his rental venture.

He wasn't happy that a murder would be committed in his parents' home, but he figured his mom and dad would understand that he couldn't go to prison.

He heard a car out front. Peering out a bedroom window, he saw Sutton's sedan pull into the driveway.

He opened the door as his accomplice shuffled across the front walk, his shoulders hunched and his head on the swivel.

"Stop acting like a crook," Haywood hissed. He pushed open the screen so Sutton could enter.

Stepping inside, he exhaled. "I thought you weren't here. I didn't see your wheels out front."

"It's in the garage so we can put Buckner's body in it without the neighbor's watching."

"Are you still sure this is what we have to do. If we knocked off the gir—"

"I told you before if we have to, we can do her later down the road. If she winds up dead now, they're gonna come talk to us after hearing from Buckner."

"Yeah but Buckner's partner—"

Haywood rolled his eyes and sighed. "Again. She's going to be humiliated when it comes out that she's been boning devoted Roy Buckner. After her husband and kid were killed, she developed a drinking problem. I know this because the chief told me before he sent her to me. We'll be sure she gets plenty drunk to the point of alcohol poisoning, which will be ruled accidental."

"Glen, I'm not sure. It's so risky. And why isn't Justin here. He's as much a part of this as we are."

Anger coursed through him. "Because the last thing we want is to tie ourselves to Justin any more than we already are. You don't like my plan, what have you got, huh?"

"Seems to me if we take out the girl...maybe something we can't be connected to..."

He sighed with impatience. "Did you get the girls contact info?"

Sutton nodded and retrieved a piece of paper from his wallet and handed it over to him.

What a fucking idiot. "If we kill the girl now, they'll be pulling you out of your house in front of your wife and kids so fast—"

The other man held up his hands in a sign of surrender. "Okay! How's this gonna go?"

"You're going to call Buckner. You'll tell him you hear he's looking into a cadet camping trip at the beach. Tell him that you want to give him the facts before he gets the wrong impression."

"What if he wants to bring his partner?"

"Today is their day off. If he suggests bringing her, you can say you've heard he and his pretty Asian partner have been getting pretty up close and personal—something you know his wife would find interesting."

"Is that true? That's too much. The great Roy Buckner has been servicing his co-worker. I doubt *Mrs.* Buckner would approve." His smile was replaced by a frown. "He could bring the Asian chick and not tell us."

"Jesus Christ, Duane. If he shows up with her, we'll kill

her too. We'll make it look like a murder-suicide." He raked a hand through his hair. "We have to roll with whatever happens."

Sutton stared at him, knowing there was no other way.

"Make the call, Duane."

84

AMBER

For the first time in over a week, Amber and Roy had the same day off. After her shift with Dave Wilson, she raced home, excited to tell her husband about finding a stolen car and the ensuing pursuit.

She entered the house, and all was quiet. *They must still be asleep.*

In the kitchen, she grabbed a small glass of milk and a couple of cookies, quickly downing them. Tiptoeing down the hallway, she made her way to her bathroom, where she showered and let the warm water wash over her.

She couldn't believe the difference it made working with a partner who was willing to train and not intimidate her.

They'd been driving down Roscoe Boulevard, and she spotted an older sedan with a male at the wheel and a female passenger. She didn't know why, but she got a funny feeling about the car.

She'd run the license plate, and the vehicle came back as stolen. She told Wilson who'd asked her to double-check the plate. When she confirmed she'd run the right license plate, he'd praised her work, then laid out the game plan.

"You're going to radio for backup, but use your personal radio, not the car mic. Keep your eye on the occupants, but don't fixate. Pretend to be looking at other vehicles. Go ahead and call for backup."

It hadn't taken long for another unit to pull behind their black and white, and as soon as Wilson had turned on the lights and siren, the suspects sped off at a high rate of speed.

They'd chased the car for almost ten minutes before the driver lost control and crashed into a tree. The driver and passenger were taken into custody without incident.

The supervisor who'd arrived at the scene told her she'd done a great job on the radio relaying their position during the pursuit.

Wilson had chimed in and told the female sergeant that Amber had spotted the GTA herself.

In the shower, as she toweled off, she grinned. "I can't believe I get paid to have so much fun," she whispered to herself.

There was a light tap on the bathroom door. She opened it.

Roy stood there. "Hi, honey. How was your night?"

"Great. I worked with a cool partner and I got my first G-ride."

He smiled and nodded. "Good for you." He leaned in to give her a quick kiss.

Stoked by the memory of her adrenaline-filled pursuit, she stepped a little closer and dropped the towel and extended the kiss.

He pulled his head back and looked at her.

"I'm not sure how far I can go," she whispered, "but let's find out."

Later, as she lay in his arms, she silently cried tears of joy. Once again, they were husband and wife.

"Amber, I love you."

"I love you too, Roy. I think I'll be sleeping here from now on," she murmured as she drifted into blissful sleep.

85

SUTTON

Haywood handed him the piece of paper with the phone number.

With a slight shake to his hands, he set the phone on speaker and dialed. "Is this Roy Buckner?"

"Yeah, who's this?"

"Duane Sutton, your wife's TO. We need to talk."

"About what?"

"Well, I'll bet you don't want your wife's hard work in the academy to go to waste."

Out of the corner of his eye, he saw the captain using his index finger to make slashing motions across his neck. *He was ad-libbing, and Haywood didn't like it. Tough shit. He didn't like Glen's plan at all.*

There was a pause on the line. "Is she struggling on the street?"

"No. Nothing like that, but I'm sure you'd like it to stay that way."

"Stop jerking me around. What do you want?"

"I know you're taking a look at a cadet camping trip from some time back. I have some information you might be interested in knowing."

"Go ahead."

He looked at the captain who paced nearby, shaking his head. "No. I want to talk to you in person."

There was another pause on the line. "It's my day off. The earliest my partner and I can meet you is on Thursday."

"No. Just you."

"Hey, I work with a partner. Either she comes or you can take your information and shove it up your ass."

He looked at Haywood, who nodded.

"From what I've been hearing, your mama-san hasn't had any problem *coming* since she started working with you." He paused for effect. "It would be a real shame if Mrs. Buckner had to find out about you and your geisha's special relationship."

More silence on the phone.

"Where and when?

He gave Roy the address to the rental. "One o'clock. Alone. Deviate from the plan, and I'll be sure your little bride doesn't pass probation, and she gets the full details about you and your lotus blossom."

Buckner's response was to hang up on him.

Sutton grinned and turned to Haywood.

It took him half a second to register his old buddy holding a gun with a suppressor on the barrel. "What the fu—"

Haywood pressed the trigger.

86

HAYWOOD

He wasn't the best shooter in the LAPD, but Haywood was good enough to shoot his friend and kill him.

He wanted to feel bad, but the thought that Duane could tie him to more than the partying at Zuma Beach meant his buddy had to be eliminated too.

Once Sutton hit the floor, he sprang into action. He moved over to the body and tucked a plastic keychain holding a key to the rental house in Sutton's pants pocket. Next, he eyeballed where he'd been standing when he shot Duane and dropped the throwaway gun there.

All these years he remembered his first training officer's warning. *"I've treated this gun very carefully. I didn't touch it without gloves. I put it in this plastic bag so the fingerprints of the last gangster to hold it will be on the hook for whatever crime the pistol is connected to. Don't take it out of the plastic bag unless absolutely necessary, and wear gloves loading ammo into the gun."*

By this time, he wasn't worried too much about an innocent man going to jail over the murder he'd committed. He figured whoever had held the gun last with an ungloved hand would be long gone or in prison.

After checking that the front door was unlocked and the drapes were closed, he used his experienced eye to examine the crime scene. Afterward, he snuck out the rear, leaving that entrance unlocked as well. He slipped over the fence while the Sheltie sounded the alarm—her owner oblivious in front of a blaring TV.

He dashed between the houses and hopped into his car. He needed to get home and shower so by the time the proverbial shit hit the fan, he looked totally innocent.

87

———————

AMBER

Amber, still half asleep, reached to Roy's side of the bed to touch him and verify the lovemaking they'd shared was real and not an incredible dream.

Her eyes popped open when she realized he wasn't beside her. The she glanced at the clock—twelve thirty.

Of course he's not still in bed. He slept all night. She listened for any sounds of him or Gage. Everything was quiet.

She slid from bed, threw on a robe, and wandered into the kitchen. As she suspected, there was a note on the kitchen counter.

Amb—

I'm sorry. I had to go to work. Gage is at pre-school. I'll call you later.

Love,

Roy

P.S. - This morning was amazing, but we'll take things slow.

She smiled. He knew she'd had a big breakthrough this morning.

Hoping he wouldn't be gone too long, she made herself a cup of coffee and headed to the bedroom to shower. She'd collect Gage from preschool, and they'd play until her husband came home.

88

———

ROY

Roy drove to the address he'd been given, his mind racing. How had Amber's training officer found out about him and Katie?

He thought about his wife and how this morning they'd finally made love. If she ever found out about him and Katie...

How did Sutton know he and Katie were investigating the cadet camping trip? He hated to think it, but could Amber have said something to tip him off?

He considered calling Katie to back him on his meeting. It was stupid to go alone, but the training officer held the advantage. He had the goods on Roy.

The neighborhood he'd been directed to was filled with small mid-century homes that boasted sleek clean lines with geometric angles.

He parked his car about thirty yards away from the target residence. A silver sedan was parked in the driveway.

He exited his car and walked toward the house. His phone rang. Amber. He didn't want to answer her questions now, so he ignored the call.

He needed to talk to Sutton. What info he was willing to give up about the cadet camping trip—and how he planned to blackmail him to keep his affair with Katie quiet. He had no doubt the two situations were now connected.

As he reached the front porch, he noticed the neighborhood was particularly quiet. The birds weren't even singing.

He knocked. No sounds came from inside the residence. He knocked again, this time a little harder. Still nothing. He glanced at the front window, but it was covered by draperies. He rang the bell—his cop instincts telling him something was wrong.

With no response, he tried calling the other man's phone. The call went to voicemail. "Hey, it's Buckner. I'm out front. Where are you?" It occurred to him this could be some kind of setup.

Wound up and frustrated, he gingerly tried the front doorknob. It was unlocked.

He opened the door. "Hello? Sutton?" He glanced over his shoulder at the cemetery-quiet neighborhood. He slid his Glock from his holster and pushed inside.

"Sutton? It's Buckner." Still nothing. "Police Department!"

With his gun at a low ready, he stepped through the small living room toward the kitchen. In the den, he saw a man down. Blood stained his shirt, and there was no rise and fall in the chest to indicate he was breathing.

"Hey. Can you hear me?" He didn't know for certain it *was*

Amber's TO, but it was a pretty safe bet. His heartbeat pounded in his ears.

He quickly cleared the location, ensuring no one would spring out from being hidden to attack him. He rushed back to the downed victim, dialing 911 while he did so.

"This is Officer Roy Buckner." He gave the dispatcher his serial number and the address. "I need an RA for a male with a gunshot wound to the chest. He's approximately forty-two, not conscious or breathing. I'm starting CPR. I also need a supervisor and two units."

He put his phone on speaker and set it on the floor. He checked the prone man's airway, then began chest compressions.

89

HAYWOOD

Finally—his work cell phone rang.

"Haywood."

"This is Lieutenant Niles from West Valley Division. We've got a 187 with an off-duty LAPD officer as the victim. The person reporting is another cop."

He made sure to sound like the information was fresh to him. "Who's the dead guy?"

"A P-3. Duane Sutton."

"Shit. I worked with him years ago. Is the PR the doer?"

"We're not sure. He's not giving us a whole lot of information and asking for a defense rep from the League and telling us to call Internal Affairs."

He nodded. *Smart.* "PR's name?"

"Buckner. Roy Buckner."

"You're joking, right?"

"Uh...no. You're probably remembering his wife—"

"No, I'm not talking about what happened to her. Roy Buckner works for me at RHD."

There was a slight pause. "Ohhhh."

"What's the address? I'll respond and get a team out there."

The lieutenant gave him the address to his rental property.

Remember, sound puzzled. He spoke slowly as though he was processing info. "Say the address again."

She repeated the address.

He sighed heavily into the phone, then spoke in a clipped tone. "Roger that. I'm on my way."

90

———

KATIE

Katie was enjoying a late start to her day off. She'd slept in and was having coffee and watching television when her phone rang. It was Roy.

"I guess it's true. There *is* no rest for the wicked," she said into the phone.

"Sutton's dead. He called me this morning to meet him at a house in West Valley Division."

"Wait, what?"

"Sutton's dead. When I got here, he was on the floor dead from a gunshot wound. I'm not talking to anyone, but I've told them to call IA. I don't have much time. No doubt Haywood has been notified. They'll want to talk to you— probably today. Print out our statements from yesterday and bring them with you. Don't give them to anyone other IA— especially our boss."

"Yeah, yeah. Are you all right?"

"Yes, but I've got to go. Can you let Amber know I'm working? They'll be taking my phone soon."

"Sure." She could hear someone in the background talking to him.

He said nothing and disconnected.

She sat for a second, thinking. Why hadn't he called her to go with him to the meeting? Who would kill Sutton? Araceli? Her brother? *Haywood?*

Her heart pounded. She'd better get cleaned up, but she also needed to call Roy's wife. How much should she tell her?

She dialed the Buckner's house phone.

"Hi Amber, this is Roy's partner, Katie Nanako."

"Oh, hi." His wife sounded wary.

"He asked me to contact you and tell you he's going to be tied up at work for quite a while."

"Why isn't he calling me himself?"

There was sharpness in her tone that Katie wasn't surprised to hear.

"I'm not with him, I don't have all the answers, but your training officer has been shot and killed."

Amber gasped. "What? That's crazy. Roy didn't shoot him, did he?"

"Of course not. He found the body."

"How?"

"He didn't say. There was no time." She needed to get off the phone. "Listen, the whole thing about the cadet camping trip is going to blow up. You might want to arrange for childcare, because they'll want to talk to you probably sooner rather than later, since you brought the story to your husband."

"Okay. Should I call anyone? My captain or something?"

"I wouldn't. Wait for them to contact you. Once they do, be sure to ask for a League attorney before you give them any information. Oh, and be sure to tell the truth. The department forgives many things but lying isn't one of them."

"Okay. Thanks."

Katie hurried to the shower. *This investigation is turning into a real shit show.*

PART X

91

ROY

Roy noticed it hadn't taken long for Haywood to arrive at the crime scene, but the officer in charge of the crime scene had kept his boss from talking to him.

He'd told the sergeant that Internal Affairs needed to be called because there was more to the situation than a cop's murder, and he would *only* talk to someone from IA.

Roy had never been on the suspect side of a criminal investigation, and he didn't like it. After being transported to West Valley Station where he was given a gunshot residue test, he was placed in an interview room, and left to sit for hours. They were probably writing warrants to search his home and seize his car. They'd taken his phone before they transported him to the station.

One of the patrol cops who'd brought him to the station

came in to see if he wanted something to drink. As the officer closed the door, he glimpsed his captain being led down the hallway.

Although the interview rooms had soundproofing tiles, he could tell that someone had been situated in the space next to him. *Haywood?*

After what seemed like days, a homicide detective from West Valley came in and introduced himself. Roy didn't know him.

"I'm told you want a League attorney and to talk to someone from IA. They're both on their way. But I've been sent in here to obtain a statement from you while things are fresh in your mind."

He shook his head. "I'll wait to tell my story to IA, and I won't do it without a League attorney."

He didn't have to wait long. The League attorney, Dion Puckett, arrived and Roy advised him they needed to talk someplace else because he was afraid his boss was next door and might overhear what was said...and that could be a problem.

Puckett excused himself, and a few minutes later, Roy was led to the station's conference room.

Comfortable now, he told his attorney about Amber's arrest of Antonio Lima and his allegation that Sutton had raped his sister, Araceli. He brought Puckett up to speed on his wife getting the logs, and the interviews he and Katie had done afterward. "My partner has the statements we wrote up yesterday."

The attorney gave him a hard look. "Why didn't your wife or you go to a supervisor?"

"Amber barely has a week out of the academy. It was *her* TO being accused by a gangster. Put yourself in her shoes."

"Okay, so your wife comes to you for advice. Why the hell didn't you go to a supervisor?"

Roy ran a hand through his hair. "Who was I going to go to? Haywood?"

"You could have gone above him. That's going to be a problem. Nanako will take a hit for it as well."

"Whose side are you on? We were trying to catch dirty cops."

"Make no mistake, I'm on your side. But I need to tell you where they're going to find fault with what you've done." Puckett shifted in his chair. "So, what happened today?"

He related the phone call from Sutton and what he'd found after arriving at the designated location. "He was dead when I got there. I'm being set up."

"By who?"

"My first guess would be Haywood."

"What about the third officer. What was his name?"

"Justin Lowe. Actually, Nanako and I interviewed him on the homicide we're working. The victim was LAPD—his brother Adam. He worked Topanga Division."

"That's weird. Do you think there could be any connection?"

"Maybe. Katie—Nanako and I haven't had time to figure it out. We got distracted by the cadet thing and haven't hit the Lowe case very hard."

"Is there anything else I need to know?"

Roy folded his arms across his chest and bit his lower lip while shaking his head. "My partner and I...we, um..."

"What? Spit it out. Are you screwing her?"

He shook his head. "I was, but that's over now. And somehow Sutton knew it. That's how he got me to meet with him without Katie. He told me to come alone or he'd tell my wife."

Puckett made notes on his yellow legal pad. "How long have you been having the affair?"

"It's not an affair. We had sex twice. My wife...Amber... she's had some difficulty since—"

"Look, man. I remember what happened to your wife and what she experienced, and I'm sorry that happened to her." He rolled a pencil between his palms. "You can put lipstick on a pig, but it's still a pig. You and Nanako were having an affair. How did Sutton know?"

"I have no idea."

"How did he learn you were looking into the cadet campout?"

He shrugged. "No clue."

"Is it possible that your wife found out about your affair and in retaliation told him about it *and* the cadet investigation?"

"Absolutely not. She is the one who came to me with the info about the cadets. She set up the meeting between me and Antonio Lima. She's as invested as Katie and me to bringing the misconduct to light."

There was a knock on the door.

Puckett answered and pulled the opening wider to allow a statuesque brunette wearing a navy pantsuit to enter.

The attorney turned to him. "This is—"

"Sergeant Lacey Galloway, Internal Affairs Group, Criminal Investigations Division." She produced two business cards out of her pocket and slapped them on the table in front of each of the men.

She sank into a chair across from him at the conference table and looked directly at Roy. "Tell me why I'm here."

92

HAYWOOD

Haywood tried to quell the acid building up in his stomach as he waited in the interview room.

He'd thought he had the situation all worked out, but how many other cops thought they were smart enough to get away with felonies and now sat in the joint? *But you got away with murder once...and you can do it this time too. You're smarter. Of course, the fact they "asked" him to come down to the station for a "quick" interview meant they already knew the house where the body was found belonged to him.*

He rose and started pacing the tiny space. Any second, he expected to see his team of RHD detectives he'd called to investigate the homicide.

The door opened. He exhaled. They were here—except instead of his two RHD detectives he expected, it was a male and female detective he didn't know.

The male detective entered with a half-smile and an outstretched hand. "Hi, Glen. We've met a few times, Gunner Ferrari from West Valley Homicide. This is Detective Lacey Galloway."

"Oh, right. Right." he said, giving the D-III a cursory handshake. He nodded at the female.

"The chief has decided to let West Valley take the Sutton homicide."

"That's bullshit. This is the murder of a policeman. RHD always handles cop homicides."

The female spoke. "Not when the homicide scene is a house owned by the officer in charge of Robbery Homicide Division."

Haywood waved his hand in annoyance. "Instead of jumping to conclusions, why don't you ask me what you want to know?"

Ferrari nodded. "We will. Give us a few minutes." He turned to go out the door, then paused. "I'm sure you've got an RHD team on the way. Give them a call and tell them we've got this one."

After he'd called his detectives and told them the chief had given the homicide to West Valley Homicide, Detective Ferrari returned.

"We're all set."

"Good. Let's make this happen."

Ferrari told him that he was free to leave at any time and they were merely gathering information.

He gave a sardonic smile but kept his tone friendly. "I understand how this works detective."

"Outstanding," said the female detective. "Start at the beginning of your day. When the body was discovered, your office was called. You weren't there. Where were you?"

"At home. I wasn't feeling well."

"Was there anyone there, or anyone who can verify you were there?"

"I live alone. I doubt my neighbors keep tabs on me. Although I texted my adjutant, Darnell Wiggins and told him I wouldn't be in today."

"Are you sick now?"

"I won't lie. My stomach is still upset, and I feel like I got hit by a bus. But other than that, I feel fine."

Ferrari looked concerned. "Do you feel well enough to continue the interview?"

Galloway shot Ferrari a look of annoyance.

"Sure. I can finish."

"Then, let's get started," Ferrari said. "Tell us about your day—from the time you got up until you arrived at your rental home."

"There really isn't much to tell. I texted Wiggins I wouldn't be into work, and then went back to bed. I was asleep until I got the call about the homicide."

Galloway shifted in her chair. "Do you know why Duane Sutton was at a house that you own?"

"Not really. Years ago, Duane and I were pretty tight. At some point, I'd given him a key to that rental. I have several properties, but that house is the hardest one to rent so a lot of times it's empty."

"Why would you give him a key to a rental?"

He affected a lopsided grin. "The place is furnished. Sometimes Duane needed a place to go for a Code X day."

"You gave him a key to *your* house so he could screw

someone who wasn't his wife?"

"I don't live there, Detective Galloway. It's a rental I own."

"Did he call you or text you that he was going to use your house?"

"He called me Monday night. We shot the shit for a bit, but he didn't say anything about using the rental."

"Did he ask if the residence was rented or anything that would give you an indication he wanted to use it?"

Haywood shook his head. "Nope. I had no clue."

Galloway cleared her throat. "Is there anyone who would want him dead?"

Haywood feigned a pained expression. "I can only tell you that Sergeant Wiggins, my adjutant, heard Buckner talking on the phone. I don't know who he was talking to, but he threatened to 'tune Sutton up.'"

"When was that?"

"Late last week. I'm sure Darnell would remember better than me. He only told me about it because he wanted to alert me to the fact that Roy might have anger management issues."

Galloway leaned forward. "Did you contact Sutton with that information?"

Haywood shook his head. "No. I didn't take it very seriously. Obviously, I was wrong."

"Is there anything else you want to tell us?"

"Duane was a policeman and my friend. I want you to catch whoever killed him and throw his ass in prison."

Detective Ferrari leaned back in his chair. "We thank you for coming in, Captain. As you know, we may have to ask you more questions as the investigation continues."

"Not a problem. I've got nothing to hide."

93

AMBER

Amber canceled the appointment she and Roy had planned with Doctor Stevens. Via voicemail she explained neither of them could make it. To cover all the bases, she sent a text message as well.

Then she called her mother and made arrangements for her parents to pick up Gage from preschool. They hadn't been happy, but she couldn't worry about that now.

She flitted around the house, mindlessly cleaning waiting for her phone to ring. When it did, she jumped and tried to sound casual. On the other end of the line was a detective from West Valley Homicide.

"Mrs. Buckner, we'd like to talk to you about your partner, Duane Sutton. Could you come to West Valley station?"

"What's this all about?"

"We'll explain that when you arrive."

"Am I in some kind of trouble?"

"No. We're investigating a crime, and you may be a witness."

"When do you want me to come?"

"How about now?"

"Okay. Give me a few minutes and I'll be on my way."

On her way to West Valley station, she called the Police Protective League and got a lawyer en route to meet her.

After checking in with the clerk in the detective lobby and sitting down, she knew word must have leaked that something big was going down. Officers and detectives increased as they passed through the lobby while doing their work. They eyed her with curiosity.

Unfortunately, because her kidnapping had been such big news, she was often recognized by strangers.

A tall man, who was easy on the eyes, appeared from the depths of the detective squad room. Their gazes met, and she knew he was a bigwig in the department, because she'd seen him giving media interviews on TV. But she didn't know his name.

As he approached, he took a call on his cell phone. "Yeah, I'll be there soon." He grabbed a notepad from the vacated desk of the receptionist who'd gone to alert detectives Amber had arrived.

While his head was down, she overheard his side of the conversation. She tried to figure out who he was.

"Well, I'll tell you one thing. I wouldn't want to be Buckner. His affair with his Japanese partner is coming to light. Looks like they suspect him as the shooter in this murder, too."

Jolted from scanning the man, she tried to catch her breath. *Roy was having an affair?*

Of course he is. Why are you surprised? You suspected it—and now this guy has confirmed it.

"I don't know how much evidence they've got, but from what I'm told, his story is weak." The man listened, jotted something down, and ripped the page from the notepad. "Okay—on my way."

He disconnected the call. Walking past her, he smiled and bobbed his head in greeting before walking out the door.

94

ROY

Roy liked Galloway's energy of no nonsense and confidence. She'd returned his questioning to an interview room where his statements would be recorded.

He laid out everything to her and Ferrari that he'd told his attorney.

Galloway let him talk without interruption but would occasionally jot down some notes in a folio she'd brought.

When he was done, she leaned back in her chair. "Well this is one hell of a mess."

"Tell me about it," he replied.

She looked him straight in the eyes. "You know your wife will find out about the affair, right?"

"That can't happen. It has nothing to do with the investigation."

She made a face. "I understand. But the fact that your

wife's training officer used the affair to blackmail you into meeting him alone will come out."

He lowered his head and ran his hand across his forehead. *This is what happens when you think with the wrong head. When Amber finds out you've been unfaithful, it will kill her.*

"So, this is the way it's going to go down," Ferrari said. "West Valley Homicide will handle Sutton's murder, and IA will investigate the beach party allegations." He glanced at Puckett. "We'd like to have Roy's phone. We're writing paper for it now."

Puckett spoke. "Let us know when you have the warrant and we'll turn it over."

Ferrari made a face. "We'll do that."

Galloway looked at him. "We've got your partner en route. We'll walk you out."

The group filed out and walked single file down the hallway to the lobby.

Amber sat on a wooden slatted bench. She looked at him.

His heart dropped.

Her eyes were flat and filled with pain. Somehow, she knew.

Galloway made a beeline to his wife. "Mrs. Buckner?"

Amber nodded, her gaze never leaving his.

The IA sergeant introduced herself and Ferrari. "Come with us and we'll get you situated where you're more comfortable while you wait for your attorney."

Mechanically, she rose and glared at Roy as she brushed past.

95

GALLOWAY

Lacey Galloway was glad to unofficially be teamed up with Ferrari. The criminal division of IA was slammed with cases, so even though the cadet allegation was high priority, she'd been sent to investigate this case alone. She welcomed Ferarri's help with the cadet rape case, and she'd helped him however she could on Sutton's murder.

Do more with less. The popular mantra had been part of the LAPD for decades. At least Ferrari appeared competent and willing to join forces with her.

They'd interviewed Amber Buckner, skirting the relationship between her husband and his partner—for now. She'd given Lacey contact information for both Araceli and Antonio.

The bombshell she'd surprised them with was the story

of how her training officer had sexually attacked her in the car wash rack at the station.

With over a decade on the job, Lacey knew how hard it would be to be on probation and have your training officer take such advantage. On the other hand, it sounded like the officer had held her own utilizing the vacuum hose nozzle.

They'd also questioned Katie Nanako, who'd provided them written copies of the statements she and Roy had written the day before.

Although interviewed separately, both women used the same League attorney.

After both women left, she and Ferrari sat in the homicide office with the two teams of detectives he had working on the homicide.

"Did you see how nervous Nanako got when we asked her how well she worked with her Buckner?"

Lacey chuckled and nodded. "She was waiting for us to delve into it more deeply. And I think Amber knows about the affair. Whenever we mentioned Roy, her answers got more clipped."

"We don't need to press the issue with either of them," Ferrari said. "If it turns out that either woman becomes a suspect, we can sprint down that road."

Lacey tapped her pen on the table. "The pair I want to talk to is Araceli Espinosa and her brother. I'm going to give them a call and get them down here—hopefully, tonight." She looked over at Ferrari. "Maybe you can sit in with me for the interviews."

"Yeah sure, and we need to chat with Justin Lowe," Ferrari noted. "It seems like he's potentially connected to both cases and flown under the radar. Let's bring him in here tonight."

He looked at two of the detectives seated in the small office. "Will you go pick him up?"

They nodded, and then one detective spoke. "Yeah, and so you know, we're waiting on a call from SID regarding prints on the gun."

Ferrari grimaced. "Probably wiped down. But why didn't the suspect take it with him? Why leave a perfectly good gun there?"

The other detective shrugged and shook his head. "We're waiting to see if SID got anything off the ammo."

"Maybe we'll get lucky," his partner said before they walked out the door.

Lacey looked at Ferrari. "I'd like to catch a break on these cases. How about you?"

96

AMBER

As Amber drove home from West Valley Station, silent tears slid down her cheeks. *How could you sleep with someone else?* Her stomach clenched as she imagined her husband and Katie naked and writhing together in bed.

I finally got to the point where I felt safe enough to have sex with you, and I find out you've been sleeping with another woman.

That's not true or fair, she thought. Before this morning, she hadn't been available to him sexually. Katie didn't have the hang-ups that tormented her. It had been almost two years since she and Roy had sex. How long was he supposed to wait?

What to do now? Could she forgive him? She wasn't sure. It was like just getting out of a full body cast only to be hit by a train. Most marriages didn't survive sexual betrayal.

She pulled her car into the garage next to his truck. They needed to talk it through.

Entering the kitchen, she found him at the counter making salad. On the stove, spaghetti sauce simmered. Next to the sauce pot, a cookie sheet with garlic bread was staged to go into the oven minutes before the meal.

"I'm home."

He turned to her, his face pale, his gaze searching hers.

"How did it go?"

"Okay. They asked about Antonio, the logs, and what happened the night Sutton and I went to Araceli's house." She set her purse down. "We need to talk."

His expression changed to one she'd never seen before. Fear.

He picked up his beer bottle and moved to the kitchen table and sat down.

She sat across from him.

"What did you want to talk about?"

"While I was waiting to speak with the detectives, another detective came to the lobby. He must be department brass. I've seen him before on TV. The man was on his cell phone. I don't know who he was talking to, but he said you and Katie were having an affair. Is that true?"

Roy exhaled and held his head with both hands. Then he looked up at her. "I was afraid you'd find out. We slept together—twice. It's not an affair—and it won't happen again."

The silent tears returned.

"I'm so sorry, Amber. I shouldn't have let it happen. I was feeling—"

"Horny? You needed to get your rocks off, and Katie was

available and willing?" She relished the bitterness in her voice.

"No. It wasn't like that. I was feeling...rejected and unloved. I know that isn't fair," he hastened to add, "but that's the truth."

She stared at him. Finally, she found some words. "I understand the physicality of what happened...but you say you felt unloved. I might not have been able to have sex with you, but you think I didn't love you?" She shook her head. "Since when do men equate sex and love? I thought only women did that."

"Now what?" He sounded miserable.

"I'm not sure."

"Do you understand? Can you forgive me?"

Don't make promises you can't keep. "Probably not."

97

GALLOWAY

One of Ferrari's detectives poked his head around the door frame. "We've got Lowe in interview room two. We're gonna grab a bite. You guys want us to bring something back?"

"No thanks, I'm good," Galloway said.

Ferrari also declined, then looked at her. "You ready?"

Once in the interview room, Galloway assessed the former policeman.

In his mid-forties, no one would mistake him for a cop today. His pasty complexion and rounded beer gut signaled he wasn't very active. Of course, she knew he'd been hurt in an accident.

She noticed how he rubbed his right leg. She wondered if it really hurt or was it an act to garner sympathy?

Ferrari began the interview. "Mr. Lowe—may I call you Justin?"

"Sure."

"I'll bet you're wondering why you've been brought here. We're investigating the homicide of an off-duty police officer, and we believe you knew him."

"I saw on the news that someone had been killed. Who was it? The media didn't say."

"Duane Sutton," she said.

Either Lowe was an excellent actor, or the shock on his face was real.

"You remember him?"

"Uh, yeah. We worked at Topanga together."

"In what capacity? Patrol?"

He nodded. "We were often partnered together. We got tired of all the political BS that went with working the field, so we looked for a position to get us off the streets. We wound up in the CRO office together—mostly with the cadets."

Lowe frowned. "Why would you think, after all these years I would have knowledge about Duane? I haven't seen or talked to him since the time of my accident."

Ferrari nodded. "Okay. Do mind telling us where you were yesterday?"

Lowe jerked his head back. "Come on. You can't seriously believe *I* killed him."

Galloway smiled at him. "You know it's a standard question we have to ask."

He made a face. "I was on a plane coming home from Vegas. You want my boarding pass?"

Ferrari rolled his pen between his palms. "Do you have it on you?"

The retired cop grabbed his phone and tapped at the

screen, and with a flourish, turned the device to where they could both see his flight's electronic boarding pass."

"Now that we've got that formality out of the way, let's talk about that point in your career...when you worked with cadets. Who else worked in the CRO unit back then?"

A wariness crept into his expression. "What does that have to do with Duane's murder?"

"We're not sure, but it's come up in previous interviews."

"*What's* come up?"

Ferrari leaned forward. "What kind of activities and programs did you and Duane do with the cadets?"

Justin's gaze bounced between her and Ferrari. "Come on. You guys have been with the department long enough to know the assignments that cadets do."

She smiled at him. "Did you ever go on field trips with the kids, Justin?"

"Of course we did."

"Camping trips...say to the beach?"

"Yeah. So what?"

"One of the female cadets is alleging that Duane sexually assaulted her at a beach camping trip."

"Whoa, I have no knowledge about the sexual assault of a cadet," he said, leaning back in his chair. A look of comprehension filled his face. "Ohhh, you think maybe the girl killed him? Wow."

Ferrari picked up his pen. "Do you remember going on any beach camping trips with the cadets?"

Justin tilted his head and closed his eyes while he thought. "Yeah. At least one. Maybe two. I'm pretty sure the beach campout was an annual thing."

"Who was in charge of the CRO Unit then?"

"While I was there, the sergeant was Glen Haywood."

Galloway took over the questioning. "Do you remember a point at the end of the campout where you, Duane, and Glen stayed behind with some of the cadets?"

Justin shrugged. "No. I won't say it didn't happen, but I can't remember that specifically."

"What would you say if I told you that sexual assault allegations have been made against all three of you: Duane, Glen and you?"

Justin crossed his arms. "I'd say this interview is over. You want to talk to me again, you'll need to go through my lawyer."

An hour later, fortified with mugs of coffee, Galloway and Ferrari prepared for Araceli Espinosa and her brother, Antonio Lima.

"I found it interesting that Justin Lowe was willing to talk about Sutton's murder but the second you pressed him about the potential rape, he lawyered up," Ferrari said.

"That's because he didn't kill Sutton but he's dirty for the rape." Galloway brushed her dark hair from her face. "We should interview the girl before we question her brother," she said. "Even though we've got the story she told Buckner and Nanako in their statements, *we* need to hear it from her."

Ferrari nodded. "Yeah, and if she or her brother killed Sutton, I think she's more likely to break than Antonio."

"Do you believe either of them did it?"

"No. I'm leaning toward one or both of Buckners. Amber might have killed him in retaliation for the incident in the wash rack at the station...or Roy did it as revenge for the same incident."

"Yeah, but somehow the cadet thing is related to the

murder. It seems like both things are connected. I got Haywood's phone records, and like he said, he talked to Sutton on Monday night."

"We should have a better understanding once we interview Araceli and Antonio."

Listening to Araceli's account of the beach party and the sexual assault, the girl's story was solid—almost word-for-word of what she'd told Buckner and Nanako, and they'd written in their statements.

"Tell us about the drive-by shooting death of Teresa Pineda," Ferrari urged.

"I can't really help you there. I'd been recruited to work for my pimp. When Teresa was killed, I was working in Oakland. I hated it up north, and I hated my life." She gave a wry smile. "I wanted to come home. Antonio helped me. He's always been my big brother and protector."

"If he was your protector, how did you wind up with a pimp?"

Araceli sighed. "Antonio was sent to prison. I needed money and someone to watch out for me."

"Once you got back to the neighborhood, did you hear any rumors about Maria Gonzales's death?"

Araceli shook her head. "No, but she'd been dead for several months. No one was talking about it anymore."

After a short break, they had Antonio sequestered in the interview room.

Ferrari introduced himself and Galloway to the gangster.

"The reason we've asked you here is because we're investigating a homicide."

Antonio raised his hands in a defensive manner. "I don't know nothin' about no murder."

She smiled at him. "I'm glad to hear that. Tell us where you were yesterday."

"Me? Uh, yeah. Let me think." He thought for a second. "I slept until about noon. I headed over to Lanark Park about one thirty looking for my homies. No one was around, so I returned home."

"Can someone confirm any of that?" Ferrari had his pen poised above his notepad.

The gangster shrugged. "Nah. My mom was out with the baby runnin' errands all day. She didn't get back until about four." He tilted his head. "Who got whacked?"

She looked him in the eye. "Officer Duane Sutton."

Antonio's head jerked upright. "No shit?"

She nodded. "No shit."

"He's dead? Wow. Couldn't have happened to a more deserving guy."

"Did *you* kill him?" Ferrari asked.

Antonio shook his head. "No, no, no. You're backin' the wrong horse. I'm not the one who did it—but I wish I had."

98

ROY

It was still dark outside when Roy awoke from a night of sporadic sleeping. While the Sutton homicide was investigated, he'd been assigned to his home. There was no need for him to drive to PAB.

He lay staring at the ceiling. He had to fix things with Amber.

Once the murder investigation started, he knew his dalliance with Katie would come to light. He'd hoped to tell her himself before she heard it from someone else.

Who the hell would be dumb enough to talk in the detective lobby about witnesses in a homicide? And who could possibly know about him and Katie?

As his thoughts flowed, it came to him. Haywood. Roy didn't understand *how* his boss knew of the affair, but it all made sense. "*That's* why she recognized him," he whispered. "He gets his face on TV every chance he gets."

He grabbed his phone from the nightstand and searched for the department organizational chart that included photos of the upper echelon of the LAPD. Once he found the captain's smug smile, he got out of bed to find his wife.

While the house was in darkness, he heard noises coming from the kitchen.

She stood at the counter, making coffee.

Gage sat in his highchair, fingering Cheerios and sliced banana from a plastic bowl into his mouth. "Daddy."

Roy smiled. "Good morning, Son. You're up early. How's our Mommy doing?"

She shot him a sharp look. The dark circles beneath her eyes told him she'd had a rough night too.

He held his phone so she could see the screen. "Is this the guy you overheard in the lobby yesterday?"

She looked at the photo, then looked at him. "Yes. Who is that?"

He pressed his lips together. "That's my boss, Glen Haywood."

Her eyes widened and she gasped. "Do you think he meant for me to overhear him?"

He scoffed and nodded. "Yes, I do." His mind was overrun as connections and motives fell into place. "He's trying to frame me for your training officer's murder." He could feel his face and neck flush at the persecution.

"You need to call the detectives and tell them."

"Tell them what? That someone is framing me?"

She sipped her coffee. "Yes."

He was silent for a few seconds thinking. "No. We need to

let the investigation play out. If I start throwing Haywood under the bus, it makes me look more guilty—like I'm looking for a scapegoat."

She added creamer to her coffee. "How did your boss know about you and…and your partner?"

He grabbed a mug from the cabinet. "No clue. But remember what I told you last week? Cops are the biggest gossips in the world. When coworkers are…intimate, people sense it—especially cops. We're trained to watch body language and look for signs of deceit."

She bit her lip. "The whole department will know you cheated on me."

His shoulder's slumped. His transgression would humiliate her. "Yeah, I think that's true."

"So, thanks to you, for the *second* time in my life I'll be sexually mortified for the world to see." Tears filled her eyes. "I can't forgive you for that, Roy. You know the shame I've carried since my kidnapping. I'm taking Gage and leaving you. I hope your partner was a worthwhile lay, because it's cost you everything. I can't be in a marriage where there is no trust—and obviously, I can't trust you.

She whirled away and stormed out of the kitchen.

He stood in shock as she marched through the house.

"Da-da? Mama cry?"

99

AMBER

Amber was worried. About a half hour after Roy confirmed with her that Haywood was the person who'd divulged his misdeeds with Katie, he'd gotten dressed in a suit as if he was going to work.

He stormed out to the garage, and she ran and followed him. He was getting into his pickup.

"Remember, you wanted to let the investigation play out," she called. "Don't make things worse."

He'd gunned the truck's engine and tore out of the garage.

Gage sat on the couch in the family room, watching cartoons.

As she showered and dressed, she felt mired in mud. She was nauseous from Roy's betrayal, and her mind whirled with the worries of the fallout of Sutton's murder.

Hurrying back to check on her son, she found him in front of the television singing and dancing along with an animated blue bear.

Needing to gain control of her life, she grabbed two suitcases from the closet and began to pack her clothes.

100

―――――

HAYWOOD

Haywood woke up at 4:00 a.m. with a sense of dread. He'd screwed up big time. As much as he hated to admit it, the dead guy had been right.

The girl, the one witness from the private beach party he, Sutton, and Lowe had orchestrated, needed to be killed. She could still tell the story and sink his reputation, career, and everything he'd worked his whole life to achieve. There had to be a way out.

His foresight to secure the girl's address and phone number was brilliant, providing she hadn't lied when she provided her info for the ADW report. After seeing the address, he knew the house was in a poorer section of the Valley.

You can go into the office, then go home sick again. It won't seem strange since you were out yesterday. Besides, you should probably grab your old Vice driver's license and credit card in your alias name. You may need it.

As he showered and dressed, he put an updated plan into place.

He drove to the police headquarters in his red sports car. Like many of his co-workers, he arrived before regular business hours and left earlier to avoid what they could of the rush hour traffic.

Walking through the RHD squad room, he saw about half his detectives were already at work. Instead of sitting at their desks, they stood in small groups speaking in hushed tones— no doubt gossiping about the Sutton homicide and Buckner's involvement.

Making his way to his office, he murmured good morning to a few and nodded at others.

Once Wiggins arrived and settled in for the day, he sought him out. "Darnell, I still feel lousy. I'm going home. Call me if you need anything."

"No problem, boss. Get some rest and feel better."

Free from the office, he drove his car to a shopping center in Burbank off the freeway and parked. He then called for an Uber to deliver him to the airport where he rented a more nondescript vehicle than his red sportster.

Once he had the rental, he made the phone call.

"Good morning. Is this Araceli Espinosa?"

"*Yes.*"

"This is Detective King from the LAPD. I'm working with Officer Buckner and Detective Nanako on the homicide of Officer Duane Sutton. We have some other questions to ask you. We'd like for you to come down to Robbery Homicide Division to be re-interviewed."

She sighed. "I don't have a car, and I can't afford the train."

"Actually, I'm on my way into the office now. Where do you live? I could pick you up and drive you downtown, and I'll either have a police unit bring you back, or the department will pay for you to take the train home."

"How long will I be? I need to be at my job at noon."

"We'll have you back in plenty of time. What's your address?"

She gave him the same address Sutton had given him.

Yes! She fell for it. "Great. I should be there in about twenty minutes. I'll be driving a black Jeep."

PART XI

101

———

ANTONIO

After a night of hanging out with his crew, smoking weed, tagging, and looking for rival gang members to screw with, Antonio had dragged himself home at 3:00 a.m. and fallen into bed.

A few hours later, through the thin wall between his bedroom and his sister's, he heard her phone ring. He looked at his watch and cursed. It wasn't even 8:00 a.m. He closed his eyes, trying to fall back to sleep.

In her room, he heard Araceli moving around with purpose. More annoying, she was loud. When he heard her across the hall in the bathroom, brushing her teeth he got out of bed.

She came out of the bathroom as he stepped into the hallway.

"Where you goin' so early?"

"Damn detectives have more questions for me. He's picking me up in a few minutes."

"*Who's* picking you up?"

"I can't remember his name. Someone from last night, I guess."

"Did they want to talk to me too?"

She shrugged. "He didn't say. Check your phone. Maybe he called and you missed it."

"In a minute. I gotta take a leak."

"Okay. If he left you a message, you'd better hustle. He should be here any time."

After finishing in the bathroom, he hurried into his bedroom and grabbed his phone. No messages.

He heard a car on the street out front.

He shoved the curtains aside and saw an SUV at the curb and his sister walking toward the heavy-duty black Jeep. Something was off.

She opened the door, then looked back at the house for a second. Then slowly got into the car.

102

ROY

Roy knew it was irrational, but he blamed his captain for the discord between Amber and himself. Yes, he'd screwed up and slept with Katie. But Haywood had no right to intentionally tell his wife about his cheating.

He seethed while driving to the police headquarters. Even though he wasn't authorized, he drove his truck into the underground parking beneath PAB. He grunted in satisfaction when he passed his boss's showy sports car parked in his designated space. After winding down a few levels, he backed his truck into an available spot and turned off the engine.

Now what? His original idea was to confront his boss, but now that he was here, what good would that do?

If you go upstairs, you'll lose your temper, maybe even slug the asshole and then you'll be arrested, booked, and you'll look like the murderer he wants people to believe you are.

Frustrated with his colossal waste of time, he started his truck and began his ascent to street level. As he passed the space where Haywood's red vehicle had been parked, he noted the space was now empty.

Pulling toward the garage exit, there were two vehicles ahead of him, waiting for traffic to clear before pulling out. The car ahead of him was a detective plain wrap with two occupants inside, but ahead of them, was the flashy red vehicle.

Where the hell is he going in his personal vehicle?

Traffic cleared and the detective ride as well as the captain's vehicle made it out onto Main Street.

Roy pulled to the exit and after letting a few pedestrians pass, shot out onto the street, amid screeching brakes and honking horns. He was positioned three cars behind Haywood.

You've got nothing else to do. Follow him and see where he's going when he should be working.

Feeling like what he was doing mattered, he followed his boss as he made his way to the Golden State Freeway. The farther away they got from downtown the easier it was to follow, but that meant there were also fewer cars to put between himself and his quarry.

When his boss transitioned off the freeway in Burbank, he knew the man wasn't going home. His boss lived on the north side of the Valley.

Where are you going?

He drove into an open-air shopping center, parked, and exited his vehicle. He was tapping on the screen to his phone as he walked to the front of a Target store.

Roy figured he was parked far enough away, that the

captain wouldn't notice his truck even though it was early, and the stores weren't open.

A few minutes later, a silver Nissan screamed through the lot and made a beeline to the lone man pacing in front of the department store. After a brief exchange, Haywood got into the car.

As the silver Nissan turned into the Burbank Airport, his heart raced. *Could he be making a run for it?*

The Nissan stopped next to the terminals, and with a friendly wave, Haywood got out. On foot, his boss turned away from the airline buildings and marched toward the car rental structure.

He's renting a ride? Interesting.

He sped through the parking structure, quickly parked, and sprinted to the multi-story garage where cars were rented.

Wishing he'd thought to grab a ball cap or had some luggage to blend in with the travelers bustling about, he put on his sunglasses, removed his tie, and unbuttoned the top few buttons of his shirt.

Peering around a pillar, he watched as his boss handed over ID and a credit card to rent a car. Once his boss picked out a black all-wheel-drive SUV, Roy snapped a photo of the vehicle being sure to include the license plate. Then he sprinted back to his truck. There was only one way out of the parking garage, and he had to be in his truck and in position to follow before his boss left the airport. If he missed him, he would slip away.

He drummed on his steering wheel as the woman ahead of him struggled to use her credit card to pay for parking. "Come on, come on."

She finally finished, and he quickly paid and accelerated to the circular road that returned to the airport. Driving double the speed limit, he zipped along until he got into view of the ramp where rental cars descended to join the traffic exiting the airport.

Now he slowed to a crawl, itching to see the black SUV coming down the concrete ramp. The sloped surface was empty.

His gaze searched the line of cars closest to the rental structure, while he waited for the signal to change to exit the airport. Midway in the line was a midnight, boxy SUV, but was it the one containing Haywood?

Quick. Make up your mind.

Roy gunned his truck and sped to the tail end of line of cars turning right. *He's not heading to the 5 Freeway. Where is this idiot going?* He ignored the blare of horns from irritated drivers as he ran the red light to keep up with the SUV he prayed contained his boss.

Taking Vineland north to Sherman Way, the black vehicle drove west, heading into the heart of the San Fernando Valley.

Morning rush hour traffic filled the streets with weary-looking drivers—most sucking down coffee while they drove.

With the morning flurry of activity, it wasn't hard to follow the black boxy vehicle. At one stoplight, he was able to compare the plate on the truck with the picture he'd taken with his phone. He let out a heavy sigh. He had the correct vehicle.

After driving through the neighborhoods of Van Nuys, Reseda, and Winnetka, he had an idea where Haywood might be going.

The farther they drove; the more convinced he was that his boss was heading to the residence of Araceli Espinosa. Once they turned off Sherman Way, it was harder to follow him—there were fewer vehicles on the move.

He dropped back almost two blocks, now certain of the destination.

Sure enough, his boss turned on the street where Araceli lived and glided up to the curb in front of her home.

A hundred yards away, he pulled to the curb as well. He watched as Araceli got into the black SUV.

He was up to no good. As soon as the vehicle was on the move again, Roy followed.

As he approached Araceli's residence, his attention was diverted by Antonio leaping off the front porch, shirtless, and with shoes in hand.

Roy sped up, and screeched to a stop and rolled down the passenger window.

Antonio's face registered relief when he recognized him.

"Get in! Hurry!"

Antonio jumped into the truck, and Roy sped down the street to put eyes on the SUV again.

103

KATIE

The night before, when Katie had been interviewed by the IA Sergeant Galloway and West Valley Homicide Detective Ferrari, they'd informed her she was being assigned to home until they cleared her of any wrongdoing during their investigation.

She needed to fill her time, and she couldn't help but feel that she and Roy had missed something important—some information that connected the murder of Adam Lowe and the sexual assaults at the beach.

The common denominator was Justin Lowe. She opened her laptop and found the emails that she routinely emailed herself of her reports as a backup.

She reviewed the witness statements chronologically that they'd written. There had to be something that they'd missed.

Since Roy was ordered to stay home, too, she wanted to

call him and ask him to look over the statements as well. She glanced at the clock.

It was after nine. Katie tried calling Roy's cell.

It went to voicemail. She wasn't surprised and didn't leave a message. She'd gotten a quick glimpse of him as she was being led to be interviewed the night before, when she was questioned by Detective Galloway.

He'd been in another interview room, and his expression was as hard as granite and one of his legs bounced as though charged with electricity.

At the time, she'd wondered if the shrewd detectives had left that door ajar for her benefit, so she could see him distressed to throw her off balance too.

When Galloway and Ferrari asked about her partnership with Roy, she'd been anxious, but the detectives didn't give any indication they knew about the affair. She'd hoped it wouldn't come out but was practical enough to realize it eventually would—especially with the scrutiny of a murder investigation.

She reread Justin Lowe's interview and hadn't found anything unusual.

She re-read his sister-in-law, Brandi's statement—and one comment jumped out at her. *Not long before Adam's death, Justin got hurt at work. Hit by a drunk driver. Then his mother died. Because of his injuries, he had to quit being a policeman. Eventually, he got a boatload of money.*

It got Katie wondering...could *this* be the reason Adam Lowe was killed—and was Justin behind it?

104

HAYWOOD

Haywood drove his rented SUV while the girl sat mute in the passenger seat. His Glock rested in his lap. The pistol had sealed the deal in getting the stripper in the car once she realized who was picking her up.

Every time he slowed the vehicle, the gun was in his hand so she wouldn't consider jumping out. Oddly enough, she didn't seem distressed or even looking for a way to escape.

He cleared his throat. "I'm not going to hurt you."

She turned her head slightly and gave him a look that translated to *you're full of shit.* She turned her gaze straight ahead.

"No. I mean it. I want to pay you to keep quiet. Money. A lot of it."

Another shift of her eyes went back to him, containing a

flicker of interest—then she returned her focus to the traffic on the road.

"Look. What happened was a long time ago. We thought you girls *wanted* to party with us and have fun."

She sat in silence. Seconds later, she didn't look at him but spoke softly. "We were underage minors who were good girls—children. We were in the cadet program because we hoped to make something of ourselves—maybe even become cops."

Yeah, yeah, yeah. But you downed those drinks and let us remove your clothes pretty fast. He maneuvered the SUV onto the Simi Valley freeway.

"You were our advisors, our mentors, and we looked up to you. We didn't want to disappoint you. It was very confusing for us."

Okay, that was years ago. Get over yourself. You work as a stripper giving hand and blowjobs in a back room.

"Like I said, I want to make it up to you. I can't undo what we did to you girls, but what if I gave you fifty thousand dollars to help ease your pain?"

A mocking smile played at her lips.

She had him by the balls and she knew it.

"Obviously, your pain is deeper than I realized. One hundred thousand."

She turned her head to look out the window.

Stupid bitch. You just signed your death certificate, sweetheart...but I can play this game too.

"Look. I haven't got the cash to pay you any more than that in a lump sum. How about this, I pay you a grand monthly?"

She kept her head averted.

He sighed. "Two thousand."

"Two bills a month *plus* a Corvette."

He laughed. "I want to make this up to you, but I'm not made of money. I can only do so much."

"Then I guess I'll be sharing my story."

Don't be stupid. Let her think she's winning. It doesn't matter. She's sealed her fate. "Okay, a Vette too."

She turned her face to him and smiled.

"But..." he said. "We should close the deal with a private celebration, and I know the perfect place."

105

ROY

The few seconds spent allowing Antonio into his truck had almost caused him to lose Haywood and Araceli.

In the passenger seat, the gangster struggled to pull his shirt over his head so he could fasten his seatbelt.

Roy maneuvered his truck slow and steady through the morning rush-hour traffic until they were about six cars behind the black SUV.

Antonio bent to tie his expensive sneakers. "Who's got her?"

"My boss." He gave a sidelong glance to his passenger. "You're not strapped, are you?"

The kid's shoulders slumped and he made a face. "I barely got out of the house with my fuckin' shoes, much less a gun."

"That's good, because I'm not sure how this is all going to turn out, but you've got to let *me* handle it."

Antonio recounted the conversation he and his sister had that morning. "She said he was taking her for further questioning. He's not questioning her, is he?"

"I doubt it."

"Why'd he snatch her?"

"He was one of the three officers on the beach trip."

The gangster's gaze shot to the black vehicle and narrowed.

They drove in silence as he followed the car onto the Simi freeway. *I'm taking Gage and leaving you. You know the shame I've carried since my kidnapping. I hope your partner was a worthwhile lay, because it's cost you everything. I can't be in a marriage where there is no trust—and obviously, I can't trust you.*

Haywood. It was *his* fault that Amber found out about his affair with Katie. Roy didn't care that it was irrational to blame his boss. Rage controlled his actions, and he was losing everything, and his captain was the reason.

His boss had destroyed his personal life and was ruining his reputation by framing him for the murder of Sutton. There was no doubt in his mind that the man he was following had killed Amber's training officer.

At that moment, a sense of calm came over him. He would kill Haywood. Why not achieve full revenge? He had nothing left in life.

Roy was sorry he'd impulsively picked up Antonio. He didn't need a witness for what he was planning. Maybe he could have the gangster recover his sister and drive off in his truck, leaving him and his boss alone.

"He's getting off the freeway," Antonio hissed.

Beads of sweat emerged on Roy's forehead, and even the back of his hands. Was he really contemplating murder? Yes. He was.

Once Haywood turned off the Santa Susanna Pass onto the fire road, Roy knew exactly where he was going. He was driving Araceli into the desolate hills to kill her.

"Okay," Roy said. "You're in charge of getting your sister, putting her in my truck, and taking off. Don't worry about me. Grab her and go. I'll deal with the guy."

"You're gonna smoke him."

His gaze shot to the gangster.

"I'll back your play. You might need me."

Roy shook his head. "No. Rescue Araceli and get the hell out. I'll take care of the rest."

106

HAYWOOD

He exited the freeway at Rocky Peak Road and drove the SUV onto the Santa Susanna Pass, a small two-lane roadway that connected the Simi and San Fernando Valley's through the boulder-strewn hills dividing them. He only drove far enough to turn onto a dirt fire road that ran along the ridge of the two valleys.

They'd only driven about fifty yards when he came to an obstacle of two cement pillars on each side of the road with a heavy chain suspended between them. Next to the pillars, purposely stacked boulders prevented vehicles from going around the obstacle and continuing on the path.

Years ago, as a young policeman, while working the grave-yard shift, one of his partners showed him this road as a perfect location to catch an hour or two of sleep when things were slow. At the time, he thought it would make the perfect location for a murder. Back then, all the late-night cops had keys to the padlock that secured the thick chain. Now he'd have to improvise and put the barrier to the test.

He gripped the wheel tighter. "Hold on," he yelled, stomping on the accelerator.

The stripper gasped.

The SUV sprang forward briefly jolting when snapping the chain.

A plume of dust trailed their breach as they jostled along the uneven compacted soil. He continued driving for another mile and a half before he stopped the car, shut off the engine, turned to her, and smiled.

"Now doll, why don't you show me what you've learned about pleasuring men since you're all grown up?"

107

ROY

As he drove past the security chain to the fire road, Roy saw several of the links on the ground. "Geez, he broke through the security chain with his car."

Antonio grunted, his gaze steady on the remnants of the trail of dust lingering in the air.

"There are a few side trails to this main one," he said. "As we get close to them, see if you can tell by the tracks if he left the main path."

"Got it."

He hoped he and Antonio would be there in time.

The farther they got into the foothills, the more the dirt road deteriorated. Roy slowed his speed as they bounced along climbing the hillside. He didn't want the captain to see a dust trail from his truck and know he'd been followed.

"I'm going to stop short of the crest of the hill. We'll have the high ground, and I want to see what we're going into."

Antonio nodded.

As soon at the pickup came to a stop, both men got out of the truck and climbed to the ridge. Roy led, and as he got close to the rise, he dropped to a squat.

The gangster did the same.

The black SUV was about two hundred yards ahead, stopped in the middle of the path.

"We won't have much time," he said. "We're going to fly down there—balls to the wall. I'll stop almost parallel to that big bolder on the left. Do you see it?"

"Yeah."

"I'll jump out of the truck and run to the boulder and use that for cover. My guess is that Haywood will get out of the SUV—the only trouble is that I don't know which side. Let's hope it's the driver side. I'll try to draw his attention toward me at the boulder."

"What am I doing? Standing around with my thumb up my ass?"

"He won't be expecting you. See the smaller boulders on the right side of the road? I want you to use those for cover, and while I deal with Haywood, get Araceli, run back to this truck and drive off."

"You might need my help."

"I'll be fine. Drive to where you've got cell service and call 911. Tell them an officer needs help on the fire road off Santa Susanna Pass and Rocky Peak Road. Got it?"

The gangster gave a quick nod.

"Okay. Let's hit it."

108

HAYWOOD

Semi-reclined in the passenger seat of the SUV, Haywood moaned as the girl serviced him with her mouth. Pressure had built, but he didn't want to finish that way.

"Stop."

Startled, the girl retracted.

"Straddle me." He knew it was dangerous to give her that physical advantage, but he had his pistol in his hand ready to shoot her if she made a wrong move.

The stripper started to position herself, but her gaze fixated on something behind their car.

"What is it?" He struggled to sit up.

"A coyote. It's nothing." She pushed him back into the seat and bent her leg to ease herself onto him.

He watched the girl's tits waggle in his face as she rode him. "That's it, baby. Faster. Faster."

She gasped and moaned loudly, while talking dirty to him.

The girl was good. God, he loved young ass.

He thrust and groaned in complete release.

The girl waited a few seconds and then uncoupled and pushed herself over the center console and onto the driver's seat.

He frowned and opened his eyes. "Christ. You couldn't wait a few seconds?" He smirked. "I was enjoying the afterglow."

"I need to pee. Can I get out and go behind one of those big rocks?" She bobbed her head to the right side of their vehicle.

He moved his gun to his left hand, then reached between the seat and the door to move the passenger seat to an upright position.

A quick assessment of the area determined it was just as good as anywhere to kill the bitch. He could drag her body between the small boulders, and if Mother Nature did her job, the girls remains might not ever be found.

"Yeah. Give me sec to zip up."

The girl opened the driver door.

"I *told you*, give me a second," he said, pointing his .45 at her.

She froze in place.

"I'll come to you." He opened the passenger side and got out.

109

ROY

Roy couldn't be sure, but he thought Araceli had seen his truck as they blazed toward the idle black SUV.

From her motions, it was obvious she and Haywood were having sex.

He worried what Antonio's reaction would be.

"Remember, I'll deal with the man. Grab your sister and drive like hell out of here."

"That dip shit has her fucking him!"

"Antonio. Focus. We've got to get her out safely. That's your job. Don't slam the truck door getting out."

Roy rolled to a stop and bailed from his truck and ran to the cover of a massive boulder.

He searched the rocks on the other side of his truck and glimpsed Antonio slip behind the largest one.

Araceli was in the driver seat.

The upper part of Haywood's body rose from a reclined position. He was talking, then he opened the passenger door.

Damn! I should have gone to that side.

He left his position of cover and sprinted to the left side of his pickup. He used the engine block for cover.

The captain walked around the front of the SUV, then crouched after spotting Roy's truck.

"Haywood! Police! Drop the gun!"

His boss fired at him.

Roy returned fire but had to shoot high. Araceli was still in the driver's seat of the SUV, and she was positioned between him and Haywood.

"Move to the other seat," the captain yelled to Araceli.

The girl didn't shift.

Cursing, Haywood fired two more shots at him and then ran to the driver's door of the SUV and yanked it open.

Roy raised his gun and fired two more shots, one of them catching Haywood in the left shoulder.

Undeterred, his boss yanked Araceli from the SUV and flung her to the ground and jumped into the driver seat.

From the corner of his eye, Roy saw Antonio run toward the black vehicle, gun in hand, and firing while on the move.

He laid cover fire to distract from Antonio's approach.

The gangster flung open the passenger door, fired a couple of rounds, and then leaned inside and put the pistol to the back of Haywood's head and fired two final shots.

Roy ran to Araceli. "Are you hurt?"

"No. No, I'm okay."

Antonio skidded around the corner of the SUV, his sister's clothes in hand. "She okay?" He dropped the garments next to her.

Roy nodded and then opened the driver side to confirm his boss was dead. The gangster had done the job well.

Araceli stood and pulled on her clothes.

Antonio grabbed her and hugged her.

Roy looked at Antonio. "I thought you weren't packin'."

"I lied. It's *my* job to take care of my family."

He gave the gangster a hard stare. "I didn't need your help."

"Hey, man, chill. I saved you. Don't kid yourself. I saw it in your eyes. You planned on killing him one way or the other—even if that meant shooting him in cold blood. That's not who you are." The gangster shrugged. "For me, knocking somebody off is a regular day at the office." He grinned. "You're welcome."

EPILOGUE

Two days later...

Roy spotted Katie in a booth by the window of the cafe. He plopped onto the bench seat across from her.

She tilted her head. "How are you holding up?"

He scoffed and shook his head. "Lousy. She came back yesterday and packed up Gage's crib, more toys, and a bunch of her personal stuff."

"I'm really sorry."

"I am too. She's getting an apartment. She's not bluffing. We're through."

His partner sighed.

A waitress brought coffee and took their breakfast order.

He added creamer to his cup and stirred. "So, tell me about the Lowe case."

Katie nodded. "While you were being all heroic and rescuing Araceli, I reviewed the Lowe file. Brandi McGee had mentioned something about Adam's mother dying and Justin getting a boatload of money.

"That got me to thinking how convenient it was that Adam died right before his mother." She stirred sugar in her coffee. "I telephonically re-interviewed Brandi. I did some research on the Lowe's, and it turns out their mother came from a wealthy family. But with Adam's murder, all that money flowed to Justin." She tilted her head and pointed her finger at him. "*That's* how he was able to afford that multi-million-dollar home in the hills."

"Can we prove that Justin killed his brother?"

"No. In fact, it's physically impossible. Justin had been hit by that drunk driver and was in the hospital. But guess who two of Justin's most frequent visitors were."

The server brought their food, and Roy took a bite. "Sutton and Haywood."

Katie smiled. "Yep."

"So, the two of them killed Adam Lowe for Justin Lowe? Why? Why would they do that? Did he pay them off with that *boatload* of money?"

She shook her head. "We subpoenaed all their financials, and any money Justin Lowe got from his settlement and inheritance stayed with him."

Her smile turned into a wide grin. "We know that last day of the cadet campout, Adam Lowe drove to Topanga Division and signed out the Youth Services van. We have the vehicle sign-out sheet."

"So?"

"The detective from IA, Lacey Galloway, and I believe the three CRO cops were too hammered to drive home from the beach. We suspect Justin called his brother, Adam, to pick them up so they could bring the female cadets back to their houses."

"Okay. But how does that translate into Sutton and Haywood shooting Adam outside his house?"

Katie nodded. "Galloway and I think Adam Lowe knew, or at least suspected what had gone on at the beach and threatened to expose the three. It was a few days later that Justin was hit by the deuce. It worked out perfect for him. He couldn't actively be a part in killing his brother, but he could coerce his buddies Sutton and Haywood to do it by telling them Adam was going to blow the whistle on them."

"It sounds like you and Galloway have been busy, but do you have any proof of any of this?"

She smiled. "We're working on it, but we're waiting on you to get your ass back to work to sweat it out of Justin Lowe. Any clue when that's going to be?"

"As soon as the department doesn't look at me as damaged goods."

"Trust me on this one partner—we exposed dirty cops who sexually abused police cadets, and I'm pretty sure we've solved the decade-old murder of Adam Lowe. We'll put a case together showing Justin had his brother killed *and* nail him for sexual assault. That makes us damn fine detectives—and nothing close to damaged goods."

AUTHENTIC CRIME...ARRESTING STORY

Damaged Goods came about because I wasn't through with Amber and Roy Buckner. In the previous book in the series, *Collateral Damage*, the Buckners went through horrific experiences. There had to be after-effects of those adventures. Those developments are revealed in *Damaged Goods*.

I also wanted to showcase some of the experiences that a female probationary police officer might experience—at least back in my day. While overly dramatized in this story, there were grains of truth in some of Amber's experiences.

Just gathering all the equipment officers need during their shifts, for a brand-new probationer was challenging—and they have even more equipment now! I knew of a training officer who proudly stated he looked for opportunities to get his female partners into physical altercations "to see what they're made of." I had an officer or two try make advances while I was on probation, but I was like Amber—so focused on doing a good job, I didn't have time or the desire for any shenanigans—although the shenanigans won me over toward the end of my probation, and I've been married to Mr. Shenanigan for twenty-five years.

In the late eighties/early nineties, (when I was on probation) things were a lot easier than the women who came before me. And I think that's how it goes as the years go by. The challenges may change, but the young people coming through the ranks don't know how it used to be.

While Amber's experiences held elements of true experiences, rest assured that the main villain's problem-solving skills are a figment of my imagination.

Two side notes: During the course of writing *Damaged Goods,* I was told that LAPD has disbanded their Cold Case Unit. Knowing that the department often makes changes and then changes back again, in *Damaged Goods,* I've left the Cold Case Unit downtown in RHD.

Also, at this time there is no Academy Award given to casting directors. However, during my research I read that there are signs the Motion Picture Academy may be considering adding such an award.

Don't miss out on any of my new releases. Sign up for my newsletter and get the fast-paced story, A Deadly Second Chance—a tale inspired by a true LAPD SWAT incident, and the prequel to, *A Deadly Blessing,* Book 2 in my *Deadly Thriller* series. Sign up for my newsletter at www.KathyBennett.com

I'm sure other readers would like to know what you thought about *Damaged Goods.* Please consider leaving a review about this story of healing, betrayal, and murder.

Warm regards,

Kathy Bennett

SNEAK PEEK OF DAMAGE CONTROL

DAMAGE CONTROL

AMBER - 1

Tick. Tick. Tick. Amber Buckner listened to the steady beats from the clock on her shrink's desk. They mirrored the palpitations of her heart.

"I think I made a mistake leaving Roy."

Doctor Angela Stevens glanced at the yellow legal pad on her lap. "And you guys have been separated for what...about eighteen months, right?"

She nodded. "Yes."

The doctor crossed her legs. "So why, after a year and a half, have you changed your mind?"

"I've had time to reassess everything that's happened to us. The Seth Farley thing, me becoming a cop, and Roy's affair."

"Okay, so you've taken another look at all those things. How has that revaluation changed your view?"

Amber sighed and cast her gaze around the room, then returned her focus to her shrink. "Being a cop changes your perspective...on just about everything. Before my kidnapping, when I worked as a Neo-natal ICU nurse, I faced plenty of pressure, physicians yelling, babies not breathing, mothers panicking. During my nursing days, I often made life and death decisions. And that stress was real and critical." She readjusted the pillow under her left arm.

"When I became a police officer, I knew interacting with the public was necessary, frustrating, and dangerous. But I had no idea that the *real* frustration, mental strain, and anxiety would come from inside the department itself. Being a cop—especially in today's world—is a no win situation."

She looked into the other woman's eyes. "You might find it surprising that I feel some compassion for Farley. He thought the LAPD had wronged him. That wasn't true, but now with my experience as an officer I can see how he might have believed he was targeted." She rubbed her hands together.

"I've also realized that I'm not Farley's only victim in our family. My husband suffered too. Not only by the after-effects of my abduction, but the guilt he must carry from other officers and innocent citizens being killed. He was under the weight of that whole mess while still working as a cop...and becoming a father—something he never wanted to be." She blew out a breath, relieved she'd been able to articulate her thoughts.

Angela nodded. "Okay. How does all that stuff you've just said relate to uncertainty that it was the wrong decision to leave your husband?"

"Because now that I wear a badge, I can see how he needed...relief."

The doctor smiled. "Do you think all police officers who face extreme stress or hardships on the job and in their personal life need relationships outside of marriage to cope?"

"I can't speak for them. I only know that Roy is a decent man. Yes, he cheated on me. He said it was only twice, and I believe him. Back then I wasn't there for him sexually, and he found someone who was and hurting as much as he was not afraid to be intimate. I don't like it, but I understand why it happened. I've forgiven him, and I want him back."

ROY - 2

On Thursday morning, Roy Buckner moved with purpose. He wasn't used to having his three-year-old son at his apartment on a workday.

"Okay, buddy, finish your Cherrios and apple slices. We've got to get going. Daddy will be late to the office.

The little boy clutched a handful of cereal and jammed the contents of his hand against his open lips. Most of the oat circles fell onto the table.

"Good job, Son." He smiled. "Don't be afraid to use your fingers to put the Cherrios into your mouth."

Gage reached for his sippy-cup and swallowed several gulps of milk. He grinned, then grabbed an apple slice and bit off a bite.

"You keep eating. Daddy has to go brush his teeth and put on a tie."

A half an hour later, they were on their way to Balboa Nursery School. As they traversed the morning traffic, he pointed out orange buses packed with kids, sleek sportsters, and traffic guards, shepherding youngsters through the traffic.

"Powice," Gage said, pointing at a black and white ahead in the lane next to them.

"That's right, Son. Those officers probably just came on duty and they'll be working the whole day—even past the time Mommy comes and gets you."

From his safety booster in the back seat, the toddler clapped his hands.

"Mommy'll pick you up this afternoon. You'll spend the night with her, and then Daddy will come for you sometime tomorrow morning. How does that sound?" Roy glanced at his boy in the rear-view mirror.

The toddler nodded.

As he pulled into the parking lot of the pre-school, he wondered how his little one was effected by the screwy schedule he and his wife Amber kept.

After walking Gage inside and into his classroom, he couldn't help but feel better.

The three-year-old threw his arms around his father's legs, tilted his head up for a kiss, and as soon as he finished, the toddler ran to join a group of boys building a tower of wooden blocks.

Back in his pickup truck, knowing his three-year-old was safe and happy, Roy shifted his thoughts to his caseload of sex offender registrants.

Several of the detectives who worked Valley missing persons were coming to meet with him. In the past four months, three young boys had disappeared. His position as the head of **sex offender registration made him the logical first stop. He hoped he could help.

ROBYN - 3

Robyn McGee bustled down the hallway of her green cottage-style home in lower Bel Air—a gated enclave of the rich and famous in Los Angeles.

She carried several bags of boys' clothing, along with several others containing toys.

Behind her, the weekly housekeeper, struggled to keep up with two large bundles of bedding.

"Irma, I can't wait for you to see the bed the props department made for the little boy I've adopted. Logan will arrive in the next few days and there's so much to do!"

"I'm so happy for you, Miss Robyn." As soon as they entered the guest bedroom that was transformed into a train enthusiast's wonderland, Irma set her burdens down. "Oh, this is wonderful. What a treat for a young boy."

She moved to the bed, crafted to look like a train locomotive. She rubbed her hand on the bright blue wood forming the cab of the engine where the mattress lay waiting for sheets and a bedspread. Beneath the bunk were two drawers on each side with rounded facings painted to resemble locomotive wheels.

"See this?" Robyn said. "Did you notice how they designed a mural on the wall to appear like the train was coming out of a tunnel?"

"The room is magical. I'm sure your new son will be very happy." The maid pulled the bedding from the bags. "I'll get these sheets and bedspread in the washer. I'll have the room before leaving today."

Robyn dumped toddler jeans and shirts adorned with dinosaurs onto the mattress and began pulling off tags. "Do you have time to wash his news clothes, too? I don't know how much he'll be bringing from the foster home."

"Of course, Miss. We'll have everything ready for Logan."

"Excellent." She glanced at her watch. "Oh gosh, I've got to go to my office. I have a meeting with a couple of actors coming over to read for some small parts."

"I'll handle this. You work."

With a nod of her head at the maid, she strode down the hallway to the other side of the residence.

After winning back-to-back Oscars for casting two Academy Award Best Picture films, she'd allowed herself to splurge, and had an office built at the far end of the house. The architect had designed a separate entrance so thespian hopefuls weren't traipsing through her home. Big-name actors were always welcomed into her her private quarters.

She enter her workspace through the door attached to the butler's pantry. She flipped on lights, and opened the blinds, then poked her head outside and waved frantically at the gardener who wore hearing protection against the whine of the leaf blower.

ABOUT THE AUTHOR

Hi there!

I'm Kathy Bennett.

A little about me—I worked for the LAPD for twenty-nine years. I was a civilian employee for eight years, and I served twenty-one years as a police officer. While most of my career was spent in a patrol car, I also worked at the police academy as a firearms instructor, promoted to the position of a field training officer, and then worked in the "War Room" as a crime analyst. I promoted again, this time to the position of Senior Lead Officer—where I was in charge of a basic car area within a geographic division. I've done a few stints undercover and was honored to be named Officer of the Year in 1997.

In my spare time, I started writing romance books. However, I wasn't really cut out to be a romance author—I'd forget to write the romance, but I was always killing off one or more characters. After a few years, I realized I'd better write what I know: Authentic Crime... Arresting Stories. (Yeah, that catchy phrase is a part of my brand.) One of the books in my Deadly Thriller series, *A Deadly Blessing*, was chosen by Barnes and Noble as one of the best original books of the year.

I live in Idaho with my husband and soul mate, who is also a retired LAPD officer. We have two entertaining and energetic Labrador retrievers, and one cat who is perfect in every way. I like to garden, exercise, and spend time with our daughter and her family. Life doesn't get much better than the one I'm living.

I'm always interested in my readers. Drop me a line and tell me a little about yourself or what you thought about *Damaged Goods*. You can reach me here: kathy@ kathybennett.com, and know that I *do* write back—and it's me—not an assistant.